endure

The Survival Series
Book Two

Amber R. Polk

Endure

Cover design by ARP Publishing
Stock Photo from Depositphoto
All Rights Reserved.

ISBN- 978-1530371723

For Matthew.
The youngest love of my life.
I'm so proud to be your mom.

Chapter One

"*Roni, come look,*" *Jacob said, smiling up at me with his emerald green eyes shining and the wind bouncing his curly blond hair against his forehead. His tongue peeked through the empty space where his two front baby teeth had been, making it impossible not to return his smile. He was such a beautiful boy and I couldn't refuse him anything. I set my glass of iced tea on the porch step and stood to follow him when, in an instant, he was twenty feet away.*

"*Veronica! Come on,*" *he called, waving his chubby fingers.*

I started toward him, excited to see whatever it was he wanted to show me, but with each step forward, Jacob moved farther and farther away. My eyebrows furrowed and mouth quirked to the side, trying to figure out what game he was playing. His giggle echoed all around me.

"*Jakey wait up!*"

"*Find me, Sissy,*" *he giggled.*

1

In a blink, I was standing in the middle of the snow-covered orchard. The bare trees bent with the weight of the ice covering the limbs, giving them an eerie look. A chill ran down my spine as I spun around, trying to catch sight of my baby brother. He shouldn't be in the orchard all alone. I needed to find him.

A lump on the ground at the back of the orchard caught my eye and I began to feel the heavy weight of fear fill me. I closed my eyes as dread took over. Something was wrong. Very wrong. But I didn't know what it was and was terrified to find out.

When I opened my eyes, I was standing over a lifeless body. Jacob's lifeless, adult body. His faded green eyes stared blankly into the sky, blood covering the front of his shirt. I took quick, shallow breaths, feeling the bile rise in my throat, choking me.

"Roni," the young Jacob said, standing next to me as he put his tiny, cold hand in mine. "Why did you leave me alone? Did you love him more than me?"

"No, Jacob. No! I love you so much," I said, falling to my knees and pulling him tightly to my chest.

"Then why did you let him hurt me?" he whispered in my ear.

I violently jerked awake, my knee crashing into the steering wheel, sending a jolt of pain through my leg. Pain I deserved. Pain that wasn't nearly enough to numb the gaping hole where my heart used to be. Blinking my swollen eyes open, I stretched my limbs. I ached not only from constant trembling from the cold, but from three nights sleeping in the cab of our pick-up truck.

There I went again, saying ours.

There was no ours. Not anymore.

My little brother was dead, and Luke, the man I stupidly fell in love with, murdered him.

Jacob and I had lived two years on our own after the plague hit and killed the majority of the population, including our parents. Surviving hadn't been easy, but we had each other and our parents' apple orchard to keep us alive. We'd even managed to find a way to have happiness in the life we were left.

That was until Luke—supposedly—stumbled onto our property. In an instant, our lives changed. I thought it was a change for the better.

I had been an idiot.

I was still an idiot.

Lifting myself to a sitting position, I stared through the windshield into the dark night, trying to block any thoughts of Jacob from my mind. If I was going to make it long enough to find Luke, I had to keep my wits about me. If I let myself ruminate on Jacob for too long, my mind would become paralyzed. I couldn't fail now. I hadn't protected Jacob while he was alive, but I was sure as hell going to make the man we put our trust in pay for what he did.

Cupping my hands close to my mouth, I blew hot air into them, momentarily thawing my fingertips. The day had been sunny but, when the sun disappeared, cold had set in and the cab of the truck was my only protection from the elements. I couldn't turn on the engine for the heater. The noise would carry in the soundless realm, and I might as well put a flashing neon sign on the truck saying *woman alone*, if

I did. What I needed was a blanket to cover up with at night, but I hadn't thought about it while packing to leave home to hunt down Luke. Instead, I packed water, bullets, knives, guns, and a lighter.

You know, the necessities.

I reached down and plucked a bottle of water out of the open duffel bag resting on the floorboard and took a sip. I put the water away and lie down on my side, arm tucked under my head, staring at the dashboard. I wondered if anyone would find the orchard one day and have a life there. I hoped so. Once upon a time, love and happiness filled the walls of that home. It needs to be filled with joy again someday.

I had almost burned the house down before I left. I went so far as pouring gasoline on the porch but couldn't bring myself to light the match. My dad built it for my mom and it deserved a better fate than to be burned to rubble by my hand. One day, it might be the home of another family and I didn't want to be the one who took it away from them.

Maybe when they found the house, my sweet chickens would still be around. They were good little chick-a-dees. At least for now, they would free-range roam around the farm and pick the remnants of my garden clean. I hoped whoever found them would be good to them.

I closed my eyes, already knowing it was going to be hell to get back to sleep. Instead of putting effort into a losing battle, I went over the plans for the day. I had to wait for daybreak before I could get back on the road. Headlights could be seen for miles away, and I wanted to stay as invisible as possible. That tip was courtesy of dickhead Luke. I grinned and knew if anyone were around to witness it, I would look like a crazed lunatic. It was ironic; the skills he taught me were now aiding me in hunting him down and killing him. He deserved every ounce of suffering I would inflict. No, he deserved worse.

I had loved him. *Loved* him. He was gorgeous to the point of breathtaking, with beautiful silver eyes that melted me with a look. He was also protective to the point of stifling and said all the right things at the right time to keep me in line. I think the worst part of his betrayal was how safe and loved I felt with him there. He knew exactly how to play me. I had been so completely overwhelmed with happiness, having found someone as great and beautiful as him in a disastrous world, that I let it blind me to who he really was.

I felt like my reason for surviving the plague was to take care of Jacob and Luke.

Luke pretended to love us. To love me.

I should have known better.

Like I said, I was an idiot.

I shifted in the seat, trying to get into a more comfortable position, which was impossible, but my body's natural reaction was to at least try. First thing to do at sun up would be to find a blanket. I also needed food. I had absolutely no desire to eat, but if I wanted to be able to run if the need arose, it was essential to stay fed and hydrated.

Hopefully, I would find some sort of indication proving I was actually on the trail of Luke and the army men with him, and not miles out of the way. If I had to drive all the way to Atlanta—where Luke was headed—I would. Though, it was vital for me to find him before he reached

Atlanta. Once there, it would be exponentially harder to locate him and much less likely I would be able to get close enough to kill him. And I wanted to be up close and personal when I killed him. I wanted him to know who was responsible for ending his life. *The piece of shit.*

He would feel the full meaning of "hell hath no fury like a woman scorned."

With that lovely thought on my mind, I drifted back to sleep and into sweet nothingness, free of the reminders of my failings. When I woke again, the morning had just barely arrived. I sat up and took the few minutes still needed to let the sun come up enough to be able to drive without the aid of lights to pull out the map of Arkansas.

Using a dirty finger, I traced the line of the roads to find the best possible route to the next town. My best guess was it was about a thirty-minute drive from where I was, and if the size of the dot on the map were any clue, it was a very small town. This was a good thing. More than likely, I could find something to eat and a blanket, but I probably wouldn't run into anyone. Not that I didn't think I could handle myself when I inevitably did run into someone. I just didn't want to take out the extra time to have to deal with it. Any second I wasn't moving forward, Luke was getting further and further away.

Folding the map, I shoved it into the glove compartment and looked out the window. Feeling confident enough that it was safe to get back on the road, I opened the door and hopped out. I stretched my aching limbs before walking around and climbing into the bed of the truck. Three faded-red gasoline canisters were tossed precariously about the bed. I kicked at two, already knowing they were empty, and picked up the third and last of the gasoline.

Looked like I forgot a very important component of traveling, which I needed to look for immediately or I wouldn't be going anywhere.

With a sigh, I hefted myself and the canister over the bed of the truck and to the ground. After opening the gas cap, I lifted the gasoline and started pouring it in. Within seconds, my arms began shaking. My heart started to beat quicker and my breathing slightly labored just with this simple task.

"First things first, you're finding food," I told myself. My stomach growled in answer. "Okay, you can shut up now. I'm working on it."

Emptying the last drop of fuel into the tank, I tossed the empty canister in the back of the truck and closed the gas cap. I did a quick survey of my surroundings before opening the door of the truck and climbing inside. I started the engine and backed the truck away from the trees I'd used as added coverage. Shifting into drive, I slowly made my way from the bumpy field to the paved road, which would lead me to the next town and to food so my damn stomach would shut the hell up.

Once I reached the smooth pavement, I reached over and turned on the stereo. There had been nothing but static for more than two years, but Jacob had a wide variety of CDs and it helped to keep me awake and prevent my mind from wandering where I didn't want it to go. I put in a greatest hits of the 80s CD, sadly knowing every word to every song. I wished I could blare it and sing at the top of my lungs like I used to as a teen, but I wouldn't be able to hear anything around me and I also didn't have the energy to spare.

As if on cue, my stomach clinched painfully. I tried to remember the last time I had eaten anything. It had to have been the day after I hit the road and today would be day four away from the orchard. Well, hell. No wonder I was weak and shaky. Three days without food would make anyone feel like a slug.

"Dumbass." I shook my head at my own ignorance.

My eyes kept moving from each window and to the rearview mirror, making sure I had an eye on everything going on around me. As the miles passed by, it was hard not to notice the stunningly beautiful scenery. Tall trees wrapped around the hills and valleys along both sides of the road, making the road feel like a wide tunnel. I bet when spring fully came in bloom and the trees were bursting with leaves it would be flat-out majestic. *Not that it matters to me*, I reminded myself. I didn't plan on being around for the spring bloom.

Coming around a curve, I slammed on the brakes, screeching to a halt. Out of freaking nowhere, I was in a town. No joke. There were vast amounts of trees, then all of a sudden, there I was amid buildings and houses. Fully alert, my heart pumped wildly as I debated what to do. I couldn't see anyone, but that didn't mean there wasn't anyone around. No road blocks, which was a really good sign.

I lifted my foot off the brake and turned on the first road to my right, parking alongside a rundown consignment clothing store. Turning off the truck, I pulled out the keys and stuffed them in my pocket. I reached down and took a handgun out of the duffel bag before zipping the bag and throwing a jacket over it and exiting the truck. I decided it would be best not to lock the doors; it would be easier to get back in if something went wrong. I pushed the driver's side door closed with my hip to keep the sound to a minimum.

Standing still, I listened for any hint people could be close. Besides the wind blowing leaves around, all was quiet. Quiet wasn't exactly a good thing. It meant either no one was around—which would be good—or they were waiting for the perfect time to introduce themselves. Which would undoubtedly be bad.

I had no desire to make new friends today. Or enemies, for that matter. And if I heard one banjo I was getting the hell out of there.

Keeping my hand tight on the handle of the gun against my thigh, I moved to the front of the building and did a visual sweep of the area. Across from the consignment shop was an old gas station with a tire shop attached to it. Chances were it would have a vending machine or a rack of junk food I could pillage. Biting my bottom lip, I wondered if it would be wise to try to cross the street considering it would leave me in the open for at least twenty seconds. Twenty seconds wasn't a long time, but plenty of time for a sniper to take me out.

Quit being a baby and go, my stomach cried.

Be smart, Sis, Jacob's voice said in my head.

I closed my eyes and gritted my teeth at the sound of his voice. "Both of you, leave me the hell alone."

Stepping a few feet away from the building so I could see what was next to the consignment shop, I kept my eyes darting from one place to the next. Faded words announced the building as Benny's Diner. I moved to the front door and peeked in before trying the door. Of course, it was locked.

I sighed and my stomach growled its annoyance as I audibly growled my own. Turning, I scanned the area once more, paying close attention to the windows of the houses, but not a curtain or blind had moved an inch. Was it really a possibility the town was deserted or everyone was dead?

Yeah, it *was* possible.

Just highly unlikely.

I walked back around to the side of the building where the truck was parked and stopped at the entrance of an alley leading behind the buildings. I moved around until I found the second door. Testing the handle, it immediately gave.

Bingo.

Raising the gun as high as I could without making my arm shake like a rubber band, I opened the door wide enough to let the sunlight disintegrate the shadows of the room. I really wished I had a flashlight, but beggars can't be choosers, and my stomach was begging.

Hurry up! my stomach screamed.

My lips tightened across my teeth in frustration as I stepped across the threshold and into the back of the diner. The first thing that came into view was a rack of canned foods, but instead of going straight to the food like my gut begged, I did the smart thing and secured the area first. Another thing dear ol' Luke taught me.

Once it was all clear, I walked my bitching stomach to the rack and pulled down the first can and walked it to the back door. I held it up to the light to read the label.

Black-eyed peas.

Oh, yum!

"I deserve this," I mumbled before walking back to the kitchen and rifling through the drawers for a can opener. Once I found one, I yanked an armful of cans from the shelf and left the diner, closing the door behind me. I walked to the truck, my eyes constantly scanning, then tossed all but one of the cans to the bed of the truck and kept one with me to eat down the road.

Deciding it would be best if I stayed to my current side of the street, I looked toward the road behind the diner. There were a few houses and cars relatively close by. Maybe I could find fuel in one of them, and there was bound to be a blanket in one of those houses. Guessing it would be safer to walk than to have the extra noise of restarting the truck, I pulled a gas can from the bed of the truck and headed out.

Making my way to the first house, I walked to the backyard, looking, but not finding a water hose. I kept going to the house next door and moved to a jog when I spotted a hose hanging on a hook. Setting the canister down, I pulled a pocketknife from my jeans and cut a long section from the hose. Closing the pocketknife, I shoved it back into my pocket while searching the area.

Always watching.

Always scanning.

Always on alert.

It was unbelievably freaking tiring, not to mention annoying!

It didn't help that my hands were shaky and my bitch of a stomach wouldn't shut the hell up. *Why can't this be easy? Why can't Luke just be found so I can kill him and finally die already?* Nothing ever freaking went my way.

I took the hose and canister to the first vehicle and opened the gas cap. Shoving the hose in until it hit the bottom, I put my mouth over the other end and sucked hard. I continued sucking until I heard bubbling and felt the fuel coming up the hose and quickly moved the hose into the top of the canister, letting it fill.

Yes! Finally. A freaking break.

Oddly enough, this town hadn't been cleaned out like the rest I had passed through in recent days. I scrunched my eyebrows. Did that mean the bastard and his band of thugs hadn't come this way, or did they just not stop? With all the supplies they stole from *my* home, they definitely had plenty to eat. Which meant the only thing they would need to stop for was fuel, and there was obviously still fuel here.

Shaking the hose, willing it to flow faster, I shifted from one foot to the next. I needed to hurry before they got too far ahead.

After I filled both canisters, I did a little B & E into the nearest house, taking the first blanket I found. I rushed back to the truck with both of my hands full. Tossing the gas can into the bed of the truck, along with the cut hose, I jumped into the truck throwing the blanket to the passenger side. Once I did a quick inventory to make sure everything was in the duffel bag, I shoved the key in the ignition. It was either habit or a sixth sense, but I looked into the rearview mirror. When I did, I sighed, knowing the run of good luck I had had with the fuel and the food had come to a screeching halt.

The rearview mirror pointed to the front of the tire shop where a man stood with a shotgun resting casually on his shoulder, the barrel pointing toward the sky. He seemed cautiously relaxed yet his eye squinted watchfully, unlike the woman who was next to him hopping and waving her hands above her head while smiling. Smiling!

With my eyes still glued to the rearview mirror, I tried to turn over the engine, but nothing happened. The freaking truck was dead. Trying not to show any outward sign of emotion, I gripped the steering wheel until my knuckles hurt.

Dammit!

Doing my best not to lose my shit, I kept my eyes on the mirror while reaching over and picking up the handgun, placing it on my lap. Biting the inside of my bottom lip, I tapped the side of the gun with my finger. They weren't moving. The woman was still grinning and oddly, still waving. The guy was resting a hand on the girl's shoulder. Possibly to keep her back? I wasn't sure.

What the hell is going on?

The way I saw it, I had two choices. I could get out of the truck calmly and see why in the hell this woman was waving like a loon, or I could come out guns blazing and hope for the best. Though, if I went guns blazing, I doubted I could figure out what these people obviously did to my truck. And there was no way I was leaving without Jacob's truck.

If I played nice, yet smart, I might weasel out information from them, too. They could even know if Luke's convoy came through recently.

Deciding my options were limited, I let out a defeated breath and opened the truck door.

"Time to meet the locals."

13

Staying close to the bed of the truck for cover, I stopped before reaching the tailgate. No way was I going to put my body in clear view until I knew what they wanted. They started to move forward. The woman—who couldn't have been more than twenty—stayed next to the man, but her excitement hadn't dwindled in the least. The man, who looked to be close to my twenty-six years—maybe a few years older—had a hand on the woman's forearm, keeping her close to him. Both looked like normal, everyday people, except the man had one hell of a shiner on his left eye.

I waited, not saying a word, but I didn't have to because the cute, blonde young woman started talking as soon as they crossed the street. The guy put a hand out to stop them about twenty feet away from me.

"Hey there! I'm Daisy and this is Josh," she said with a rainbow wave and an abundant Southern twang. "Hope we didn't scare you." Without acknowledging her, my gaze shifted from her to the man standing to her side, but Ms. Bubbles went on. "You headin' to Canaan?"

Tilting my head slightly, I moved my eyes back to her. This was not a town I recognized from the map and I'd studied every town this side of Little Rock. "Doesn't look like I'm going anywhere, does it?"

"Sorry 'bout that," she said with a grimace. "Josh will get you fixed right up in a few."

Suspicions confirmed, my anger rose, but I tamped it down. My head felt fuzzy and black spots were dotting my vision. I absolutely didn't have time for bullshit. I needed to eat and drink something before I fell flat on my ass, perfect for the waiting vultures to pick my bones clean.

"Josh, how about you go ahead and fix it up right now and I'll be on my way?"

Daisy looked up to Josh and his lips thinned. He did not look happy, but Daisy went on. "The thing is… we need a favor first."

My eyebrows shot up. "Do you now? That's interesting. Does Josh speak?"

Laughing like I'd just told a hilarious joke, Daisy said, "Well, duh. We thought it would be best, since you're a woman and I'm a woman, that I do all the talking so you don't get, you know, intimidated."

Smiling, I said between gritted teeth, "The thing is, Josh doesn't intimidate me." Daisy's smile dropped a few inches and Josh's body went still. "What's this *favor* you want so I can be on my way?"

Daisy's hands rested on her narrow hips. "Well, I need a ride to Canaan."

My eyebrows shot skyward. "You need a ride… to Canaan?"

Daisy nodded with another smile.

"And exactly where *is* Canaan?" The spots were getting bigger, blocking parts of my vision, so I casually leaned against the side of the truck, waiting for her response.

She turned to Josh and smiled. I noticed their hands were clasped together now. They were at ease, with each other and with me. Odd. Or not so odd if they're used to seeing new people. "You're not from 'round here, are you?"

Again, I didn't answer, but I did pinch my lips together. I'd be damned if I gave a stranger information about myself. I'd made the unfortunate mistake with Luke and I wouldn't do it again. This was a new world and new rules applied. Anything and everything which could be used against us, would be.

"Canaan is a new town. Well, it was an old town that's new again if that makes any sense? Everybody goes there to get stuff now. The people are real nice and help everyone they can. I bet you'd really like it there. Everyone likes it there," she said, trying to sell me on the place.

So, Canaan had a marketplace. Luke had told me there were communities forming areas like that across the country, forgoing larger cities which held too many dead bodies and too large of an area to keep protected from looters and such. At least it was one thing he told me that was the truth. I would bet everything—not that I had anything to bet—Luke and his thugs were headed there, if not there already. No doubt to trade some of the food they stole from my home for more fuel or ammunition.

I imagined they used a lot of ammo killing innocent people along the way.

"How far away is that?" I asked, blinking away the rapidly increasing spots in my eyes. This needed to be settled, fast. I needed to sit down.

"'Bout a half a day away, I guess," she answered looking to her partner. He nodded his agreement. Her eyes sparkled in awe at Josh, like his nod said remarkable things, before turning back to me. "We have some people already there who can bring me back. Josh can't leave the house unprotected and it would save on gas. See, we're planning on moving to Victory, a little town outside Canaan, but we have a lot of stuff to move with us so it's takin' some time. Oh, and we could give you food and I'm real good company. I'm Daisy, by the way. Did I already tell you that?"

Ignoring the question and the queasy feeling in my stomach, I stated, "And you'll fix my truck."

Josh nodded an affirmative. I was seriously beginning to doubt his ability to speak.

"So you'll take me with you to Canaan then?" Daisy asked.

Thinking about the nasty black-eyed peas tossed in the floorboard, I curled my lips. Some food that didn't taste like a horse's ass would be good, and I could probably pry additional information from her about Canaan. If Luke was there, I didn't want to accidentally bump into him when I wasn't prepared. I looked back to her bubbly face and smiled, feeling like my face was about to crack from the unfamiliar movement. "Sounds good."

"Let's go get you something to eat and Josh'll get your truck fixed right up." Daisy walked right up to me and held out her hand.

Did she expect me to hold her hand? Not going to happen. Instead, I put the gun in the waistband of my jeans and turned to Josh. "I'm going to assume you don't need my keys to get the truck fixed since you didn't need them to keep it from starting, right?"

"Don't need them, but you'll need to move the truck over to the gas station in a few so I can fill it up and load the back." His voice was deep and gruff, like he didn't use it often. With Daisy around, I assumed he didn't get much of a chance.

Walking backward to the door of the truck, I opened it. "I need to get my bag first."

"You don't need anything in that bag right now," Josh said, stepping closer in warning.

Obviously, he'd checked out the inside of the truck and knew I was packing enough heat to take out ten men. Giving him my best deadpanned look, I reached for the bag and pulled it out. "I hope not."

Chapter Two

Scraping the rice and beans from the bottom of the bowl, I lifted the spoon to my mouth and chewed the last bite while watching Josh load the back of my truck with supplies they intended to trade at the market. Placing the empty bowl on the counter where I was perched close to the door, I hopped down and moved to the window. For the first time in the past few days, I didn't sway or get lightheaded.

Daisy took Josh a bottle of water and gave him a quick kiss while wearing her ever-present smile, before coming back inside where I waited. "Did you get enough to eat?"

"Yeah, thanks. Hey, did a group of cars come through here recently? A military looking truck could've been with them."

For the first time since I meet her, Daisy's mouth moved to a frown and, I'll be damned, she looked angry. "There was a group came through yesterday. One of those jerks was the one who punched Josh." She shook her head. "They were stealing the gas when Josh found them. One of the guys forced Josh inside here, told us to stay quiet. Josh argued with him, but the guy said to shut the hell up before we got hurt. Josh pushed him and the man hit him. Then he walked outside, argued with someone, and then left."

It had to be them. Daisy and Josh might not have realized it, but they were lucky to be alive. She was lucky Josh hadn't been ripped from her life like Jacob had been ripped from mine. "What did the guys look like?"

"The one who came in here and hit Josh was big, real big, like a football player. Short, dark hair. Pretty eyes. If he hadn't been such a jerk I would have thought he was hot. Not as hot as Josh, of course," she said, her eyes widening like she'd just betrayed her man.

Luke. It had to be, but why would he tell them to keep quiet? It didn't make sense, but did anything Luke did really make sense? Maybe he planned to come back, apologize for hitting Josh and worm his way into their fold, entice Daisy away from Josh, make her fall in love, and then destroy everything they had.

"What time of day did they come through?" I asked, ridding my mind of images of Luke with another woman.

She shrugged. "I don't know. Probably around noon." Daisy studied me for a moment. "Why are you asking? You're not with them, are you?"

"No, I came across them before and just want to stay clear of them." This was true, not the whole truth, but all the truth she was going to get out of me.

My explanation must have been enough to ease Daisy's mind because she changed the subject. "Are you sure you got plenty to eat? I can make more before we go."

"I'm good," I said before stepping out of the shop and into the warm sun. I walked to the bed of the truck, opposite of Josh, and looked inside. It contained five closed boxes. I almost asked what was in them, but I really didn't care. We needed to hit the road. Being a full day behind Luke didn't sit well with me.

Josh added another box then rested his forearms on the truck and considered me with understandable trepidation. "She's a good girl."

I nodded, agreeing with him because from everything I had witnessed so far, she was. Poor girl didn't know how life was anymore, but sadly, one day she would certainly learn. "I can see that."

"She's naïve," he clipped. "She trusts too easy."

I swallowed and nodded my awareness. "I used to be like that, too."

His eyes bore into mine, cold and severe. "I want her to stay that way."

I understood him perfectly. He loved her just the way she was and didn't want me changing her. I wasn't the one he had to worry about. "She's safe with me."

Daisy bounced up to his side, her happiness breaking the tension emanating across the bed of the truck. He instinctively wrapped his arm around her shoulders and pulled her close to him, just like Luke used to pull me close. My throat tightened and I looked away. "Ready?"

"Road trip!" Daisy declared, raising both hands above her head.

Fighting back an eye roll, I walked to the truck and climbed inside, taking out the gun and placing it in my lap. I forced down the lump resting in my throat as I watched Josh look down at Daisy and run a thumb across her cheek before bending down and kissing her. Daisy leaned back and said something to him, making him smile. The smile morphed his entire face. It made him softer, gentler, and well, attractive.

He walked her to the door and helped her inside. He gave her another quick kiss and nodded to me before taking a step back. Nodding in return, I started the engine and got us on the road before they could make a fuss about parting. It didn't take long for Daisy to turn her bubbly personality my direction.

"You gonna tell me your name, or do I have to give you one?" Daisy asked kicking off her shoes and crisscrossing her legs in the seat.

"Roni, well, Veronica," I told her flatly, keeping my eyes on the road, hoping to deter her from further conversation.

"Veronica," she repeated. "That's a pretty name."

Reaching over, I turned on the stereo, hoping she would get the hint that I wasn't down for a game of twenty questions. Alas, she did not. Instead, she raised her voice above the music. "How old are you?"

Pretending I couldn't make out what she was saying, I shook my head and kept my sights straight ahead. Daisy reached over and turned the music down.

This was going to be one hellacious long trip.

"I *said*, how old are you?" She smiled bright as the freaking sun. Too bad I didn't have any sunglasses.

Okay, I guessed the only way to get through to her was directly. "Listen, Daisy, you needed a ride and I needed to find out more about Canaan. You seem like a sweet girl and all, but I'm not in the market for small talk."

Her face visibly slacked and her eyes dropped to her folded legs, making me feel like I kicked a puppy. "Yeah, I understand."

After at least an hour of silence—even through refueling the truck—I tried to think of a way to ask about the market without sounding like a total asshole. I should have handled her with a little more care if I wanted to get information out of her. Not to mention what happened to me wasn't Daisy's fault, and she was probably going to get disappointed by more than her fair share of people and I didn't want to be one of them.

"How long have you and Josh been together?" I asked, trying for a cheerful voice, which ended up sounding like my lungs were full of helium.

Daisy turned from the window and faced me with deserved suspicion. Dammit.

"About a year." She turned and stared out the window again.

"That's a long time," I said, because at Daisy's age, it was. "How did you two meet?"

This time when she turned to me, some of the gleam was back in her eyes. "I was at college when it all happened and my mom came and got me from Texas. We were on our way back to Alabama when we got a flat just outside town and we didn't know what in the world we were going to do and wouldn't you know it, he happened to drive by. He was so handsome and sweet. It was like cupid flew right over me and let loose a whole bunch of arrows. He must've got hit, too, 'cause we were in love right there on the side of the road."

"That's sweet," I forced out. *Oh, this poor girl. She is more naïve than I first thought.* "And where's your mom?"

"She's at the market in Canaan. She just loves Josh. Well, she does *now*. That took a while, but he managed to win her over." Daisy's smile was bright again.

Good. This was good. We were finally going to get somewhere.

"Your mom's at the market?" I asked, keeping my tone light and conversational.

"They left yesterday morning," she said with a nod. "You're gonna want to stop in the next town. I know people there."

"Uh, *what*?" My eyebrows shot up. That was *not* part of the plan, but the sun was beginning to set and we did need to get settled for the night. Just not with her "people." "I don't think that's a good idea."

She laughed. "Stop being such a worry wart. We always sleep at the lodge in Victory when we're coming through. That's how we decided we wanted to live there. They're good people. Just trust me on this."

Trust me.

Trust me. The same worthless words written on a note left for me from Luke after he killed my brother. I would never, *ever*, make that mistake again. Those words didn't mean shit to me anymore. "No."

Daisy watched me, her face growing serious. She didn't look like the same young girl from a few minutes ago.

Her brown eyes seemed wiser than her appearance. "What happened to you?"

Maybe I was wrong and this girl *wasn't* as naïve as I first thought. I swallowed the bile rising in my throat and kept my eyes on the road. "Life. Life fucking happened."

After another uncomfortable minute of her scrutinizing me, she said, "How about we stop there for food and you can get a feel for them, and if you're not comfortable after that, we'll find somewhere else to sleep?" Even though it had only been maybe two hours since I last ate, my stomach growled. Daisy laughed. "See. I'm hungry, too. We're almost there. Give it a chance?"

I rolled my eyes and sighed. "Okay, but the first weird feeling I get, I'm gone. With or without you."

Daisy beamed. "Great! Seriously, you are so going to love it."

"I doubt that," I murmured under my breath.

* * * *

"You going to come do-si-do with me?" Daisy asked, moving both hands up and down while shuffling her feet around in an odd mix between river dance and hillbilly stomping. If I weren't freaked way the hell out, I would probably be laughing at her. Instead, I had my back pressed to the wall, staying close to the exit while observing everyone around me.

Twelve people—not including Daisy and me—were there. Young, old, male, female, and they were all laughing and having a great ol' time. I could've been wrong, but I was pretty positive I was also the only one carrying a gun. Daisy begged me not to bring it in, but I refused to leave it behind. In the end, we compromised and I concealed it in the waistband at the back of my jeans.

The home, which Daisy called "the lodge," was large; I guessed it might have been the mayor's house or someone equally important in town because it was by far the largest home I saw around. Daisy told me it was where everyone gathered for meetings and meals or when peaceful people needed a place to sleep for a night or two. I thought it sounded creepy and half-expected there to be some sort of cult or commune waiting to brainwash me to become one of them.

See all the smiling faces, I hadn't yet disproved that theory.

Daisy had gone in first and after just a few minutes, poked her head outside and waved me in. At that point, I was nearly nervous enough to drive away, but I sucked it up enough to at least check it out and maybe get a bite to eat. Even before I walked through the door, a sound stopped me dead in my tracks. A sound I'd forgotten ever existed and never thought I would ever hear again. It was the beautiful sound of children laughing, filling the air like music. Once the shock was over, I went inside, only to be shocked yet again. People were milling about, preparing for dinner or talking amongst themselves. A few waved and they all smiled at me, not an ounce of trepidation from them. No one came up to me, though. Probably by Daisy's beseeching. I was appreciative, because I was beyond freaked out.

But when the kids smiled at me, I couldn't help but smile back.

Within minutes of walking inside, I was shown to the bathroom where a washbasin sat filled with water for me to clean up for dinner. While scrubbing my hands, I only glanced at the mirror, not recognizing my reflection and not really caring that I looked like I had been homeless and unkempt for months rather than days. I *was* surprised the children hadn't screamed bloody murder at first sight of me. With them in mind, I took my hair out of the ponytail, used my fingers to comb it, and refastened it.

By the time I made it out of the bathroom, Daisy had made me a glass of lemonade from a powder mix and a bowl of deer stew, complete with potatoes and carrots. I ate in the corner of the room, where I stayed until Daisy tried to talk me into a hoedown.

"No, I am *not* dancing with you," I said with wide-eyed horror.

Plopping down next to me, Daisy and I sat in silence while listening to the thrown-together band of a guitar, harmonica, and spoons. Yes, I said spoons. "You okay with staying here?"

Instantly, any relaxation I had managed to muster in my corner of the room vanished. "I don't know."

Releasing an exasperated sigh, she nudged my shoe with hers. "I know it's hard for you, and I'm not asking you to tell me why, but if you don't want to stick out like a major sore thumb in Canaan tomorrow, you're going to need to chill way out. They have security there who will literally follow you around like a lost puppy if they feel like you're up to something, or in your case, if they're worried you're about to go on a mass murdering spree and slaughter everyone." She said the last part gently as she patted the top of my hand like she was concerned I might snap any second.

I blinked slowly, letting her words sink in. *Shit. Security?* Remembering my reflection, I could see how people might think I could go nuts because, well, I *could* go nuts at any time. The thing I hadn't planned on was security stalking around and I should have anticipated it. "Do they have some sort of checkpoint or something?"

Daisy nodded. "Uh huh. It's not a pat-you-down sort of thing unless you're giving off the heebie-jeebies vibe." She looked me up and down like she fully expected for me to receive a pat down.

Could I do it? Could I pretend to be or feel like a normal person anymore? Guess there wasn't much of a choice if I wanted to get to Canaan and catch up with Luke.

The music slowed down and two sets of couples moved to the makeshift dance floor and swayed closely together. My heart constricted at the intimacy, and I looked away from the couples and back to Daisy. "I'm ready to get some sleep. Where do I go?"

With a sad smile, she stood and looked down at me. "Whatever it is, eventually, it will get better."

It was time to practice the whole "act normal" thing, so I smiled and nodded. "Thanks, Daisy."

She led me to a small bedroom with a twin-size bed on the second floor. She lit a kerosene lamp perched atop an antique oak dresser with a mirror, illuminating the room. The bed sat on hardwood planked floors and a couple of oil paintings hung on the stark white walls. The single window was adorned with heavy green curtains, giving the space a cozy feeling. With the lantern lights and the décor, it felt like stepping into another century.

Daisy left but returned shortly with another woman. They carried a basin of hot water, toiletries, a nightgown, and clean clothes for the next day. Daisy advised me to go ahead and throw out the clothes I currently wore and the people there, including her, had gifted what I might need.

I think it was her sweet way of saying, *Please take a bath, we all think you stink.*

Murmuring my thanks, I locked the door behind them and began removing the clothes from my too-thin frame. The same clothes I had worn four days ago when Jacob was ripped from me. The same jeans with brown stained knees from the pools of my brother's blood I'd knelt in on my living room floor. Once naked, I dipped a washcloth in the basin of water, added soap, and began to scrub. I even took the time to wash my hair.

Before a few days ago, I wasn't like this. I cared about how I looked and, well, smelled. The last thing I wanted was to slow myself down with trying to find a place to clean up during the day and when nighttime came, it was too dangerous to even attempt. Not that I would have tried even if it would have been safe. There wasn't a point in caring anymore, not when I would be dead in a few days. *Hopefully.*

What I looked like didn't begin to come close to how I felt. I felt dead inside—the marrow of me replaced by hard bitterness. So why would I care how I looked? All of the soap in the world couldn't remove the filth in my soul.

But Daisy was right. Unfortunately, I *had* to care right then. If I didn't, I would get noticed and not in a good way. I had to do whatever it took to bring him down.

Slipping the too-large nightgown over my head and onto my freshly scrubbed body, I crawled into bed and pulled the covers over me. Comfort surrounded me in its tight, oppressive embrace, trying to suffocate the sourness coursing through me. Within seconds, I couldn't breathe. I didn't deserve to be comfortable when my brother was dead and it was my fault. Dear God, they didn't even leave his body so I could bury him next to our parents.

How could he lie in rest? How could I?

I choked back the tears I felt coming but refused to allow myself the fulfillment of mourning him with tears. I squeezed my eyes shut and took deep breaths, willing myself to be a stronger person. Before I realized what was happening, I fell asleep only to be jolted awake by dreams of Jacob's dead body asking me how I could do this to him. With shaking limbs, I pulled the quilt to the floor and lay beneath the soft fabric. The wooden floor was cold and painfully hard through my nightgown, biting into my skin. It was exactly what I needed and nothing less than I deserved.

Chapter Three

The next morning, I was up before the sun, as usual. My neck and back were stiff, but I didn't have any more nightmares once I found my way to the floor. I would rather sleep in discomfort for the remainder of my days if it meant I didn't have to suffer as many nightmares.

After making the bed, I dressed in the clothes Daisy left for me, which had to be hers because the jeans fit almost perfectly at the waist, but I had to roll up the bottoms to keep them from pooling on the floor. The shirt was a light blue fitted t-shirt with an animated penguin on the front.

It was cute. I was not.

Loosely braiding my clean hair in front of the mirror, I scrutinized the dark circles under my eyes. Today was show time and I looked like a well-accessorized zombie. Sadly, my current look was about a hundred times better than it had been just twenty-hours earlier. Taking a peek at the water basin, I cringed at the dark water. Picking up the dirty water, I tiptoed to the bathroom, took care of business, and used the dirty water to flush the toilet. When I made it to the kitchen downstairs, I was surprised to find an older woman—probably in her late sixties—standing over the kitchen island, rolling out dough. At this early hour, I imagined everyone would still be in bed.

Glancing in my direction, she pointed the rolling pin she held toward the stove. "There's hot water on the stove and we have instant coffee, or if you're a tea drinker, we got that, too, but it's that nasty Earl Grey. How in the world Earl Grey made it to the south is beyond me. To me, if it ain't Lipton, it ain't tea."

"I'll just have the coffee. Thank you," I forced myself to say and made a cup of coffee, adding three heaping scoops of sugar. I wasn't much of a coffee drinker, but anything was better than water. With the long day ahead of me, the added caffeine was welcomed. Sipping the coffee, I moved to the island to watch the woman work. "Is there anything I can do to help with breakfast?"

She gave a huff of a laugh as she placed discs of dough on a baking sheet and put them in the wood stove. "There's always something that needs done around here. Do you know how to make powdered eggs?"

I faked a smile, testing it out, and picked up a cardboard canister which had a photo of three eggs on the front and directions on the back. "I think I can handle it."

"Good, I appreciate the help."

As I started the eggs, I was informed the woman's name was Lydia and she had a husband, George, who'd also survived. She wore a mother's ring with three birthstones in it and I didn't ask, but I guessed her children had fallen with the rest of humanity. Yet, there she was, cooking breakfast for strangers while telling stories about all the people of Victory. I couldn't begin to fathom how she was still functioning. What kept her going? Was it because she still had her husband, or was she just that strong?

Am I just that weak?

Already knowing the answer, I put the cooked eggs in a bowl and worked on turning powdered gravy into something edible. Lydia picked up a metal triangle and started banging the shit out of it with a little metal stick. Without stopping the assault on my eardrums, she walked to the back door off the kitchen and opened it. Within minutes, I could hear people closing in like a herd of cattle. Footsteps came from above, doors opened and closed, and happy voices filled the air.

It didn't take long for the kitchen to fill to capacity. I was glad to see how everyone waited for the children to make their plates and head to the dining room before they all dug in. Each and every last person either said "thanks for helping with breakfast" or "good morning." I wasn't sure how to act, but I didn't care for the extra attention. Daisy was the last one in line. Her smile was too bright for morning and her eyes sparkled.

It didn't take a rocket scientist to decipher what she was thinking. She assumed I was having some sort of social breakthrough and coming out of the dark place I had been. What she didn't understand was the darkness surrounding me was so thick it swallowed any light before it could reach me. These people were more than likely decent and the kids were wonderful, but my acceptance of them wasn't even a fraction of the hurt and anger filling my core. No, this socialization was just practice for my end game.

Moseying up beside me, she handed me a plate and told me I looked much better. I feared she would get emotional and try to hug me so I quickly moved around the island to fill my plate.

With our plates made, we walked side-by-side to the large table in a gigantic dining room. The kids sat to the side at a smaller table, laughing and eating. The adults were basically doing the same thing. There was enough room for us to sit on the bench; she went in first, and I sat on the edge.

The food was surprisingly tasty for being a meal of basically powder. Lydia's biscuits were the star, though, and far better than any I had ever attempted to make. I pulled off piece after piece, dipping them into the gravy, barely giving myself enough time to breathe between bites until I finished them off.

"Daisy, did you have any trouble with those guys who came through yesterday morning?" a friendly-looking guy from further down on the opposite side of the table asked.

My hand froze halfway to my mouth and my back went ramrod straight at the question.

"Not too bad. They were jerks, but left pretty quick," she said with a shrug then raised her head to the group. "I'm guessing they stopped here, too?"

"Stopped on the road asking how much longer 'til Canaan, then took off. Thank the heavens," a pretty, dark-skinned woman I put in her early forties said, "Did not get a good vibe from that bunch, that's for sure."

It had to be them.

I skimmed the children's table and thanked the heavens Luke and his thugs hadn't decided to come inside. There was no telling what could have happened if they had and the thought of these innocent kids being stuck in the middle churned my stomach.

"At least the big groups have stopped coming through," another said, but I was still looking at the children's table to notice who.

There was my opening to gather more information and attempt to figure out what was really going on compared to what Luke had told me. "Big groups?"

Lydia's husband, George, spoke this time, "Military, and most of them weren't exactly friendly. Biggest group had about fifty in it I'd say, and they decided this would be a good place to stay for a few days. By the time they left, we had nothing left, and I mean absolutely nothing. They even made a few of the young men go with them." He shook his head in disgust and ran a hand through what little hair he had left. "It's a damned shame."

Luke had told us General Wells liked to acquire strong, able-bodied men along the way to fight for them. No one knew who they were fighting or for what ridiculous cause, or at least Luke hadn't let me in on the information if he did. My best guess was Wells was a power hungry wannabe emperor.

One thing I *did* believe was General Wells had taken Adam, Luke's younger brother. Adam had Addison's Disease and had to have medicine to survive. General Wells would withhold the medicine from him if Luke didn't do his bidding.

Again, I spoke to the group, "Was there a young man with them who might have been taking medicine a lot or maybe tired a lot? Tall, dark hair, named Adam?"

All of them nodded in unison, smiles on their faces. My stomach lurched and my heart skipped. Luke had told Jacob and me so many stories about Adam, and his struggles with Addison's, that we cared for him without ever meeting him. I even went so far as to make him up a room at the farm for when Luke returned with him. I was truly glad he was okay. It wasn't his fault his brother was a liar and a murderer. I tried not to dwell on the fact I would be taking his last family member away from him, too.

"He's such a sweet young man. You know him?" Lydia asked.

"I knew his brother," I said, then took my empty plate to the kitchen before any more questions could be asked.

Cleaning my plate, my mind couldn't stop thinking about what killing Luke would mean for Adam. Would the General refuse to give Adam his medicine if they didn't have Luke working for them? If what Luke told us about the asshole was true, then no, he would probably toss Adam out to fend for himself.

There was an entire duffel bag full of his medicine still at the farm. Luke had collected the medicine on his journey from Colorado when he'd found us on the orchard. If Luke was being honest, he had planned to get Adam away from General Wells and would need enough medicine to keep Adam alive when he did. This was the *only* thing I believe he had been truthful about.

Biting my lip and rolling my eyes, I made a decision. I would either give Adam a note with a map telling him about the medicine and the farm, or I would take him there myself before I died. It was what Jacob would want me to do. It was what I *had* to do.

"Roni, you okay?" Daisy asked, pulling me from my thoughts.

Drying my hands on a towel, I nodded to her. "We need to get going."

"Sure... sure. I'll get my things together and meet you at the truck." She scratched her head for a moment and looked anywhere except at me. Wringing her hands in front of her, she finally looked at me. She opened her mouth to speak, and then closed it before shaking her head and walking away.

I had no idea what she wanted to say, but I was grateful she chose not to say anything or ask questions.

Heading back to the dining area, I murmured a thanks to everyone for their hospitality before making a mad dash outside before anyone could start a long session of goodbyes. I refilled the gas tank while Daisy stood on the front porch giving hugs and promising to be back in a few days.

This is the exact situation I tried to prevent.

Jumping in the truck, I started it up and pulled the handgun out of my waistband, placing it in my lap. I tapped impatiently on the steering wheel until Daisy opened the door and climbed inside. She barely managed to get the door closed before I put the truck in gear and hit the gas pedal.

"Lydia gave us a treat for the road," Daisy said, holding up two cans of soda. "She said if you tell anyone, it'll be the last one you get."

"Think it's still good?" I asked, my mouth watering at the thought of the acidy suds.

"Oh, yeah, they're still good. Lydia sneaks me one every time I come through. Sometimes I make up reasons to come through just so she will slip me one," Daisy told me, pulling the tab and handing me the drink.

Taking a sip, I fought back the urge to close my eyes as the sweet liquid invaded my system. Taking another sip, I couldn't stop a moan. Daisy and I both laughed. It felt foreign against my ribs, almost painful, but in a good way. Back when I lived in Tulsa, before the plague, I used to get sore muscles from that once-a-year workout, then got a massage two days later because I couldn't move—hurts, but feels good at the same time. If I'd let myself forget, our trip would've felt much like the road trips my friends and I used to take. Sadly, forgetting wasn't possible.

"How long will it take us to get to Canaan?" I asked, setting the can of soda into the cup holder.

"'Bout forty-five minutes," Daisy answered, pulling off her shoes and crisscrossing her legs in the seat. "What are you doing in Mississippi, anyway?"

We were in Mississippi already? Must be just over the border; guess I hadn't paid enough attention to how far we had gone. "Looking for someone."

"Oh? A family member?" She took a sip of her soda and went on. "We get a lot of people come through looking for someone."

"No. I don't have any family anymore. Just need to find someone," I said low, shifting in my seat.

"Yeah, I guess I got lucky. I never knew my dad and didn't have any siblings." The cab was quiet for a few minutes before Daisy cleared her throat. "You know, I met Adam while he was staying at the lodge. He was a sweet guy. I liked him."

Not liking where the conversation was going, I kept my eyes on the road and my mouth shut. I should have kept quiet about Adam at breakfast. It wouldn't be good if it got around that someone was asking about him. Luke might hear about it before I could dispense my revenge.

"I take it you know his brother?" She wasn't looking at me, and I wasn't sure if it was intentional or not.

"I used to," I said between tight lips.

"Did you date him or something?" she asked, her tone light.

"Or something," I clipped.

Daisy pumped a fist into the air. "I knew it! I remember Adam talking about his brother. The way he talked, his brother was the most amazing man on the planet."

Gripping the steering wheel tightly, I took a few seconds to control my temper and not show any emotion. I swallowed and let out a slow breath. "He would do anything for his brother."

Including killing mine.

I contemplated bursting her happy little bubble and telling her he was more than likely the same man who gave Josh the black eye, but what would it actually accomplish? It wouldn't take a rocket scientist to figure out who I was searching for if I did. Anonymity was my best option, and I wasn't going to do anything to screw up my best shot of catching him. In the current situation, low key was the *only* way to go.

Realizing she wasn't getting anything else out of me, Daisy let out a resigned sigh and changed the subject. "When we get to Canaan, I'll introduce you to my momma. She's a nurse and has a medical tent there to help people as much as she can since we haven't been able to find a doctor anywhere around, but momma is pretty much a doctor, anyway. She's one of the smartest people I know."

"I would like that, but I don't think I'll have time. I'm already a day behind, and I need to get a few things done in town before heading out," I explained.

If Jacob were alive, he would have loved the chance to meet and maybe learn from her mother. Hell, he would probably want to help her see patients and consider himself fully interned and ready to open his own medical tent by the end of the day.

"Well, maybe on your way back you can stop by and meet her then." The frown pulling on her face made her disappointment evident.

Dammit.   Seemed like I was getting good at disappointing her. "Yeah, I'll do that," I lied.

"Good." She sighed. "Man, I miss Josh already."

I gave a weak smile, remembering the same feeling just a few months back, before my life and everything in it went to hell for the second time. I was so in love, my world revolved around Luke. He was everything I never thought I could have. He had been living with us for a few months when it came time for him to leave to get Adam from the General and bring him back. I thought my heart was going to implode from the amount of constant pain I felt when we were separated.

I endured six weeks of continuous worry and longing before I saw him again. When I did, I wished he would have just stayed away. He took everything I hoped to have and everything I ever was and shattered it into pieces.

"I bet he misses you, too," I forced out, knowing it was what she needed.

"He'd better," she said with a dreamy smile.

At Daisy's insistence, we played multiple games of *I Spy*. It was torture, but it kept Daisy's mind busy enough to keep from asking personal questions. For the majority of the trip, I stayed relatively calm until vehicles began to come into view. On instinct, my hand went to the gun and my foot pressed harder on the gas pedal.

"Don't worry We're close to Canaan, so there will be more traffic."

Daisy was right; the closer we got, the more and more people we saw. And the more people we saw, the more I wanted to pull my gun out in preparation of defending us.

By the time we reached Canaan, my heart was racing, my palms were sweaty, and my shoulders ached from being so tense. Daisy directed me where to pull in line for the checkpoint. While in line, I stowed the handgun in the waistband at the back of my jeans and looked around. People milled about in every direction, waiting their turn to either get into town or carrying bags and boxes out. I felt like I was in an alternate universe where people were happy and life moved on while I was still living in the previous week.

It didn't take long to make it to the front of the line, and my anxiety to hit an all new level of high. One of the guards, equipped with a gun strapped on a belt at his waist, walked toward the truck. My hands itched to reach for my own gun, but instead, I rolled down the window with a silent prayer that it would go better than my expectations.

He bent his head and smiled. What was it with everyone smiling? Was there really that much to smile about? "Hey, ladies. Daisy! Hey, girl, how are you doing?"

"Hey, David. I'm good. This is Veronica, but she goes by Roni," Daisy introduced me.

I fought back the urge to close my eyes and groan. Last thing I wanted was my name spread around here. It was imperative to keep a low profile. I had to act normal and pretend I *wasn't* on a mission to assassinate my former lover. *Why hadn't I given Daisy a fake name?* "Hi. Nice to meet you."

Giving me a crooked smile, he leaned into the window frame. He was an attractive man. I guessed he was Hispanic, or at least had Hispanic in his lineage, because he had beautiful caramel-colored skin and chocolate-colored eyes. He was probably around my age, maybe a few years older. If I was honest with myself, he was on the really attractive side, but he was a man, so… that alone was enough for me to steer clear. "Nice to meet you, too."

"We have a bunch of boxes in the back. The usual." Daisy pointed a thumb toward the bed.

He leaned back without moving his arms. "Are you two staying in town tonight?"

"I am. Roni's not sure yet."

Inhaling deeply, I smiled and he winked at me. "If you decide to stay, you two should come to Rita's tonight. Daisy knows where it is."

Without waiting for an answer, he moved to the bed of the truck and opened a box, taking a quick look before telling us we were clear to proceed. I put the truck into drive and followed Daisy's directions to the next stop, which ended up being an unloading dock. Daisy jumped out and walked to a woman seated behind a table set up under an eave. They spoke and Daisy signed a paper on a clipboard before the woman gave her a plastic number. Daisy went inside the warehouse and out of view before coming out pulling a wheeled pallet with a makeshift handle.

The town appeared to be functioning quite well and I was impressed. I hopped out of the truck and started unloading the boxes from the back onto the pallet. Once finished, Daisy wrapped her thin arms around my shoulders and pulled me into a hug. *This is it.* I would probably never see her again. No, there was no probably about it; I would never see her again. She was a sweet girl, and I hoped she beat the odds and lived a great life full of love and babies—the life I once thought I had a chance at having.

Daisy pulled back and pinned me with her eyes. "You know, if you change your mind, Mom's tent is on Lincoln Street. I know she would love to meet you."

I gave her shoulder a squeeze. My chest tightened and I took a deep breath. I needed to get away from her; I didn't want a goodbye, either. "I'll try, but I really need to hurry and get back on the road."

"I know. Just… just be careful." Gripping her hands in front of her, Daisy's eyes welled up with tears. "Roni… whatever it is that you're going through, we're here for you when you're ready. Please don't do anything you can't take back."

Clearing my throat, I looked over her shoulder. "I'm fine, Daisy. Really."

"You really can be." Daisy pursed her lips. "You know where to find me."

Taking the handle of the pallet, she tugged until the wheels began to move. She walked down the road, sun shining down on her, her hair glowing like a halo. My breath hitched, so I put my hands on my hips, closed my eyes, and leaned my head back, letting the sun warm my face. I took a deep breath and my stomach dropped. It was a feeling I'd had many times before, and I trusted my gut.

Luke was there.

I could feel him like a heavy coat on my back.

My eyes flew open, searching the crowds. People laughed, couples held hands on the streets, children bounced a basketball, but no Luke. At least not anywhere I could see, but he was close. I would bet my life on it.

Pulling the keys from my pocket, I got in the truck and started it. I needed to find a place out of view to hide the truck since Luke could recognize it with one look. Driving around the block, I paid close attention to the faces and vehicles, searching for him. Finding a place to park close to a former printing company, I stopped close to an oversized dumpster, keeping the truck from view of passersby.

Keeping my eyes on my surroundings, I climbed out and pulled an extra handgun out of the duffel bag. I took a backpack and filled it with the gun and canned foods Daisy had left for me. Tugging on a hoodie, I hefted the backpack on my back, locked the truck, and started down the road.

It hadn't taken long to find the hub of the town; all I had to do was follow the noise. I found an empty picnic table and sat down so I could be an observer without attracting attention. I pulled a can of soup from my pack and opened it. Using a plastic spoon, thanks to Lydia, I began eating the cold vegetable soup. It tasted pretty terrible without being heated, but I kept shoving in one bite after the next. It served its purpose and that was all that mattered.

What I needed was a plan. The sun would be setting in the next few hours and I wasn't sure what the nighttime rules were in Canaan, so I needed to get moving. Picking up the empty soup can, I tossed it into the trash next to the picnic table. Looking from left to right, I wasn't sure which way I should go. My best bet was to look for the Buick Luke had been driving and see if it was still there. If I found it, I could use a trick out of Josh's manual and disable the car so he couldn't drive away.

Moving forward, I stopped a middle-aged couple and tried not to compare them to my parents. "Sorry to bother you. I'm new to town. Can you tell me if there's, like, a hotel or something here?"

The man smiled down at me. "There's a few. If you're alone, though, you want to stay away from the one on Dodson. There's a bar in it and it can sometimes get a little…

out of hand. There's a couple of places on… Honey, what's that street called by that antique shop?"

"Elm Street." The woman pointed past my shoulder. "It's about two blocks that way."

"Thank you," I told them, turning and walking toward the direction the woman pointed. I walked around the corner and smiled.

All I have to do now is wait for the sun to go down and find Dodson Street.

Chapter Four

Pulling the bill of the cap down on my forehead in efforts to hide my features, I stayed in the shadows as I made my way toward Dodson. It wasn't difficult to find the street; I was more concerned with being noticed. The streets throughout town were lit with lanterns perched on columns; I suspected the same lighting was used before electricity was discovered. It didn't cast a lot of light, but there was plenty to get around. I couldn't help but think of how much Jacob would have loved Canaan—all of these people in one place for him to meet and get to know. *Yeah, he would have loved this place.* Momentarily closing my eyes, snapshots of his smiling face filled my mind. His laugh, his hands, his eyes, his tears—all of it in a matter of seconds like a strobe of memories blinding me. I missed his smile so damned much. A smile this world was denied to ever see again.

A smile *I* would never see again.

Stumbling over myself, I opened my eyes and reached out for the sturdiness of a building. The brick skidded across my palm, tearing the skin. My chest contracted as my breathing came in quick pants. I had to get hold of myself and block thoughts of Jacob out of my head. I leaned my rear against the wall and bent forward, resting my hands just above my knees. With my head dropped down, I took slow, deep breaths until the dizziness subsided.

"You okay?" a deep, male voice asked.

"I'm fine. Thanks," I said, raising up to find three men staring at me. *Shit.* Slowly, I moved my hand behind me and gripped the handle of the gun.

"You shouldn't be out here alone at night," one of them said.

"I know. I'm meeting someone," I said, keeping my tone light and unconcerned, all the while inspecting each of their hands for possible threats. I figured I could get the drop on them if needed.

"Really? Who are you meeting?"

My mind raced and I said the first name that came to mind. "David from check-in."

"Oh, yeah? He's probably over at Rita's. Want us to walk you over there?"

Pushing off the wall, I opened my mouth to refuse when I saw it just behind them, a Buick. Luke's Buick. And it was parked in an alley across the street in almost complete darkness. Only the trunk was visible, but it was his. I knew it. I needed to get rid of these guys, quick. Luke could walk by at any second and I sure as hell didn't want him to see me before I saw him. Peeling my eyes from the car and to the three men in front of me, I smiled. "No, I'm good. I need to run a few errands first. Thanks, though."

"Well, be careful then. Most everyone 'round here are good people, but every now and then we get some assholes come through." They looked between each other and the ground. Clearly, they were concerned and didn't want to leave me alone. At any other time, I would have thought they were being chivalrous, but not now. Now, I just wanted to get away from them.

"Really, thanks, guys, but I'll be fine. I'll be quick and then I'll get to David." I pushed off the wall and walked past them, toward the music, without looking back. Rounding a corner into a dark alley, I waited until I was positive they left before sliding out and jogging toward Luke's car.

Trekking across the road, I slowed just before reaching the Buick. Adrenaline pulsed through me and I smiled but felt absolutely no joy. Scanning the area, I scurried to the driver's side door and pulled the handle; it released and the door opened. The idiot didn't lock it. Guess he thought no one would have the balls to mess with his stuff. He was correct. I did *not* have balls.

Sitting in the driver's seat, I felt around for keys but failed to find any. I opened every compartment in the front but came up empty. There wasn't so much as a piece of paper. Yet again, I wished I had a flashlight so I could see. I leaned over the front seat to the back. It was empty, but a large, dark stain covered the seat. My heart plummeted and anger burned my skin. It was Jacob's blood. Pinching my lips together, I turned and punched the dashboard before feeling around until I found the lever to the hood and pulled until I heard it *pop.* I got out and sneaked to the corner, checking for passersby before going back to the car and closing the door. I hurried to the hood and raised it.

Without a clue what Josh had taken from the truck to keep it from starting, I felt around blindly until my hand hit cables and tubes and started yanking. The blood pumped wildly in my ears and I couldn't stop a laugh from escaping the back of my throat, which sounded crazy to my own ears, but it was the first time since Jacob's murder I felt even a semblance of being alive. It just so happened the feeling surfacing happened to be on the psychotic spectrum. I shook my head. *What the hell, Roni? Pull your shit together.* When I felt satisfied the car wasn't going anywhere, I lowered the hood, climbed on, and bounced until I heard it click into place.

Jogging to the corner, I gripped the wires against my chest as I peered from left to right. Just as I was about to head across the street, I stopped. Luke prowled out of the glowing building where music was playing. Swallowing against the burn rising in my chest, it pained my soul to see how gorgeous he was. He was beautiful enough to make a smart girl turn stupid in one glance, and possessed a smile that could make her fall in love.

I used to be that stupid girl.

Not anymore.

Seconds later, a woman wearing too few clothes for such a cool night walked out behind him and called his name. He stopped and turned to her. He put his hands on his hips and she leaned in, resting her hands on his chest. He reached up and grabbed her wrists, peeling them off him, and took a small step back. I didn't want to witness anymore of Luke's exchange with his whore and anyhow, I need to leave before he turned around and caught me watching him.

Taking off across the street, I made it about a half a block away from the Buick when David rounded the corner smack dab in front of me.

What the hell? Am I a bad karma magnet or what?

"Hey, there you are," David said, his hands up and a smile on his sweet face.

I sneaked a peek over my shoulder, hoping the bill of the hat kept my face covered, finding Luke was walking away from the woman and in my general direction.

Shit. Shit. Shit!

Remembering I was still holding the wires, I shoved them in the front pocket of my hoodie and smiled at David. Call me crazy... Okay, I'll admit I *was* a little crazy, but I could feel Luke getting closer. It was that damn karma magnet working its illustrious magic. I had to do something quick or my entire plan would be shot to hell and he would live yet another day and I might not. Throwing caution in the wind, along with what little sanity I had left, I crashed into David, wrapped my hand around the back of his neck, and kissed him.

Stunned, it took him a second to react before he wrapped his arms around me, his warm body pressed against mine as he prodded my mouth open with his tongue. He was a good kisser; all gentle and caring. Poor David. He would have hopes with this kind of kiss. Hopes which would be dashed.

I was such a bitch.

No wonder karma had it out for me.

Opening my eyes, I looked to the side, watching Luke move to his car. I broke from the kiss and smiled up at David. "Good to see you again. Thank you."

I hated seeing the half-dazed look in his eyes and his goofy grin telling me he had just been smitten.

I turned and walked away. Then David royally screwed the pooch. "Roni?"

Damn Daisy for telling him my name. Damn me for telling Daisy my real name.

I began walking quicker. Turning ever so slightly, I saw Luke whip around to look at David. Dear, sweet, dumbass David called for me one more time.

"Roni, where are you going?" David asked, louder this time.

In a jog, I made it a full block away before rounding a corner and stopping. Peeking around the side, David was looking around, bewildered, and Luke was nowhere in sight. Taking in my surroundings, I realized I was in the perfect place to end it all. Luke was alone and, thanks to David, suspected there was something amiss. It was now or never. Do or die. Put up or shut up.

Taking off the cap, I scanned the road, waiting for Luke to come into view so I could lure him to the gates of hell. I was a siren and he was about to be led into the jagged cliffside. Okay, even *I* realized I was being overly dramatic, but the moment called for drama. My life had turned into a Shakespearian tragedy and the final curtains were about to be closed. I pulled out the handgun and gripped it in my hand just as a large hand snaked around my head and covered my mouth. My eyes widened and my body went stiff as Luke leaned down to my ear.

"First, I want to know what the fuck you were doing *kissing* that guy, and then you're going to explain what the hell you're doing in Canaan," he growled just before he pressed his warm lips to my neck.

Wait, he wants to know why I was kissing another man.

That's his big concern?

Waiting until his hand began to move from my mouth, I used all of my strength to send my elbow driving into his

57

gut. As he bent over, he released me, giving me the opportunity to whip around and pull up the gun. Remembering his vast abilities to get out of sticky situations, I took a few steps back to distance myself from him. When he stood, he started to take a step toward me until he saw the gun.

"Roni? What the…"

"Shut up!" There was so much I wanted to say, so much I wanted to scream, but seeing him watching me with confusion made all the words jumbled in my head. "Why did you do it?"

"I had to, sweetheart, but…"

I shook the gun at him. "Don't you dare! Don't you dare call me sweetheart."

"Okay, alright." His composed demeanor was pissing me off. He was talking to me like I was a rabid dog.

"You had to? For Adam, right? Your brother's life is more important than my brother's? He fucking *loved* you!"

"Calm down, Roni." His hands were up, the palms facing me in false surrender.

"Shut up!" I yelled. His mouth moved to a thin line and he growled. I lowered my voice, and most of the initial anger fled my pores, replaced by a bitter ache. "You didn't even leave him for me to bury."

"What?" He was shaking his head as if he couldn't understand my anger. "Roni, no."

"I said shut up." I didn't wait for him to start talking again. "After everything... everything we did for you... you bring them back to our home and kill my brother? Why didn't you just kill me, too?"

"He's not dead."

"So, now you're going to die because you didn't kill me, too. You should have killed me, Luke." His eyes locked with mine through the darkness of the alley. Then I felt it. The wealth of love I once felt, then lost, for him punched holes in my gut that could never be with anything except hatred.

One person's life wasn't meant to handle this much loss.

The loss of family. The loss of love. The loss of hope.

There was nothing left except the man standing before me who took my family, my love, and my hope and ripped it away.

Now, he was taking my humanity.

"Close your eyes, Luke," I instructed with a shaky voice.

He slowly shook his head and spoke in a pained voice. "He's not dead, Roni. He's not dead."

Numbness flowed in waves through the blood in my veins, the ebb never coming. "What?"

"I left you a note. I never thought you would think he's dead, Roni." He ran a hand through his hair. "Put the gun away and let me explain."

With the absurdity in his words, I laughed. "Oh, I get it, you sick son of a bitch. You want me to believe you again. Put the gun away so you can take it from me when my guard is down? I don't think so. Not this time, Luke. I saw you. I was in the barn and I heard the gunshots and I saw you dragging him out." My throat constricted as the memory of Jacob's limp body came to mind.

"He was shot in the leg, and I knocked him out so he would shut the hell up and they wouldn't shoot him again. That's what you saw, Roni. Jacob is alive. You know I wouldn't do that to him, to you. My God, Roni."

"Okay, prove it. Where is he?" I asked, still not believing him, but something deep inside felt like it was digging its way from the far reaches of my mind, trying to come out. But I recognized the alluring feeling—it was hope, and I was simply incapable of enduring it again. I just couldn't.

"They left yesterday. He's with Adam." I snorted, but he kept going. "I was on my way back to let you know what was going on."

I wanted to close my eyes so I could think clearly, but I didn't trust the bastard. *Is there a chance? A real chance*

Jacob is *alive?* The chances were minute. But, God help me, if there was even the smallest of chances he was telling the truth, I had to act accordingly until I found out for sure. Yet again, Luke had the upper hand with just a few words. I wasn't going to let myself believe it. Not when we had played Luke's game for so long.

If he wanted to play games, then I would be an all-star. I could force him to take me to Adam under the guise of finding Jacob before I put a bullet in him.

"Take me to him, then," I said, keeping my eyes trained on his chest. I didn't want to look at his face and have to see his lying eyes.

"I can't do that. They would hurt you, or worse." He put his hands down. "I can take you home and I'll get them both and bring them back."

"No, Luke. I don't think you really get it. *You're* not in charge anymore," I said, waving the gun in the air to make my point. "So, you have two choices. Take me to him, or I kill you now and I'll find him myself. And don't think I can't. I found you."

The dim light from the street lanterns bounced off the features of his face as he stared at me in ear-piercing silence. His jaw was clinched; the only hint he gave that he was pissed. *Good.* He'd finally realized I wasn't playing around. It was my way or the end of the road for him.

"You don't know what you're going up against."

I wasn't sure if he meant himself or the General, but either way, it was all the same to me. I would stand against the devil himself if it meant vengeance for Jacob.

So I returned the same words he said to me so long ago. "Luke, you don't know what a woman is willing to do when someone else has what she wants."

Chapter Five

Once Luke finally understood I was completely and utterly insane, he didn't fight when I escorted him from the alley with the gun to his back. "We can take my car," he said, pointing in the direction of the Buick.

"No, we can't." My mouth tipped up in the corners, feeling like I'd had one too many cups of tea with The Mad Hatter.

"They know my car. They won't think anything if I show up in it." Luke stopped and turned to me. His face was much clearer since we were under a street lantern, showing off his strong features. There was that chin I had hoped my sons would one day have.

Digging into the pocket of my hoodie, I came out with a handful of wires and tubes and shook my head. "I just don't think your car is going to start." I tossed the wires on the ground and he followed their path, staring at them, bewildered. "We'll take the truck."

"I need to get my stuff out of the trunk," he said, then turned and marched toward the car.

Rolling my eyes, I trailed behind him. "You don't need anything. I have all we'll need in the truck."

He didn't stop his progress. "I need my bag. Adam's medicine is in there."

He had to be talking about medicine he had picked up after he killed Jacob because I checked before I left and Adam's bag of medicine was still there. My worry was what else did he have in the trunk? He could have weapons, some sort of an alarm, and a dozen other things I hadn't thought of. I hurried and caught up with him.

"Wait. Give me the keys and I'll get the bag out of the trunk." I stood a distance away, not for a second forgetting how quick and powerful he was. "Toss me the keys."

Turning his cold-as-steel gaze on me, he rested his large hands on his hips. His look would undoubtedly strike fear in the hearts of most men, but not mine. Not anymore. I raised an eyebrow, daring him to challenge me. His chest rose, then fell, and he stuck his hand in his front pocket to pull out a set of keys. He watched me, his jaw ticking, before he tossed them in the air and almost directly into my opened hand.

When I reached the trunk, I waved him to the side, next to the building by the door. Lazily, he sauntered to the wall, crossed his arms over his chest, and leaned a shoulder against the brick. Satisfied he was far enough away and I could still watch his every move, I opened the trunk. There was a bag and a box. I pulled out the box first. It contained food—some of the food was from my home when he and his merry men had looted it—and bottles of water. Placing the box on the ground, I figured I could make Luke carry it, further obstructing him from trying to overpower me on the way to the truck.

Pulling out the backpack, I closed the trunk and rested it on top. Unzipping the bag was slow work, considering I refused to release the gun for any reason, but I finally managed. Reaching inside, I immediately felt the cold steel of a gun. My eyes shot to him, glaring. I pulled out the gun and stuffed it in my back waistband.

"I can see you really did need your backpack. No worries, I'll hold on to it for ya." Ignoring the shake of his head, I moved through the remaining items. There wasn't anything of immediate interest, so I slung the backpack over my shoulder and backed away. "Carry that box and let's go."

Hearing voices approaching, I lowered the gun while a group of drunks walked past us. My pulse pounded. I was sure at any second Luke was going to use the drunks to his advantage and either escape or tackle me to the ground.

Much to my surprise, he did neither.

Instead, he stood, box in his arms, staring at me with dejection in his eyes. *Dejection! How dare he.* How dare he look hurt when he'd caused this outcome. And why did he look hurt at all? He *used* me. He never loved me. I was a means to an end, a piece of ass along the way to freeing his brother.

"Let's go," I said through gritted teeth.

"You're really doing this?"

"Yeah." My eyes went a little crazy wild and I jutted my chin out. "I'm *really* doing this."

He bent his head down and shook it, like I was a petulant child he couldn't believe he was forced to deal with. I was to the point of reaching for my pocketknife to prod him into moving when he headed in the direction I pointed. His strides where wide and fast, causing me to hurry and catch up with him before he made it around the corner.

It was nothing less than a long, awkward walk back and even more awkward when I realized I hadn't thought of exactly what I would do when I got him back to the truck. Not even an hour earlier, if someone had told me I had found Luke and let him live, even temporarily, I would have told them they had lost their ever loving minds. But there I stood, ignoring him watching me while he waited to see what his next instructions were.

Did I have him drive so I could keep the gun trained on him, or did I drive so I could be sure we were heading in the right direction? I was pretty sure I was going to have issues no matter which I chose to do, so the question was which was the less dangerous of the two?

Pulling the keys out of my pocket, I unlocked the door and instructed him to put the box of food in the bed of the truck and tossed him the keys. "Get in, you're driving."

Luke let out a huff and climbed in the driver's side while I heaved myself into the passenger side. He started the truck and turned to me. "What now?"

Biting my bottom lip, I looked through the windshield to the night sky. We needed to get out of town so no one became suspicious and witnessed me holding a man at gunpoint, but it wasn't a good idea to do much traveling at night. "Just drive. I'll tell you when to turn."

He did exactly as told, which worried me some, but I wasn't giving him any chances of getting the upper hand. Once we made it out of town and on the road, I had him pull off into a campsite and cut the engine. I ordered him to take the keys out and toss them to me. Again, he did as he was told without complaint.

Now, he was watching me through the darkness of night and I was completely uncomfortable and doing my best not to show it. From the first moment I saw his face months ago, he had a captivating hold on me. He was like a fire blazing in the middle of a blizzard; I wanted to be close to feel the warmth, but I would eventually burn.

Next to me was the man I thought I was going to spend the rest of my life with and oddly enough, I still would. My life was just going to be vastly shorter than I had imagined a week ago. A week ago, I trusted him with everything. A week ago, my brother had trusted him, too. We were wrong.

And damn it all, he was still beautiful. It was so freaking hard to look at him and know the man I believed him to be was just a wicked façade. I was nothing more than a means to an end. The thing was, I just couldn't stop wondering, why target us? Why kill Jacob? Why say Jacob was still alive? All of it. Just why? I wouldn't ask, though. Asking would be fruitless. He wouldn't tell me the truth and even if he did, I wouldn't know the difference.

"I've missed you," Luke said, breaking the silence. Each word was like a clap of thunder in the silence of the cab. I closed my eyes and pretended *those* words, in *his* voice, didn't cut me deep. "The past seven weeks have been a living hell without you."

Oddly enough, I felt lonelier at that very moment than I had in my entire life. When I refused to react to his words, he continued. If he said much more, I wasn't sure I could keep from shooting him. "I was on my way back to you tonight. Everything went to shit last week. I'm so sorry for what happened, but…"

My head whipped around and I yelled, "Went to shit? Everything went to *shit*? You brought them to our home and *killed my brother*! And you call that going to shit?"

"I told you, he's not dead, sweetheart."

Unable to control myself, I laid my head back and began laughing. This sorry son of a bitch. "That's what you keep saying."

He shook his head and ran his hands over his face in frustration. "Because it's true."

There it was again—the twinge of hope trying to break free. If I wasn't afraid he would overtake me, I would have closed my eyes. I didn't want to be there. After days of hunting and planning to get where I was, I desperately wanted it to be over. "We'll see."

"You know I would have never brought them there if I had a choice."

"Stop." I sighed. He was the master of manipulation. On the short trip to the campsite, he'd probably already devised a fantastic story which had him being the tortured hero who had no choice. The pathetic thing was I was afraid I would believe him, even knowing better. "I don't want to hear it."

His full lips moved to a thin line and he shook his head. Slouching in the seat, he moved his legs until his feet were in the same floorboard as mine. He leaned his back half against the seat and half against the door, crossing his arms over his chest. Guess he was going to take a nap.

"Must be nice to sleep so easy," I murmured half to him, half to the world.

"It's going to be a long day tomorrow. I need to sleep and so do you," he said, his eyes remaining closed.

"I bet you would love for me to go to sleep, wouldn't you?" I glared at him, even though he couldn't see me through his lids. "Don't even think about trying to get the gun because I *will* shoot you."

"Then don't sleep." he said on a sigh.

"Trust me, I won't."

"Okay… then don't."

"I won't!"

"Shut up, Roni."

"You shut up, asshole," I maturely retorted while flipping him the bird.

****

"Sweetheart," Luke whispered in my dream. I smiled as I waited for his hands to touch me. "Sweetheart, wake up." *This must be Christmas morning.* It was one of my favorite dreams. Any second, I would open my eyes and Luke would be holding up the Polaroid camera he had bought me. It was my most favorite possession. Something nudged me, dragging me from the bliss of my dream. I wanted to bask in the dream, the memories of happier times, but the nudging wouldn't stop.

I hadn't yet fully awakened when realization of what was really happening hit me. I simultaneously jumped up and threw myself back and away from the threat, knocking my head into the window. His hands were up while I felt around in the seat for the gun. Finding it on the seat between us, I grabbed it and pointed it at him, my heart hammering in my chest.

Disappointment shown in his eyes, and he slowly put his hands on the steering wheel but kept his eyes on me. My breathing was labored and my hands shook. *How did I let myself fall asleep? What the hell was I thinking? And why didn't he take the gun while I was asleep?*

"Why didn't you take the gun?" I asked, my voice hoarse from a combination of sleep and thirst.

His eyes pierced mine as he spoke. "Since you won't go home, I don't want you anywhere else but with me. If you need the gun to make you feel *safe*, then by all means, keep the gun. But I need to piss, so you okay with me going, or do you want to go with me and supervise?"

Glaring at him, I reached over and took the keys from the ignition before motioning for him to get out of the truck. I had to pee, too, and couldn't leave him in the truck with a bag of hidden guns. He *would* find them. "I'll supervise."

"Thought so," he said, heaving himself out of the truck. Lifting his arms over his head, Luke stretched, causing his shirt to rise up. I huffed and rolled my eyes. He was, I had no doubt, showing his abs on purpose, knowing what his abs did to me, or more like what they *used* to do to me. My eyes involuntarily moved up his body until they fell on his smirking face. Slowly, and with my own smirk, I raised my hand and gave him the bird. He threw his head back and laughed.

Blushing, I ignored him and surveyed our surroundings. We were well hidden among the trees of the campsite. "Over there."

Keeping ten feet behind him, I followed as he made his way to the nearby trees. He unzipped his pants and looked over his shoulder at me. "Are you going to watch?"

"Yep. You don't have anything I haven't already seen." Though I didn't want to see it again, I wasn't going to let him take me by surprise. He was up to something. I didn't know what, but he was a smart man, and I had to stay on my toes.

"You have *never* watched me piss, and I would rather it stayed that way."

"Oh, are you pee shy? I'm so sorry," I said in a fake-sad voice and a pouty face. He glared and shook his head before turning to look straight ahead while preparing to take care of business. "I'll stand away, but I'm not leaving."

Maybe I could take care of business myself while his hands were full. Running to the nearby brush, I hurried with my pants, holding the butt of the gun in my mouth. Yes, I knew it wasn't at all safe, but I wasn't going to take the chance of accidentally peeing on it. Once situated, I pulled the gun from my mouth and glanced in Luke's direction. He was finished and about to face me. "Don't turn around."

His profile showed a freaking sexy grin, which made me want to go punch him in the face. His head slightly moved in my direction. "I said don't turn around."

Hurrying to pull my pants back up, I kept an eye on Luke's smiling face. *Asshole.* "Come on. We need to head out."

Turning toward me, his smile was gone. *Is this it? Is this when he's going to make his move to take the gun and get rid of me?*

"No, we need to eat first."

"No, we need to go. The less time I have to spend with you, the better." I waved him toward the truck. He walked to the bed of the truck and started digging through the boxes. I ran to the bed on the opposite side and point the gun at him. "What are you doing? Back up."

Without looking up, he pulled two jars of soup out of the box. Setting them on the edge of the bed, he reached back in and came out with a lighter and a spoon. My eyes narrowed. "Did you not hear me?"

"I heard you. The next county probably heard you." Carrying his goods to an uncomfortable looking cement picnic table and benches, he set them down and began picking up pine leaves and twigs lying on the ground. Luke dumped the handfuls of twigs in the bottom of a cast iron grill that was permanently attached to the ground. He arranged the bits of twigs and leaves in a pile before holding a flaming lighter to them. Once they caught, he bent and blew gently to keep it going. "Bring me more twigs."

"No," I said in a huff. "I'm not your errand girl."

"Whatever," Luke said before quickly gathering more pieces and taking them back to the fire. When he was sure it wasn't going to go out, he opened both jars and placed them on top of the grill, stirring the contents in the jars before using the hem of his shirt to transfer them to the picnic table. Without looking at me, he said, "Sit. Eat."

"When will you learn *I'm* the one with the gun? You can't boss me around." He was such an asshole, so I told him. "You're such an asshole."

"Yep." Uncaring what I thought of him, he scooped large bites of soup into his mouth before dropping the spoon into the second jar.

He never used to say "yep" until he spent time at the orchard. It used to be a flat-out "yes." I wasn't sure why, but him using slang now pissed me off, too. The fact that he was *breathing* pissed me off. When the smell of the vegetable soup hit my nose, my traitorous stomach growled. I stomped to the picnic table and sat across from him, keeping the gun pointed at him under the table. "As long as we agree."

"Now, you eat while I talk."

Scooting the jar closer to me, I picked up the spoon and took a bite of the delicious soup. "I couldn't care less what you have to say, so go ahead and keep it to yourself."

"You couldn't care less if your plan ends up getting Jacob or Adam killed? Not to mention getting both of us killed in the process?" He laced his fingers and rested his forearms on the top of the table. "You need to use that stubborn head of yours. You can't just drive up and demand they let them go. Hell, if they see me, especially with you, we're both dead before the boys even know we're there."

He sure was stuck on making it out that Jacob was alive, wasn't he? My heart stuttered at the possible reasons why. Looking everywhere except at him, I choked down my thoughts with another spoonful of soup.

"What do you suggest then?"

"I suggest you let me take you home and I'll get them."

Shaking my head, I looked to the heavens and sighed. "We both know how that turned out last time. You fucked me in more than one way. Not going to happen, so if you don't have any *real* suggestions..."

Luke's lips thinned and his chest rose and fell with a hard breath. I couldn't help but revel in the fact I was getting under the skin of Mr. Calm and Collected. From past experiences, even when angry, he didn't overreact or blow up. I had watched him fist fight more than once and I don't think he'd even gotten out of breath. It was kind of creepy. I guessed it was part of his Special Forces training.

Was that where he learned to trick people into trusting him, to love him, so he could get what he wanted?

Whoever taught him did a damn good job. He fooled me. He fooled Jacob. Maybe he even fooled himself for a time.

Watching his strong jaw tick with frustration didn't seem as entertaining as it had just moments ago. The pain of betrayal coiled in my stomach, causing the soup to sour. I tossed the spoon on the table and stared into his steely gray eyes, waiting to hear what kind of bullshit would come out of his mouth.

After a few moments of staring at one another, he finally spoke, "They can't see us together. If they do, they'll take you from me and hold you over me like they're doing with Adam. And it would put Jacob in the same predicament. Wells wants him. I don't know why. He just does."

"He wouldn't have even *known* about Jacob if you hadn't told him about us." I slapped my palm down on the rough cement, scraping the broken skin on my hand from the night before.

Closing his eyes, he shook his head. "I didn't tell them about him, Roni. You did."

Chapter Six

My head jerked back like he had slapped me across the face. "What?! Are you a freaking lunatic? I did no such thing. I have never even met the man."

"You left a photo and a letter in my bag, right?" he asked, speaking each word slowly, like it pained him to ask.

My heart picked up speed. I'd poured my heart and soul into that idiotic letter. I told him the four of us were a family and how I couldn't wait to see my children with his beautiful gray eyes. It was full of naïve dreams when my life was destined for nightmares. "Yes."

"I didn't know about them until it was too late."

My lips parted and I stared at him without really seeing him. What was he trying to say? That it was *my* fault they stormed in and took a great man's life? *No. No. No.* Jumping to my feet, I pointed a shaking gun toward the truck. "Let's go."

He rubbed his eyes with the heels of his palms. "Dammit, Roni, please…"

"Let's go!"

Luke untangled his long limbs from the concrete bench and kept his head to the ground as he walked past me and to the truck.

Feeling suddenly queasy, I forced my legs to move forward, all the while my head pounded with the seeds of doubt Luke planted in my mind. I couldn't let them take root. Now wasn't the time to lose it. If I did, everything would fall apart.

I would fall apart.

Climbing into the truck, I dug the keys out of my pocket with shaky hands and handed them to Luke. He started the engine and quickly got the truck on the road. I stared out the side window but could feel Luke's eyes on me every few seconds. Wiping the sweat from my forehead, I closed my eyes as a wave of nausea hit me.

Taking in deep breaths through my nose, I let my shaking body slump in the seat. I needed something, a distraction, something to keep my thoughts from running away from me or I was going to lose my ever-loving mind.

"Are you okay?" Luke asked with pity in his voice.

I turned narrowed eyes his way and wheezed out, "Don't waste your concern on me. Worry about yourself." Like I knew he did anyway.

Slamming an open palm against the steering wheel, he yelled, "Why do you have to be so goddamned difficult all the fucking time, Roni? I asked you a simple fucking question. *Are you okay?*"

Am I okay? Am I okay? Seriously? He was a freaking nutcase, or maybe I was the nutcase, but either way, I was *not* okay. I wanted to scream at the top of my lungs until my heart burst in my chest, but I couldn't. It was everything I could do to hold my head up straight. Thankfully, I *did* find the energy to hold a middle finger up to him.

He said something else, but I couldn't hear the words. *What's happening to me?* Something was wrong. Really wrong. "Pull over," I managed to say before bile rose in my throat.

I pulled on the door handle just as the truck came to a jolting stop. Tumbling out of the truck, I fell hard to my hands and knees. Within seconds, I emptied the contents of my stomach for what felt like ions, but was probably more like thirty minutes. Thirty minutes was still a ridiculously long time. The gravel dug into my knees and palms, but I couldn't move. I felt Luke standing over me before I actually saw him.

Oh my God, what did he do to me? Did he poison me? Is that why he was so insistent that I eat? That low-down, dirty piece of shit.

My eyes went dark, and I felt Luke's hands come around my shoulders as I slipped into nothingness.

The sun was warm against my freezing body and a yellow light shown through my lids, but I couldn't open my eyes. Unfortunately, I could hear *him* in the distance. "Come on, baby, just a few sips." The rim of a bottle hit my lips, and I did my best to move my head away to no avail. His thick hands held the nape of my neck, tilting my head back, slowly pouring liquid on my parted lips. Knowing there was no use in fighting it any longer, I took long swallows, hoping beyond all hope, this would end quickly.

Luke dragged the bottle from my lips. "Easy now," he said, rubbing a callused thumb across my forehead.

Within seconds, my stomach cramped and heaved in gruesome waves. Pulling my knees up to my chest, I laid on my side in the fetal position, squeezing my eyes tight. I tried to hold off, but I couldn't stop the vomit from coming up. The last thing I felt before everything went dark again was Luke's hands caressing my hair.

Damn him. He won.

****

The truck was moving, and my body was stretched out across the seat, my head on Luke's thigh. My breaths came in short bursts, each more painful than the last.

Why am I still alive? Why is he putting me through this torture? Why not just shoot me? Strangle me?

Anything would be better than the burning pain controlling every nerve in my body.

Peeling my dry eyes open, I saw Luke's face concentrating on the road, the sun shining brightly, casting a light around him. Like an angel. He was the angel of death, sending me home to be with my family. And I *really* wanted to go home.

"Thank you," I whispered, since it was all my throat would allow to pass my lips before closing my eyes and losing myself inside the hopelessness once again.

****

Opening my eyes, I was incased in darkness, the pain still brutally fierce. Was I dead? I didn't feel dead. No, I felt everything. Was this purgatory? Was this my punishment for loving someone enough to allow him to take away the one person I was granted life to protect?

"Jacob?" I called out to the darkness, praying he would find me and guide me out.

I reached out into the obscurity and felt a hand cover mine and my heart swelled and the pain numbed. This time, when I closed my eyes, I smiled.

****

Blinking my eyes open, I squinted as I took in my unfamiliar surroundings. Swallowing, my throat felt dry and raw as my eyes darted around the small room. Using my palms, I pushed myself into a sitting position. My head felt fuzzy, and for the life of me, I couldn't remember how I'd ended up where I was.

Okay, I was in a clean bed and if the zebra print comforter and the boy band posters on the wall were any clue, I would guess I was in a teenage girl's room. The full sized bed was pushed against the wall to the right and a nightstand was to the left making the most of the small room. On the nightstand set a half-empty bottle of water and a bottle of pain reliever. The most surprising discovery was the 9mm gun resting next to the water bottle.

I held my breath and listened to the sounds of the house. Other than the wind blowing outside, all was eerily silent.

What the hell is going on?

Pulling the blanket down, I found my legs bare and my upper half wearing an oversized tee without remembering taking off my clothes or putting on the shirt.

Someone brought me here.

Someone changed my clothes.

And I knew exactly who that someone was, but where was he?

I rose on weak legs, holding my arms out to balance myself. It felt like I hadn't walked in weeks. Slowly, I padded across the hardwood floor and put my ear to the door to listen again. Nothing.

I turned and moved to the thinly covered window. Hooking a finger at the edge of the curtain, I pulled back just enough to peek through. From this view, I learned several things: I was in the country. I was on the ground floor facing a driveway. The driveway was empty. My truck was gone.

The asshole drugged me, brought me here—wherever here is—changed my clothes, and left me.

Luke left me. And with a gun. He was the cruelest and strangest man I had ever met. I glanced around the room looking for my shoes, but didn't see them. Putting both hands in my hair, I squeezed my eyes shut trying to think through the fog. Luke was still making my life ridiculously difficult.

I needed to get out of this room and figure out what to do next. To do this, I first needed clothes and gosh, my throat burned. Picking up the bottle of water, I smelled it before taking a small sip. It felt good against the back of my throat, so I took a few more sips. Still holding the bottle, I moved to the dresser and opened the drawers and dug around for a pair of jeans. Placing the bottle on the dresser, I pulled out a pair and checked the size before sliding them up my bare legs and fastened them. They were a little loose, but not so terribly that a belt would be needed. Next, I went to the closet for shoes. I picked out a pair of tennis shoes, but just looking at them could tell all the shoes were going to be far too small. That didn't stop me from trying and feeling like an evil stepsister while doing it.

Giving up, I tossed the shoes back into the closet and stood, my legs wobbly. I hoped there would be a pair that fit in another room. With shallow breaths, I leaned against the wall and tried to steady myself as sweat beaded on my forehead and my vision blurred. *Whoa, this wasn't good.* How would I manage to get back on the road when I could barely manage to walk around a room without wanting to pass out?

As I reached for the bottled water, I heard a door close from somewhere within the house and footsteps followed. Stepping lightly, I moved to the nightstand, retrieved the gun, and walked to position myself behind the bedroom door. Spots dotted my vision and I did my best to control my breathing. The door opened slow at first, then swung wider and pushed into me. Hiding behind the door hadn't been my brightest plan.

Luke stuck his head around the corner, his hard eyes softening as he took me in. "Roni, what are you doing? You need to be in bed."

"Get back!" I shouted as I shoved the door into him.

He released the door and took a big step inside the room. My body was too weak to stand any longer, so I stumbled to the bed and sat on the edge, resting the gun on my lap.

"You need to lie down."

"What happened? Where the hell are we?" I asked, keeping my eyes on him as he leaned a shoulder against the wall and crossed his arms over his chest. "Where are my shoes?"

"Lie back down and I'll get you something to eat," he said with a lift of his chin.

"You need to stop telling me what the hell to do and answer me."

Though my eyes were hard, my resolve was waning. Luke had obviously taken care of me while I was poisoned, but on the other hand, was he the one to poison me? I shook my head knowing full well Luke hadn't poisoned me. It wouldn't make since to poison me just to stow me away in a house instead of killing me. I was all for conspiracy theories, but that would be going too far, even for me. Resigned and utterly exhausted, I slid my body up the mattress until my back was against the wall.

Luke pushed off the wall, picking up the water bottle and handing it to me. I took it and untwisted the lid as he sat on a pink beanbag. "I think you got food poisoning from the soup. I brought you here," he lifted his chin, indicating the room, "and you puked on your shoes as well as the rest of your clothes."

The soup? Probably. My mom had always stressed the importance of sterilizing the jars before use and sealing them properly. Even an iota of bacteria could grow and make a person sick or even kill them.

"How long have we been here?" My voice was softer. It felt like I had only been asleep for a few hours, but my body felt like it could have been hibernating a few weeks.

"Three days, two nights."

"We need to get on the road. There's a lot of time to—"

"We're not going anywhere tonight." Luke leaned forward, folding his forearms around his knees.

"But we have to," I sputtered. If Luke was telling the truth, Jacob was alive and there was no telling what was happening to him. If Jacob was dead, then the people who killed him were getting further and further away. One way or the other, I had to know the truth. "We need to go now."

"What you need to do is lie back, relax, and try to eat something. If you can hold it down and sleep through the night, we can discuss leaving in the morning. And before you start in, you're still weak. You aren't going to be good to anyone if you can't walk or run if we need to. I haven't slept in two days, so I could use the rest, too. I'm going to cook something. Do you need anything?" Luke asked as he stood to leave.

Swallowing against a scratchy throat, I realized he was right—I was weak. What if we came to a road block or ran into the men I was looking for by sheer luck? Walking across the room and pulling on a pair of jeans wore me out to the point of seeing spots; I was no good to anyone being sick.

Plus, Luke was about to tell me something about the photo in his backpack when everything started going fuzzy. I needed to know what it was and I had a sinking feeling I wasn't going to like hearing what he had to say. Still, if it had to do with Jacob, I had to hear it. And two days without sleep? I couldn't think about that... yet.

"What are you going to make?" I asked, averting my eyes when he smiled.

"Rice and bird." When I scrunched up my nose, he laughed. "It'll be good. Sit back, drink the rest of the water, and I'll be back in a few."

Watching him walk out of the room, I wondered how he'd managed to catch a bird. Knowing Luke, he probably found a rubber band and a rock and made a slingshot. The man was resourceful and if this meal was even remotely like the meals he had cooked at home, I would eat every last drop. My stomach rolled in protest. Maybe I would just eat a few bites and go from there.

Scooting to the edge of the bed, I took my time standing and walked to the dresser. Since the jeans fit, maybe a few other things would, too. Digging through the drawers, I found a pair of pajama pants, pulled off the jeans, and put them on as fast as I could in case Luke came back. I didn't know why I cared. He had seen and touched every inch of my body before and obviously was the one to put me in the oversized shirt I woke up wearing. There wasn't anything about me he didn't already know.

Sadly, I'd spent weeks and weeks waiting for him to come home so we could spend the rest of our lives watching each other's bodies change with age. Now, thinking of him seeing my body felt wrong.

Sighing, I got comfortable in bed and sipped on the bottle of water as I took in the room. Spotting three books on the nightstand, I picked them up and placed them on my lap. The first was a book about teen vampires falling in love, sounds easy right? Well, they are from different sectors and are forbidden to be together causing them to go into hiding. Rolling my eyes, I tossed it to the side and picked up the second book. This one was about a group of cheerleaders surviving a zombie apocalypse. Thankfully, zombie mutations wasn't what destroyed our world. I couldn't imagine trying to survive while kicking zombie ass.

I tossed the zombie book across the room and picked up the last, flipping it over to read the back. It sounded like a light-hearted romantic comedy and too mature for a teenage girl, but then again, I used to sneak my mom's romance novels to my room and read them by the time I was thirteen.

Life held very little humor anymore and I sorely needed it. Thinking of Luke, I decided romance in itself was a joke. No, my life of romance was more of a tragedy like *Hamlet* or a horror story like *Texas Chainsaw Massacre*.

Luke walked in just about the time I opened the book to start reading. I looked up to find him smiling at me with his hands and forearms full. Setting the book down next to me, I moved to help him, but he stopped me with a shake of his gorgeous head.

"I got it. Just sit back." He moved to the side of the bed, his crotch about eye-level to me. Swallowing hard, I pulled my eyes away and grabbed a bowl from his hands. "This water is yours, too." He slid the water bottle from his elbow and let it fall to the bed as he sat at the edge of the bed by my feet. "Eat slowly until you know if you can take it."

"Thanks," I murmured, placing the bowl on my lap and watched him as he ate. His large hands covered the bottom of the bowl. I loved his hands. It pissed me off how much I loved his hands. It pissed me off to no end that I missed feeling the rough skin of his palms created from years of military work, as they explored my body. And his face. God, his face! The stubble across the hard line of his jaw, the fullness of his lips, the almost unnoticeable shift of his nose which only made him hotter. And his neck. That thick neck was perfect for holding on to while he pounded inside me.

Shit.

I stared down into my bird bowl, trying desperately to get the thought of him inside of me out of my messed up head

"Think you can eat?" he asked, noticing I hadn't touched my food.

"Yeah, I can," I said, dutifully picking up the spoon and shoving rice and mystery bird in my mouth. I heard him chuckle (just another thing I loved about him) as I slowly chewed.

"Feeling okay?" he asked, raising his head in my direction.

Keeping my head down, I glanced at him. "Yeah, I'm good."

We sat in silence for a moment until I cleared my throat and asked, "Before I got poisoned, were you telling me something about the photo and letter in your bag?"

Luke nodded and set his bowl on the floor before cautiously turning to me. "Is that something you think we should go into right now?"

"Probably not, but it needs to be done," I said with a shoulder raise. After a few more bites in silence, I placed the bowl on the nightstand and stared at him.

"The photo," he said on a sigh, "and the letter were found when Tucker and I met up with Major Griffin's group."

It hurt. It hurt because I hadn't told him about the letter or the photo. He wasn't supposed to find them until he was on his way and could see the photo and read my words to know I was waiting for him. I would have never dreamed his return would include a group of men coming with him to shoot my brother, take all of our food, and leave me with absolutely nothing.

Again, if Jacob was dead, why would they need to drag him away? I'd been so crazed to that point with nothing but vengeance feeding me, I hadn't thought much about what that could have meant . . . until now.

"Who's Major Griffin?" I asked, trying to keep on track and not spaz out again.

"He's the General's right-hand man." Luke moved until his legs were on the bed. It wasn't until he started rubbing my foot that I noticed my leg was sitting on top of his. I wanted to move away, but I wanted him to keep talking. It also felt amazing on my aching feet. "He's the bastard who searched my bag, no doubt on the General's orders, but I didn't know about the photo and the letter until they showed me."

I thought back to the things I'd said in the letter. Like any girl in love, there were multiple declarations of love and admiration for not only him, but his fantastic body. I wrote of the hopes we had for Jacob to be able to recreate the hydrocortisone Adam needed to survive. I wrote naïve hopes for the future we might have when he rescued Adam from the devil's clutches. The letter hadn't been a good idea.

"I should have told you about them," I said flatly before capturing his eyes with mine. "Why did you lead them to us?"

Luke leaned his head back and closed his eyes before taking a long breath. "They tied me up, knocked me around a little and when that didn't work, they pulled in Adam as incentive. They knew I would do anything to keep him safe."

I knew that, too, and understood his reasoning, but my brother's life wasn't any less valuable than Adam's.

"Before I left, Jacob and I talked. We knew they would want you both if they knew what you meant to me. You don't know how fucking happy I was that you weren't there when I got back." He began rubbing my foot again, his eyes focused on his hands. After a moment of reflection, he said, "Jacob wouldn't tell them where you were. I was terrified... *terrified* that you were going to run into the mix and get hurt or taken. Jacob was, too. They shot him in the leg to get him to talk. You know Jacob. He kept mouthing and pissing them off, and they weren't very forgiving for his lack of cooperation. He wouldn't shut up and I thought, 'this is it, they're going to kill him,' so I did the only thing I knew to do. I punched him as hard as I could and knocked him out. I don't know why, but they wanted him to begin with. They wanted *both* of you. Probably wanted you more as extra leverage over me and maybe over Jacob, but they wanted him in the fold."

There it was. I finally knew what happened. My eyes burned with tears begging to be shed, but I denied them.

"Jacob's really alive, isn't he?"

Luke's lips thinned and his eyes went soft. "Yes, sweetheart, he really is."

"This is all my fault."

Chapter Seven

"Sissy," he whispered, his tiny hands wrapped around my thigh, huddling behind me as the men closed in around us. "Don't let them take me."

"I won't, Jacob," I swore, reaching back to squeeze his shoulder, but his little body was ripped away from me. "Jacob! No!"

Jolting awake, I shot up, panting, when I felt a familiar arm wrap around my waist. I closed my eyes against the dark of the room and let him pull me down until my back was firmly secured to his chest.

"I have to get him back," I moaned, my lungs fighting to suck in air when it felt like a boulder was crushing me.

"We will," Luke assured me, his words meant to comfort. "I promise, sweetheart."

Shaking my head, I spun until I could feel his breath on my face. "I did this, Luke. Me! If I hadn't put that letter—"

"No, Roni. No." He rubbed my upper back. "You can't blame yourself for the actions of power-hungry whackjobs. We'll get him back. We'll get both of them back."

Adam was gone, too. Was this what he went through day after day, week after week, month after month, not knowing if his little brother was alive and well? He had felt the gut wrenching pain, which never diminished, like I did. The pain followed me around like a tornado, ready to suck me up, tear me to shreds, and spit me out, leaving nothing but disaster in its wake.

How could he shoulder this constant weight and not break when I wanted to crumble?

How had I not trusted him?

With nothing and everything rushing through my mind all at once, I leaned in and touched my lips to his. To my surprise, Luke jerked his head back. The room was dark, but I stared at him, trying like hell to get a sense of what he was feeling.

"Roni, I... I can't. Just..." He didn't finish his sentence. Instead, he turned me around and pulled my back to his chest, holding me tight.

I laid unmoving, staring into the dark abyss of the room, wishing it would swallow me whole. Not only had I put Jacob in danger with my letter, I put Adam and Luke in danger. My mistake could have gotten Adam hurt. Luke would never forgive me for that.

The same words tumbled around in my head, over and over.

Forgive me. Forgive me. Forgive me.

****

"Hand me the gas cap," Luke said, nodding toward the ground, his attention never leaving the truck.

Placing the empty gas can on the ground, I tossed him the cap. Like a never-ending cycle, we were going to have to hunt for more fuel. He nodded for me to get in the truck and I didn't hesitate. After the night before and my failed attempt to kiss him, we had spoken as little as possible.

What could I say? I hadn't trusted him. In just the past week I'd hunted him down, held him at gunpoint, and planned to kill him as soon as I felt it necessary. If that didn't say 'relationship issues,' I don't know what did. I was a little more than embarrassed by my actions and deserved the rejection. Did I really expect for him to fall back into my web of insanity? And that was exactly it. I was insane. How else could I explain my actions?

I didn't know everything that had happened the day they took Jacob from me, since I was too afraid to ask. *Baby steps*, I kept telling myself.

When we were back on the road, Luke pointed to the dashboard. "Can you take a look at the map and tell how much further until the next town?"

I picked up the map, opened it up, and stared at it. "Uh, where are we?" I had been too preoccupied in wondering what Luke was thinking, and what an idiot I was, to pay attention to where we were or how far we had gone.

He chuckled and pulled to the edge of the road. Leaning over, our shoulders touched as he turned the map toward him. I wanted to lean into him but bit my lip instead. "We're right here." Luke pointed to a line on the map and began to trace his finger along the line. "And we need to go here. About thirty more minutes. There should be fuel somewhere around there."

"Maybe I can find a better pair of shoes, too." I looked down at the oversized work boots Luke had found for me. If they weren't laced so tight at the ankles, I would step right out of them.

"Maybe." He turned his head, his face only inches from mine. I turned toward him, watching his full lips and remembering how they felt on my skin. Abruptly, he sat up and cleared his throat before putting the truck in gear and getting back on the road.

After a few awkward moments, he asked, "What's your three?"

Shocked by his question, I whipped my head to him. "You want my three?"

A smile spread across his face. "Yeah, what's your three?"

This was a game Jacob and I had started a few months after the plague took our parents from us. We would each say one thing useful we wished we had, one thing we wanted, and one thing we didn't miss from the old world. When Luke stumbled into our lives, we naturally included him in the game. It became a way of saying what we wanted and needed without sounding whiny and remind us there were things in the old world we were glad to be without.

"You go first," I said, still stunned he had asked. I never thought I would be asked the question again and needed a few seconds to collect myself. Plus, I really wanted to know what made him want to play this game.

"Okay, I'll go first," he said, holding the steering wheel with one hand and holding a finger up with the other. "Useful would definitely be a GPS."

"That *would* be useful." I chuckled and tossed the folded map back to the dashboard.

"Want is, hands down, a hot shower."

Images of water caressing his naked body flashed through my mind. I squirmed in the seat and peeled my eyes off him, heat filling my face. I was ashamed of myself, even though whether he liked it or not, he was mine. I just had to remind him of that.

"And I don't miss..." His hand tightened on the steering wheel, displaying the corded muscles of his arms. "I don't miss the past seven weeks of worrying if you're okay or not."

My breath caught and my eyes shifted to him. His head was like a statue, not moving a fraction of an inch. "You don't have to worry about me," I said just above a whisper.

"Not anymore," he said with a sigh. "What's your three?"

Does he mean he doesn't need to worry about me anymore because I'm with him or because I'm no longer his problem?

"I don't know." I rested my arm on the window and leaned my head into my hand.

"Oh, no, you have to. You made the rules, remember?" His tone was light, taking the seriousness out of the air. "Go."

I hesitated, and his eyebrows went up expectantly. I sighed. "Fine. Useful would obviously be a pair of shoes. Want would have to be some common sense because I've been short on that lately." I tucked my hair behind my ear and looked at his profile. "Don't miss thinking I was completely alone on this godforsaken planet."

After a beat, Luke placed his hand on my hand resting on the seat and squeezed. "I'll get him back, Roni."

"I wasn't just talking about him." He removed his hand from mine like it had electrocuted him. My heart dropped. "Look, I'm sorry."

"Roni…"

"Please, just… I'm sorry. I know I screwed up again. I shouldn't have written that letter like a love-sick school girl. I know I'm a freaking idiot. I understand that you don't want me anymore. I get it. Really, I do. I should have trusted you, but you didn't see it through my eyes. You didn't sit in that loft and watch your world slip away from you when you couldn't do a damn thing about it. So, yeah, I flipped out. I flipped *way* the fuck out, but can you really blame me?" I shook my head wildly and went on. "You were gone so long. So damn long."

It was then I realized we were stopped in the middle of the road. His body was rigid as he stared at me. "You were going to *kill* me."

Swallowing hard, I nodded, not denying it.

"After *everything*. Every night I spent with you, *inside* you, you honestly believed I was capable of walking into the house that had become my home and kill *my* brother?" His head shifted. "No, can't do it. Now I can't trust you."

Squeezing my shaking hands between my thighs to keep from reaching for him, I turned my head away in shame. Though the words stung, they were deserved.

"I *love* you, Roni, and I love Jacob and Adam. I'll get you all safe, but that's it. That's all I can give because I do not trust you not to break me in the end." Luke punched the dashboard, cracking it and causing me to jump.

The only sound was the engine idling, which only added to the uncomfortable silence filling the cab. Looking to the left, he threw the truck into gear and took off. "Storm's moving in."

Peering through the back window, the sky was filling with ominous looking clouds. Lightning flashed through the sky, followed by roaring thunder, like the clouds were screaming with the weight and would break at any second. Quietly, I raised my shaking hand and wiped away the tears streaming down my face. The pain brewing inside me was too heavy to hold, and I was being crushed beneath the weight.

The storm was already there.

****

The room was wrapped in darkness save for the light of a single small candle perched on the coffee table and the lightning continuously filling the sky. Not that there was much to see. The house had been picked clean. The two mismatched couches and makeshift coffee table were the only things useful in the place. Even those smelled a little funky, but beggars couldn't be choosers and I wasn't about to complain. Keeping my gaze at the window, I ignored the sensation of Luke watching me.

Earlier, when he'd noticed I couldn't stop the tears, he let loose a string of curse words at the top of his lungs before jumping out and repeatedly punching the bed of the truck. When he climbed back in, he was soaked and angry, but no matter how hard I tried, I couldn't stop crying. The dam holding seven weeks of tears had finally broken.

I had no idea how long we drove before he found the house and cleared it before taking me inside to wait out the storm. Luke, being the survival guru he was, made use of a tarp and set up a shower of sorts off the porch. I took a shower first. It was freezing from the cold rainwater, but it helped me get control of myself. Once the tears finally dried up, I dug through a box Luke had brought in until I found a can of coffee. Luke made a small fire on the covered porch and I managed to make a pot using a pillowcase as a filter.

There we were, drinking our coffee in awkward silence while he sat on the opposite couch, watching me. I had no clue what was going through his mind. He probably wished I had never been born or he had never found the orchard. Not that I could blame him. Hell, I had taken his already difficult life and compounded it.

"Think we're here for the night?" I asked, breaking the silence.

After a beat, he said, "Looks like it."

"Think there's any fuel around here?" I was trying to look through the sheets of rain for any other vehicles.

"There're more houses down the road I can check out when the rain lets up." He set his mug on the coffee table and blew out the candle. "Let's get some sleep."

Agreeing, I laid on the couch and observed him, stretched out on the opposite one, his arm over his eyes. With the sound of the rain hitting the house and the loss of energy from bawling my eyes out, it didn't take long to fall asleep.

I woke to the feel of warm hands on my freezing body. Luke pulled me up, rolled me over, and laid me atop his bare chest. Stunned, I lie frozen, literally, against him. *What the hell?* So I lifted my head and asked. "What are you doing?"

He pushed my head back to his chest. "Your teeth were chattering so loud, I couldn't sleep. You're freezing, so I'm using our body heat to keep us both warm. Go back to sleep."

Lying on his warm chest, my ear pressed tight against him, I listened to the beat of his heart. Steady. Strong. Just like him. He was constant, where I was a rollercoaster.

He was right, I couldn't be trusted. I had repeatedly acted with my heart instead of using my head. By writing the letter and stuffing it in his bag like a love-sick teenager, I had risked us all. Because of me, we could all be dead right then. My body involuntarily shuddered at the thought and he mistook it as me still being cold and wrapped his arms around me. And that was the kind of man Luke was. After everything I did, everything I screwed up, he still went out of his way to take care of me.

He loved me.

I sighed as I soaked in the feeling of being wrapped up in his thick arms, against his hard chest and remembering what it felt like when he made his body's sole purpose to make mine sing, and knowing I would never have that again. I was the biggest idiot left on the planet.

****

"Roni." Luke's voice pulled me from the best sleep I'd had in I didn't know how long. Before opening my eyes, I felt it. Luke was rock hard, the evidence pressed against my belly. I'm not going to lie, I wanted to grin with smugness. Actually, I wanted to rub myself against him like a cat. "You need to get up."

"Uh…" I pulled up to my hands and knees, looking down at his erection and smiled. "Guess you already are."

As soon as the words slipped from my mouth, I cringed. By the flare of his nostrils and the sound of his teeth grinding, Luke was pissed.

Shifting, he moved from under me and jerked into a sitting position. "I never said I don't *want* to bury myself inside you, Roni. I've spent the last two months remembering how it felt to be inside you. Hell, thinking of you was what got me through the days, and while I was doing everything I could to get back to you, you were spending your days hunting me down *to kill me*." He stood, his back to me, and ran his hands through his short, black hair. "Get your shit ready and load it in the truck. I'll be outside."

Stunned, I watched him yank his shirt from the back of the couch and carry it outside, slamming the door on his way out. What the hell was I thinking trying to joke around with him like that? I'd hurt him. *Hurt him!*

Momentarily closing my eyes, I pulled my head out of my ass and stood. I started gathering our items and tossed them inside the box. If I ever wanted any sort of relationship with Luke, I had a lot of making up to do. I could start by not teasing him about getting turned on by the one person he felt had failed him.

Shoving my feet into the oversized work boots, I yanked on the strings until they were tight and secured them. I clomped to the box, hefting it up, and walked out to the truck to a waiting Luke. He started the truck as I lifted the box into the bed of the truck and I jogged back to the cab and climbed inside. He backed onto the road and headed toward the nearest town. I wanted to apologize for my idiotic attempt to lighten the mood between us, but the hard set of his jaw and the squint of his eyes told me it wouldn't be welcomed kindly.

So I did the only thing possible; I kept my mouth shut and my eyes straight ahead. I figured if I did that, I couldn't make matters worse.

Watching the trees whip by, it didn't take long for my mind to wander to Jacob. Had he driven on this same path or had they taken him a different way? Was he okay? Luke said the gunshot to his thigh had gone straight through and the men had stopped the majority of the bleeding within thirty minutes of them leaving the house. It had to be painful, though, and it was the second time in the past six months he had been shot. Luke had assured me he'd spoken with Jacob the morning before I found him and he was doing fine and wasn't even using crutches.

What could they possibly want with him?

They wanted soldiers, sure, but to take a team of men and go back to the house for just one man didn't make any sense. Wells and Griffin wanted to hold both him and me over Luke's head but were fine to leave me behind and just take Jacob. Their reasons were beyond me and if I thought about it too much, I would go crazy. I needed to get the possibilities out of my head and focus on getting him and Adam out of their clutches.

Keeping my head was the only way we would all survive this. If I let panic set in, like I normally did, I was liable to do something ridiculously crazy. I needed to concentrate on the here and now and devise a way to make Luke forgive my attempt on his life. I had a feeling it was going to be much harder than the time I'd seduced him at the orchard. Seducing him wasn't really the goal, forgiveness was, but it wouldn't be unwelcomed. My plans would need to wait because houses began to appear more frequently, but I noticed there was a serious lack of vehicles in the area.

"You have your gun?" Luke asked with his eyes trained to the road. I reached down and pulled it from the duffel bag, holding it up for him to see. "We're close, so keep your eyes open."

Exit signs promised fast food restaurants, lodging, and fuel. Wouldn't that be nice? Reality promised crumbling buildings with a large side of danger.

"I would love a cheeseburger right now," he said, reading my thoughts as he took an exit and lowered our speed.

It seemed like he was past being pissed, or at least he was willing to let it go for the time being. I guessed not pushing or trying to explain myself helped cool his temper. "Yeah, that would be nice." Straightening in the seat, I asked, "What's the plan?"

"Find a neighborhood and see about fuel and shoes, then find a way around this town. It's bigger than I expected it to be." He tapped the steering wheel with his thumbs, seemingly more from boredom than nerves, but his eyes stayed in constant motion, assessing the area.

The main thing I took from his words was he still wanted to find a pair of shoes for me, which could only mean he cared. Maybe I should keep my mouth shut more often. It was doubtful I could manage it for long periods of time, but I could try it if it helped him. I had already done enough to screw up his carefully laid plans.

Passing a few neighborhoods, he turned on a narrower road and stopped at the edge of a cul-de-sac. "I'm going to clear these houses. Get behind the wheel and leave the truck running until I get back. Do not follow me. I don't need your help."

Fighting the urge to roll my eyes and argue how I was completely capable of clearing the houses, I nodded my understanding. His eyes narrowed on me. "I promise I won't leave the truck until you tell me to."

He opened the door and climbed out, waiting until I moved to the driver's side. Standing inside the open door, he towered over me, his arm brushing my shoulder as he readjusted his shirt and pulled a handgun from his jeans. "Keep your eyes peeled. If you need me, honk the horn."

"Got it," I said, ready for him to go. He paused, his eyes searching my face before taking a step back and closing the door.

I watched until he moved out of view and tried to relax. Rolling down the window, I leaned against the seat and listened for anything amiss. The sun was high in the sky, and after the rain the day before, the humidity was thick as steam. My hair more than likely resembled something like that of a witch, but a hairbrush hadn't been on my "things I need to kill Luke" inventory. Using my fingers as a comb, I tugged my ratty strands together and used a rubber band I kept around the gearshift to secure it. Looking into the rearview mirror, I grimaced at my reflection. At least it would be off my neck and out of the way.

After another ten minutes, I began to worry. Luke was nowhere to be seen. I fought with the urge to get out and look for him, but calmed myself with the knowledge that if anyone would be okay, it would be him. Also, if I got out of the truck, he would flip his lid. I'd promised I would stay put and so help me, I would even though I hated to obey.

Looking around, I wondered what had made him stop on that particular street. We had passed a dozen cul-de-sacs and streets lined with houses before he'd stopped there. The whole area seemed to be part of a subdivision. There were maybe four or five different layouts, but they repeated each other down each street. I had always heard them being called cookie-cutter houses. At one time in my life I would have loved to end up in a neighborhood like this, but now, I just wanted our orchard and my chickens.

And my guys.

I did a perimeter check, waiting to see anything unusual. He stood at the edge of the house closest to me and waved me to him. I held up two fingers upside down and moved them as if they were walking. His lip twitched and he shook his head. I gripped an imaginary steering wheel and mimed driving. This time, his lips moved to a grin as he nodded and pointed to the entrance of the cul-de-sac and walked toward it. I started the engine and quickly moved until I pulled next to him.

Walking to my open window, he nodded to the house on my left. "Pull up next to that car and we'll start getting gas."

I glanced at the seven houses and nearly all of them had a vehicle or two parked in the driveway. My heart pinched at the thought of the people who used to live in these houses and drove those vehicles. More than likely, they were now rotting corpses inside. Shaking the thought from my head, I turned the wheel and pulled into the driveway.

"Can I get out now?" I asked, sticking my head out the window.

"Smartass," he murmured before he waved me out. Climbing out, I tucked my gun into the back of my jeans. "Safety on?"

"Yes, sir." I nodded as I began to gather the empty fuel cans and handed him the hose. "Did you find any shoes?"

He nodded while cramming a hose down the tank of the truck. "Think so. There's a lot to choose from. Pretty sure we can find food, too."

"I'm hungry, so that's good."

"We need to get out of this area before we stop to eat. I don't like so many unchecked buildings around." Luke continued to work, but his eyes stayed alert.

"Want me to go find shoes and start gathering supplies while you pump the gas so we can get out of here sooner?"

"No, we need to stay together. I checked these houses, but anyone could walk over from the next street over and we wouldn't know." He pulled the hose from the car and handed it to me while he hefted the full fuel can to the back of the truck and pointed to the next driveway. "Move the truck right there."

I wanted to remind him I wasn't a helpless waif and we could get in and out a whole lot quicker if he would let me go out on my own, but it would only piss him off and in turn, it would piss me off. *Just do what he says*, I kept telling myself. *Trust his judgment on this because yours has lacked intelligence as of late.* He was Special Forces and really did know what he was doing, but when someone told me to do something, my stubborn head told me to do the opposite.

I moved the truck and helped Luke get the fuel flowing from the pick-up truck to the can. We were two for two on the fuel.

"I bet every one of these cars has gas. Think we can find a few more fuel cans?" I asked.

"We'll look. The fewer times we have to hunt for it, the better."

Replacing the fuel can with an empty one, I rose and moved to place the full can in the bed of the truck when a flash of black hair and thin limbs darted from the back of one of the houses to the next. My body stiffened, but I forced my extremities to move and set the gas can down normally. If I freaked out, I would tip off the people watching.

"Luke, come here," I said, pretending to look through the box, but instead kept my eyes on the house at the end of the cul-de-sac.

"What? I want to get this finished."

"Luke, don't react," I kept my tone normal but dropped my volume, "but we're being watched."

Chapter Eight

Luke's movements gave no indication he had heard me, so I took a chance and glanced at him. His jaw twitched. He'd heard me. Pulling the hose out of the truck, he tossed it into the bed of the truck. Coming closer to me, he tugged me to him, his hands on my hips, his chest pressed to mine. I leaned my head back to look up to him. From a distance, it would look like a simple embrace between lovers and even though I knew that to be the last thing he wanted to do, it felt good to be in his arms again.

He leaned down, his nose brushing mine as he spoke quietly, "Details."

"A woman, or maybe a girl, black hair, just ran across the backyard of the house at the center."

"Did you see anyone else?" he asked, pulling me to his chest, no doubt using the excuse to look in the area I'd described to him. I didn't mind one bit. He could use me all he wanted. Squeezing my hip, he pulled back. "Got her. I'm going to check it out. Get your gun ready and stay here."

He tried to step back, but I held onto his upper arms, feeling the tight muscles rippling beneath my hands. "Stay here? No way. I'm like a sitting duck out here."

"Fine, we don't have time to argue. You head to the east side and I'll go west and we'll meet in the middle." His eyes lazily scanned the area though his voice was hard.

"Uh, which way is east?"

He sighed and shook his head. "How the hell did you manage to make it this far on your own?"

I shrugged my shoulders, not wanting to tell him the truth. Vengeance and not caring if I died had carried me most of the way.

"Go right. I'll go left."

"Be careful," I whispered as he walked away.

Pretending his walking toward danger wasn't affecting me, I opened the truck door and pulled out the duffel bag. My hope was whoever was watching would assume we were about to gather supplies and not figure out we were trying to ambush them. I made it to the side of the house before I heard muffled noises coming from the back.

Dropping the bag on the ground, I ran around the house toward the direction Luke told me to go when I heard, "I will not be your sex slave."

"Calm down. I don't need a sex slave," Luke said. "Shit! Stop kicking me."

Gripping the handle of the gun, I slowed, pushing my back against the wall until Luke was visible. When I saw the two of them, I dropped my hand and stepped out into the open. Luke held her by her upper arms, her back facing him, but her legs were free and she was doing her best to mule kick him into letting her go. When she spotted me, her movements halted.

Her almond eyes glared at me with the hatred only a teenage girl could possess. Even with her face twisted, she was clearly beautiful. "Chāng fù."

My eyebrows flew up and I looked at Luke and he shrugged. *What was that?* The girl was Asian by appearance, but she had been speaking English a few seconds before. "I'm not sure what you said, but I'm guessing it wasn't very nice." The girl spat in my direction then yanked at her arms. "Are you alone?"

"No, I'm not, so tell your *ogre* to get his fat fingers off me before my friends come and break his legs."

Biting the inside of my mouth to keep from smiling, I looked at Luke. "Let's take this inside."

"You sick fucks, kill me now because I would rather die than give myself to you," she yelled, but her voice cracked.

My mind went back to the time men stormed our house and tried to rape me in front of Luke and Jacob. I had been terrified. I had a feeling the girl was alone and there was no telling what she had been through. "Listen, we're not some sex freaks. We just want to talk to you and then we'll let you go."

"If you're not weirdo freaks, then let me go and we can talk."

"We're not stupid, either. As soon as he lets you go, you'll run," I said, then turned my eyes to Luke who was surprisingly not giving orders. "Have you cleared this house?"

He nodded, and I walked to the back door and opened it. "After you."

"You're such a bitch," she sputtered as Luke walked them through the door.

I followed him as he walked through the kitchen and sat the girl on a couch in the living room. The living room was bright with the light from the large windows. Standing next to Luke, we looked down at the girl who was doing her best to appear angry.

"What do you want so I can go?"

"How many people are with you?" I asked.

"Ten."

"That's a lot of people. Do you normally run around alone?" I crossed my arms over my chest and she glared at me. "What's your name?"

"Stormy," she answered quickly. Too quickly. No way was it her real name, but if it's what she wanted me to call her, so be it.

"Hello, Stormy. My name is Veronica, but everyone calls me Roni. The ogre is Luke." I jabbed a thumb toward him. Luke grunted and moved to the edge of the window, giving the girl more space. "Now, how many people are *really* with you?"

"I told you. Ten. And they know where I went, so you better hurry and leave before they get here." She changed her tone, making it sound like she was actually worried for our safety. I wanted to laugh, but laughing at an angry teen would be a mistake.

"Okay, we'll wait for them. We can't walk out and be in the open if they're a threat. We'll just have to wait here and deal with it when they get here," I said nonchalantly, like I had all the time in the world. At the rate we were actually traveling, it would be weeks before we found our brothers.

I had a feeling about this girl, though. She was alone. She was alone and scared to death but doing a damn good job of hiding it.

"They'll surround the building. You won't make it out if they find us."

"I'm not worried about that. See, the ogre, I mean Luke, is Special Forces, and I've watched him get out of worse than ten guys surrounding a house." Luke looked over his shoulder to me and I winked at him.

At his impressive six foot, three inches of toned muscles, he looked every bit capable of being an army of one. I never felt safer than when I stood next to him.

"Fine," Stormy huffed. "I'm alone alright. No one is coming."

Bingo!

"Okay, that's good then." I smiled and squatted down in front of her. Her flawless, creamy skin was tinted pink on her cheeks from either anger or makeup. Being a teenager, it was probably a combination of both. "How long have you been alone?"

"What does that matter? What do you want from me?"

"I just want to know and we don't want anything from you." I brushed a falling strand of hair away from my face. "We're being cautious just like you are. We've come across a lot of different types of people and had to be sure what type of situation we were in."

"So now you know. I'm alone. Feel free to get whatever and leave me the hell alone."

Ignoring her demands, I asked, "How old are you?"

"Eighteen," she said, her head held high. I pursed my lips at the blatant lie. There was no way she was over sixteen and even *that* was pushing it. "Okay, I'm fifteen."

Fifteen? Fifteen and alone? How had she made it on her own?

"How old are *you*? Thirty?" she asked with a smirk and Luke gave a low chuckle.

"I'm twenty-six, thank you very much." I stood and pointed to Luke. "I'm going to talk to him for just a minute. Stay here, please. I don't want Luke to run after you again."

Luke turned around, his thick arms crossed over his chest, looking badass and sexy as ever. I looked down at Stormy to find her glowering at Luke. She wasn't going anywhere.

"What do we do?"

He sucked in his top lip as he watched the girl. "We could get her to her people?"

"Oh, so you found a boat that will take me to China?" Stormy asked, her words dripping with sarcasm.

"I mean people you were with, smartass," Luke told her with a shake of his head. I couldn't help it, I laughed. Luke's lips moved to thin lines.

Without realizing what I was doing, I rubbed his upper arm to soothe him. He noticed and stared down at my hand until I let it fall away. "Sorry." I turned to Stormy. "Cover your ears or something."

"Are you serious?" Her head jerked to the side and her nose crinkled like she'd smelled something bad.

"Yes, I'm serious." I raised my eyebrows until she rolled her eyes and lifted her hands to her ears. Turning back to Luke, I asked again, "What do we do?"

"She's scared to death of me," he said. His voice was low, and I could tell it bothered him that a young girl feared him.

"We can't just leave her. She's a fifteen-year-old girl. There's no telling how long she's been here alone and the next guy who comes along probably isn't going to be as good of a man as you." The thought of someone hurting her made my stomach churn.

"Fuck me," he said, running a hand through his hair. "We could take her with us and take her back to Canaan on our way home?"

The people of Canaan seemed to be good people. Actually, the town where Daisy and I had spent the night seemed even better, and I bet they would take the girl and keep her safe. *Our* trip, on the other hand, would be dangerous, but it had to be safer than leaving her there to die alone or be killed. "Can we keep her safe 'til then?"

My throat closed up at the thought of walking away from her. Unexpectedly, Luke put a finger under my chin and his thumb brushed against my lower lip. "We'll keep her safe."

My eyes searched his face and I did my best to smile. "Okay, you get to tell her she's going with us."

Leaning his head back, he said. "Fuck."

The smartass in me wanted to tell him I already tried and he shot me down, but doubted he would appreciate my humor. Instead, I turned my head around and looked at Stormy, who was still sitting on the couch with a bored expression. "I'll be your backup."

We turned and his hand went to my lower back, sending chills down my spine. His touch was nothing more than guiding me, but damn it felt good. One simple touch from his strong hand did more for me than a thousand touches from anyone else.

Stopping in front of Stormy, Luke's hand fell away and I sighed. "Can I uncover my ears now?" Stormy asked a little too loudly.

Luke nodded and she moved her hands. He squatted down in front of her, and I decided to sit on the couch but kept enough space between Stormy and me so she wouldn't feel trapped. "We think it would be best if you come with us. We can—"

"What? I don't think so," Stormy said, shaking her head.

"You're coming with us. You're not safe here and we can keep you safe." Stormy opened her mouth to interrupt him again, but he held a finger up and surprisingly, she closed her mouth. "We know of a small, functioning community that is safe and the people there would take you in, keep you safe."

Stormy's eyes were glaring, but there was something behind them, relief maybe? Even with all the attitude she was throwing around, she had to be lonely. "There are kids your age there, too," I added.

"What about my stuff?" she asked, her chin coming up a fraction of an inch.

"You can bring a few things, but we can't take much. We need to get going, though. We need to gather supplies and finish filling the fuel cans. I want to be out of here within the hour. Can you be ready by then?" Luke stood and glanced out the window.

Stormy nodded but didn't look at him. She was leaving her home and it had to be hard. I gently patted her shoulder. "Where do you stay?"

"One road over. I'll go pack my stuff and be back in a few minutes," she said, standing.

"Wait." I stood, too. "Luke, I'm going to go with her and help. Maybe I can find a pair of shoes."

His eyes narrowed and his hands went on his hips. "Fifteen minutes, then I'm coming to find you."

"Let's go," I said, and followed the smaller girl toward the kitchen. Just as we reached the back door, Luke's voice stopped me.

"Roni," he called, and I turned to him. "Be careful."

Smiling, I nodded, and then followed Stormy.

It was maybe a minute into our walk when Stormy pointed ahead of us. "That's my place."

Walking through her backyard, I noticed four wooden crosses made from what looked like broken flowerbed fence at the edge of the yard. "Did you live here before the plague?"

Stormy's eyes darted to the crosses then back to the house. "Yes."

She opened the back door and walked through. I pulled out my gun and held the barrel down. I believed Stormy was alone but wasn't going to bet my life on it. Stepping inside, the first thing that hit me was the smell of Pine-Sol. I blinked my eyes a few times, trying to adjust to the change in light, when I noticed what once was a dining room was now a well-organized food pantry. I stood in stunned silence. Stormy was a survivor.

"My room's back here," she called from the living room.

Walking through the dining room, I stopped in the living room. The place was nice and clean. I stopped at the entertainment center. The blank television screen had been painted to look like an aquarium. Little clown fish and coral were drawn by a child's hand. It was cute and innocent, and it broke my heart into pieces. I had an aching feeling she had been alone the entire time or shortly after the plague hit.

Roaming the shelves, I stopped on the family photos in various frames. A man and a woman stood behind two pre-teen boys and one little girl. Everyone in the photo had blondish-brown hair, except the little girl, who had striking black hair. She was adopted. Taking a few of the photos of her family from the frames, I tucked them into my backpack. My eyes roamed until I found a child's drawing with *Tiffany* written poorly at the bottom.

Okay, her name was Tiffany, but she chose to be called Stormy. I smiled. It reminded me of myself at her age and telling everyone to call me Jo, for my middle name Jolene. It didn't happen, though. I had been Roni since Jacob was able to speak. Veronica was reserved for when one of my parents was upset with me.

"Hurry, we're running out of time and Luke will be pissed if he has to stop what he's doing to check on us," I said, making my way down the hall to the only open door. When I saw her, I fought a laugh. She had the biggest suitcase I've ever seen, filled to the brim with clothes and notebooks. Luke was *not* going to like this.

"Do you have any size eight shoes?" I leaned against the door, watching her excitedly running through the room and tossing more clothes inside.

"Look in my mom's closet." She didn't look up but pointed across the hall while sitting on the suitcase to get it zipped.

It didn't take long to find a couple pairs of shoes that would work great. They were a size too big, but they were more comfortable than five sizes too big. Tossing the work boots to the side, I put on a pair of tennis shoes and walked out of the room and screamed when I ran into a hard chest.

"Roni, it's me," Luke said, shaking me by my upper arms.

I stopped shaking and leaned my forehead onto his broad chest. "You scared the shit out of me."

"It's been twenty minutes," he growled.

Lifting my head, I gave him a sheepish grin. "Sorry. I think Stormy is having a hard time parting with anything."

Our heads turned to Stormy, who was standing in front of three suitcases now. "I'm almost done."

Luke took a step forward. "You're done. Let's load some the groceries and go."

"I haven't packed my makeup yet," Stormy whined with her hands in her hair.

At Luke's low growl, I put my hand on his forearm. "She's a teenager," I whispered.

"Get her moving. I'm going to start loading the stockpile of food she has in this house." He turned and called over his shoulder, "Truck's parked out front."

I walked to Stormy and picked up two of the suitcases. "Do you have a big purse?" She nodded and I leaned in, "Put your makeup in that, but hurry."

Stormy smiled brightly, and I could have sworn the skies opened up and angels sang. She was stunning. The girl might have built up her defenses to prevent getting hurt and dealing with being left alone, but she couldn't hide her happiness now. My chest constricted. She *wanted* to go with us. She wouldn't be alone anymore and be safe. We would make damn sure of it. Returning her smile, I hefted two of the suitcases and walked out of the room, leaving her to spend the last moments alone to say goodbye.

When I thought I had lost Jacob and Luke, I crumbled into a bottomless hole of grief. This girl didn't. Somehow she'd endured this shitty hand she was dealt and made it. She was a fighter, without having anyone to take on that responsibility in a long time, until now.

After putting her bags in the truck, I placed the photos I'd nabbed in the glove compartment. Knowing we needed to get out of there, I helped Luke load the food that hadn't yet expired into plastic totes and into the back of the truck. "This place has been a one stop shop," I teased.

"Looks like it." He glanced around. "Did she say what happened to her family?"

"No, but there are four crosses in the backyard and," I opened the door of the truck and pulled the photos from the glove compartment, "I found these on the entertainment center."

He took the photos from me and flipped through them, his eyebrows going up at the family photo. "She's adopted?"

"That's my guess. I didn't ask."

"But she was speaking Mandarin out back," he said, confused.

"You know Mandarin?" I asked, looking up at him in surprise.

"I've been to China a few times," he told me while flipping through the photos.

"Was this on vacation or on a top secret mission?"

"I've never been on vacation."

"Oh." I scratched my head, knowing full well vacations were a thing of the past. "Do you know what she said out there?"

For the first time in too long, he smiled a real smile. "More or less."

"Well, what was it?"

He shook his head and laughed. "Ask her."

126

I opened my mouth to demand he tell me, but Stormy stepped out wearing a floral skirt, a tight gray t-shirt, ballet flats, and a sun hat, dragging her suitcases behind her. Luke shoved the photos back inside the glove compartment and stood next to me, eying Stormy.

"She looks like she's ready," Luke said.

"Looks like it," I agreed. Taking her suitcases, I handed them off to Luke before climbing in the truck and sitting in the middle. Stormy wouldn't be comfortable sitting next to a man she didn't know yet, but really, it was an excuse for me to be close to him.

Stormy jumped inside and closed the doors before twisting her hands in her lap. Glancing at her, I noticed her biting her bottom lip. She was nervous, or maybe it was sadness. When Luke got in the truck and started it, Stormy's chest rose and fell quicker. She was leaving home. Sure, she needed to leave, but this was where she had been raised. Her home was full of memories of the family she'd lost. This was all she knew.

"It'll be okay," I said low.

Stormy's chin came up. "I'm not worried."

I gave Luke a tight-lipped grin as he pulled out of the drive. We knew she was worried. Anyone would be, but Stormy would probably cut her nose off to spite her face rather than admit a weakness. She could deny it all she wanted, but I watched as she looked through the side mirror as her house faded from view.

Chapter Nine

I discovered March in northwestern Arkansas wasn't close to being as muggy as a southern Mississippi March. The air was thick and heavy, and the sun beat down on us without a cloud in sight to give a reprieve, but being able to watch Luke, I wasn't complaining one bit. His bare chest glistened with sweat as he worked, his jeans hung low on his hips as he lifted the flat tire over his head and tossed it effortlessly in the ditch. Each of his ab muscles tightened with the movement, showing off his beautifully sculpted six pack. I salivated. Holy moly, that was quite possibly the sexiest thing I had ever witnessed, and I'd had the pleasure of watching him chop wood in the winter, but this... this was something else. I grabbed a bottle of water, took a swig, and handed it to a wide-eyed Stormy.

"Wow," she said in a low whisper.

Still staring at him, I nodded. "Yeah."

"Get in," Luke ordered, using his shirt to wipe off his face and chest before tossing it in the truck and getting inside. I wanted to rub that shirt all over me. Stormy must have been having the same thoughts, maybe not about the shirt, but about his hotness, because she ran to the truck door and yanked it open. Before she could get in next to Luke, I swooped in and slid in place while Stormy tried to pull me back by the arm, but I managed to free myself from her grip.

Luke's eyebrows came down as he watched us fight for position next to him. Stormy slammed the door and crossed her arms over her chest in defeat. Brushing my hair out of my eyes, I smiled innocently up at Luke. "Ready."

His arm brushed against mine as he put the truck into gear, and I swear my lady parts cried.

"You hungry?" he asked.

Biting my bottom lip to keep from replying with entirely inappropriate things, I nodded. *Hungry enough to fight off a fifteen-year-old girl for a coveted seat next to you.* I felt starved by the nourishment he had deprived me of for so long. He was my life source and without his mouth on mine, his hands on me, I felt like I was going to starve to death.

"You feeling okay?" he asked, his left wrist on the steering wheel as he used his other hand to reach down and squeeze just above my knee.

"Yep," I squeaked out and pulled at the neck of my shirt. "It's hot in here."

He released my leg to crank up the air. "Drink some more water."

Stormy snorted and murmured, "Clueless."

Maybe sitting next to him wasn't such a great idea.

"Are you hungry?" I turned to Stormy.

Stormy shook her head, her arms still crossed over her chest. I sighed. She had to be hungry. We had driven a good thirty minutes before pulling over to map out a route that would hopefully keep us from populated areas.

Shortly after piling in and getting on the road again, the tire went flat. Since I hadn't thought to check for a lug wrench before heading out on my killing spree, Luke had to drive five miles per hour until we came upon a car that had one.

It had been the longest six-mile drive I'd ever experienced.

I'll give Luke credit, though; he kept his shit together. He didn't yell, he didn't curse (much), and he didn't punch or kick the truck when he got out. I guessed he kept his cool so he wouldn't frighten Stormy. Granted, he wasn't normally a yelling, cussing, fit throwing kind of man, but I tended to bring that out in him from time to time.

"Maybe we should stop and eat?" I asked Luke.

He leaned in and looked at the sky. "Think you two could wait another hour or two? I want to find a place for the night first."

"I can wait," Stormy chimed in agreeably.

I let out a long breath. "We're good."

Food. Shelter. Those were the number one topics and priorities these days. Honestly, I was tired of the repetition. *What are we going to eat? Where will we sleep tonight? We need more fuel. Gah!*

Once upon a time, my biggest worries were if I had enough money to pay the rent on my apartment if I bought a new pair of shoes. I looked down at the one-size-too-large shoe I'd just pilfered from the closet of a dead woman.

Times had definitely changed.

In an attempt to pass time and not worry about the next thing we needed, I turned to Stormy and asked the first question that came to mind. "So, Stormy, what's your favorite color?"

Her eyebrows shot up. "My what?"

"Color, what's your favorite? Mine's red." I smiled, ignoring the glare of death.

"Black," she deadpanned.

"Well... that's very... dark." I slowly nodded my head and Luke chuckled. "Luke?"

"You already know mine."

I did. It was blue. Royal blue, to be exact, and it looked great on him when he wore it. "But Stormy doesn't know."

"Yeah, Luke. I can't go on living if I don't know what your favorite color is," Stormy said, leaning forward so she could look past me to Luke.

Luke laughed until he saw my glare and abruptly stopped. He cleared his throat and brushed the top of his nose with his finger. "Blue."

"Thank you," I told him, then turned to Stormy again. "How about you ask the next question."

This was probably ridiculous, but it was better than awkward silence, and my hope was Stormy would feel more comfortable divulging information if we all had to answer the same questions.

"Okay," Stormy said with a wicked half-grin. "What's your favorite liquor?"

"Kentucky Deluxe," Luke sounded in quickly.

Glancing between the two of them, I rolled my eyes. "Rum."

"Kahlua," Stormy said with a clap of her hands.

Biting my lip to keep from laughing, I turned to Luke and from the line of his lips, he was suffering the same problem. I had never heard of Kahlua being in the hard liquor category, but I guess when *I* was fifteen, strawberry wine was pretty hardcore.

We continued the game until Stormy nodded off, her head resting against the window. I waited until I was certain she was in a deep sleep before getting into a real conversation with Luke. "Think she's doing okay?"

"I think so. She's comfortable enough to fall asleep."

Looking her over, she looked more like thirteen than fifteen with her mouth slightly gaping and the constant scowl on her face was gone. "We need to tell her what we're doing so she understands the danger."

He nodded in agreement. "Let's wait until we are settled for the night first."

"And us... are we... are we okay?" I asked, keeping my eyes trained on the two-lane road.

Running a hand over his forehead, he said, "We're okay. I'm still pissed, but we're fine."

"I understand," I said, nodding. "I really am sorry."

"I know," he exhaled.

The truck fell into another uncomfortable silence as I let the ramifications of my actions sink in. Leaning my head back, I moved my eyes to the shoulders of the shirtless Luke. I was never going to feel his bare skin on mine again. I was never going to hear my name on his lips as he moved inside me. Never going to hear him whisper *I love you* again. And I had no one to blame except myself.

I thought about the note Luke had left me after Jacob had been dragged from the house. It had two words: *Trust me*. Trust me. He had never given me reason not to trust him, yet I assumed the worst. Sure, it was devastating to witness from my point of view, but still… I knew better. Or at least I *should* have known better.

What I needed was to suck it up and do something about it. I couldn't give up on him, on us. No way was I letting him go without one hell of a fight. No matter what I had to do, I would prove my loyalty to him.

"Heads up," Luke called loudly enough to wake Stormy and bring me to the present. "There are a couple cars coming."

Reaching down, I handed Luke his gun before placing mine in my lap. Stormy gripped the door handle. "Do you have another?"

"No," Luke said firmly.

Seeing the fear in her pretty brown eyes, I patted her leg. "It's okay. Luke will take care of us."

"I'm not worried about it. I can take care of myself," she spat out, but her white-knuckled grip on the door handle called her a liar.

As the two cars came closer, we slowed until we were stopped window to window with them. I don't know why we didn't keep driving, but I needed to believe my own words and trust Luke to take care of us.

I inspected the cars as Luke rolled down the window. The first car had two men in it. One looked to be in his late thirties with dark blond hair to his shoulders. The passenger was older and the top of his head bald leaving only a horseshoe shaped hair left on his head. Both looked cautious but not necessarily malicious. My eyes moved to the car behind them. There appeared to be two people in front and two in back, but I couldn't determine their sex or age due to the glare of the sun bouncing off their windshield. It would be at least six against three if things went downhill. I debated if I should go ahead and give Stormy a gun, but if she didn't know what she was doing with one, she could end up hurting one of us or herself.

"You should turn around," the driver said.

"Why's that?" Luke asked conversationally, keeping the gun pointed toward the driver but low enough under the window of the truck to keep it hidden.

"Nothing but trouble that way," he said, pointing a thumb toward the road behind them. Instinctively, I looked down the road, praying more people weren't headed our way.

"What kind of trouble?" Luke asked, rubbing his unshaven chin.

The driver's eyes darted between Luke and me before giving a resigned sigh. He seemed scared and subsequently scaring me. "Men claiming to be the New Army. They're taking men, recruiting them whether they want to or not, saying it's their right to draft them. From what I hear, it ain't safe to be taking two young ladies there, either."

Luke nodded his understanding and my stomach churned. "Is it a town?"

"Yeah, for now. It's an hour, maybe an hour and a half away."

"How many of this New Army do you think there are there?"

His shoulders rose and fell. "I don't know. Twenty, thirty maybe. Could be more. I didn't wait around to get a head count, if you know what I mean."

Luke nodded absently, but his eyes stared straight ahead. My heart thudded against my chest hard enough I thought it was going to burst out. We were so close.

After a moment, Luke's tone became more relaxed and he forced a smile. "We haven't run into any trouble since hitting the Mississippi border, so you should be good. Thanks for the info, man."

"Thanks. Stay safe."

Luke rolled up the window and waited until both cars went by before taking his foot off the brake.

"It's them, isn't it?" I asked, my heart hammering away.

"Who?" Stormy asked, but I couldn't answer her.

Our guys were more than likely a little more than an hour away. What if we didn't get there in time? What if we couldn't get my brother and Adam out? What if one of them wasn't there at all? What would we do then?

Reading my anxiety, Luke patted my thigh, and left his hand there as he leaned forward to speak to both Stormy and me. "Let's find a place to settle in for the night and then we'll eat and talk."

Reaching down, I covered his hand with mine and held on tight. He squeezed my thigh and leaned into me, determination turning in his eyes. "It's going to be okay."

Not able to speak, I nodded and kept my grip on his hand. To my surprise, he didn't pull away but gently caressed my inner thigh with his thumb. I put my faith in Luke. *It's going to be okay.*

There it was again, the thing I had been denying myself.

Hope.

If I didn't keep hope, fear would take hold and consume me. Fear of what would come next. Fear of losing the people we love. Fear of being left alone. Hope was the only thing worth living for. Hope for the people I love. Hope for a better life. I had been bogged down to the point I couldn't see hope's light in the deep pit of fear. Luke was my lighthouse.

I leaned my head onto his strong shoulder and closed my eyes.

It was going to be okay.

Chapter Ten

Rolling her eyes for what felt like the thousandth time since stopping for the night, Stormy held up her dainty hand. "So you want me to stay back, on my own, *again*, while you two go have all the fun?"

We had taken turns explaining to her why we were on the road and what we were up against. Both of us assumed she would want to tuck tail and get away from us and the danger we presented her with, but no. Not Stormy. She was eager to jump right in and be part of the Rescue Squad, as she called us.

"Where do you get *fun* from that?" Luke asked with his eyebrows drawn together, his upper lip curled.

She brushed her hair over her slender shoulders. "Hello? Are you serious?"

"I'm pretty sure he's serious," I said, shoveling another spoonful of cream of chicken soup mixed with plain rice in my mouth. As far as meals went these days, it was actually rather tasty.

"You think the two of you can take on thirty men by yourselves?" she asked condescendingly.

"No, I don't plan on taking on all thirty men." Luke shook his head. "I don't plan on any issues at all because I'll be going alone."

"The hell you will." My body went ram-rod straight and my eyes bore into his through the flicker of the candlelight. He returned my glare with a raised eyebrow. "You're not going alone."

"And neither one of you are going without me!" Stormy shrilled.

"You're not going," Luke and I said in unison.

"This is bullshit. You can't go off being Captain America and expect us to wait here."

She had a valid point, but she still wasn't going. I, on the other hand, was. "You can't go, you're a child, but I *am* going."

"No, you're not," Luke said.

"I'm not a child!" Stormy stomped her foot. "I'm almost sixteen! In *some* countries I would be married with two kids."

"Stormy…" I said, trying to bite back a laugh. Her theatrics were ridiculous but refreshing.

"Fáng pí," Stormy spat out.

My eyes narrowed at her tone. What the hell was she saying?

"It's not bullshit, little girl. It's dangerous shit, and you're *not* getting involved." Luke pointed his long, thick index finger at her. Stormy shrank back, but her glare didn't waver.

"You're staying here and that's final," I said, but Luke was already shaking his head since he knew what was coming next. "I'm going."

"No, you're not." He stood and started toward the door, calling over his shoulder, "I'm going outside."

"It's not fair," Stormy whined.

"Life's not fair," I said, leaning back into the couch, exhausted from the day.

Luke was seriously crazy if he thought I was going to let him take on the troops on his own. Sure, he'd worked for them, and they probably wouldn't suspect he was there to free Jacob and Adam, but his movements would be observed. If I went with him, he could cause a distraction while I found the guys and slipped them out. Luke could get out before anyone was the wiser.

Now, all I had to do was convince Luke I was right. For some reason, I didn't think he was going to be very receptive of my ideas.

"I don't get why both of you are so against me helping. I made it on my own for a really long time. I know how to take care of myself."

I exhaled. "I know you can. *We* know you can, but what if something goes wrong and we get caught? I can deal with being caught, but I promised to keep you safe and I've had enough guilt on my shoulders lately."

Hearing my own words hit me. That was precisely what Luke was trying to do for me. He had promised me a long time ago he would keep me safe, and he thought leaving me behind was best for me. Maybe it was an impossible promise to make in the world we lived in, but I would do my best where Stormy was concerned. She was a child, I was not.

"You're strong, Stormy. You've made it all this time on your own, but I'm not that strong. I couldn't handle it if something happened to you or Luke because of me."

"Bull. You're still alive, aren't you? We're both strong, and that's why we *both* need to help."

"No, sweetheart. I'm really not." I licked my dry lips and decided she needed to know how important it was that she stay safe, for me. I barely knew her, but I had made the choice to take her from her home and take care of her until we could find a safe place for her to stay with people we could trust to make sure that happened.

"When I thought Jacob had been killed and Luke was a part of it, I lost it. I lost my soul because I let my heart be

142

shattered and I let it destroyed who I was. I felt like it was my fault because I was supposed to protect Jacob, and I'd failed him." I closed my eyes and put my head in my hands, humiliated to admit my actions that night. "I flipped my lid and went nuts. I couldn't see a life without the people I loved and I tried to shoot myself, but the gun jammed. Had the gun not jammed, I wouldn't know Jacob was alive and I would have left him alone. I would have left them all alone. I would have never met you."

I raised my head to look at her with a weak smile. "You are stronger than I am and I promised to protect you, and I *will* protect you because I'm not strong enough to handle it if you were hurt because of me."

"You really tried to die?" she asked with a hard swallow.

"Yeah, I really did." I stood, embarrassed. "When that didn't happen, I was angry at myself and took all that anger and focused it on Luke. It was the only thing keeping me alive, if that's what you want to call it." For some reason, my mind went to the zombie book on the girl's nightstand. I had been the zombie in this story. I had been the zombie.

"That's just stupid," Stormy said with a shake of her head.

I laughed. "*Very* stupid, but I never said I was a smart woman."

Stormy watched me with eyes seeing much more than a teenage girl should. "You know he's in love with you, right?"

I tried to smile, but my lips wobbled. "I know. I'm in love with him, too. It probably doesn't make sense, but I hated myself to the point I couldn't feel anything except hate and I took that out on him."

"I get it." She nodded. There was pain behind her eyes. I imagined she was thinking of the family she had lost. "Life's a bitch."

"Pretty much sums it up." Moving to her, I squeezed her shoulder though I wanted to give her a hug but worried she might hold a pillow over my face while I slept if I did. "How about I go outside and see if Luke needs help and you get ready for bed?"

"Sure," she said, picking up a pen and writing in her notebook.

Stepping out of the house onto the small concrete porch, I listened for Luke while my eyes adjusted to the dark night. Other than the light sound of a breeze blowing through the open field in front of the house, all was silent. *Figures.* Luke was like a cat; he wouldn't be heard until he wanted to be heard.

Looking to my right, I spotted Luke with his forearms on the tailgate of the truck and his head bowed down far enough to block his face from my view. "Luke?"

His head came up slowly until his face came into view. He looked pained. I took a step forward. "Luke, is everything okay?"

His eyes followed my movements and he shook his head. *Shit.* I swallowed. Something was wrong. Quickening my steps until I was next to him, I placed my hand on his arm. "Luke, talk to me. What's going on?"

I glanced around, expecting to see troops surrounding us, but I saw nothing. Suddenly, Luke's hands cupped my face. Startled, my eyes widened, and before I could ask him what the hell was going on, his lips crashed into mine. He pushed my mouth open with his tongue and took control before I realized what was happening.

One hand wrapped around my neck as the other snaked around my back, slamming my body against him. This kiss. This kiss was filled with so many emotions it was hard to hang on to one before another pushed it away. Hurt. Anger. Fear. Regret. Love. It was everything between us and I felt it all.

I didn't know what flipped the switch inside him, but I wasn't about to stop whatever was happening to ask. If I did, he might let me go and it would be a fall I couldn't stand up from again.

With little effort, Luke lifted me until I could wrap my legs around his hips, his hardness pressed against me. He walked us to the far side of the truck, out of view from the house, never removing his lips from mine.

Pushing my back against the door of the truck, he leaned back and ripped my shirt off me before owning my mouth again. His strong hips held me in place while his hands stroked and caressed my breasts. I couldn't help but be a little embarrassed at the state of my body, especially my breasts. They were a victim of the mistreatment I had inflicted on myself over the past few weeks, but if he noticed, he didn't show it.

Wanting to feel his skin on mine, I bunched his shirt in my hands and pulled it up and over his head. As soon as his hands were free, Luke gripped my hips as I grinded myself against him. He growled and my body responded with a shudder.

Releasing my legs and lowering me to the ground, he unbuttoned my jeans and pulled them down. I kicked off my shoes and yanked away my pants before I was wrapped around him again. His pants were at his knees and his thickness pressed against my heat. Luke held me hovered over him, but he didn't enter me. Instead, he brushed a thumb over my swollen bottom lip as his hand held my neck and chin still. It was gentle, but it was possessive, and it got my attention.

"Don't *ever* try to leave me again," he whispered, fear piercing his words. Luke was rarely scared.

The hurt in his eyes was blurred by the tears filling mine as I nodded.

"Say it, Roni. Promise me you'll never try again," he said, this time with more force, but the raw fear was still there.

"I won't leave you. I promise." I leaned down and kissed the palm of his hand.

In one movement, he slid deep inside of me, his hands biting into my ass. I laid the back of my head against the cold window, exposing my neck as I arched my back. His strong arm wrapped around the small of my back and his mouth covered my nipple, sucking hard before working his way to my neck.

"Look at me," he said, moving himself in and out of me in torturously slow motions.

Raising my head, I found his eyes. Seeing the varying emotions burning behind them, my heart grew to the point I thought it would burst inside my chest. "Luke," I whispered, not knowing how to take away whatever pain he was being tortured with.

"You're mine. You'll always be mine," he commanded. "No one gets to take you from me. No one, Roni. Not even you. Don't ever fucking do or try that again."

That's when I knew he'd heard me admit to trying to end my life. I never wanted him to know my shame for this moment that almost never was. Tears streamed down my face as I faced him with my humiliation.

"I'm so sorry." I shook my head. Grabbing the back of his head, I pulled my body flush to his and kissed him with everything I had, trying to communicate all the wrongs I wanted to make right.

Losing all control, he pounded inside me, over and over, beating away all the pain and replacing it with more of a reason for living. Feeling him move inside of me felt as natural and right as breathing. It wasn't just sex. It was him forgiving me. With every movement he told me he loved me. He told me I was his. And I was safe. With every thrust, my pleasure built until I was on top of the world ready for the freefall back to earth. Our kisses became frantic, my heels digging into his ass as I fell. My body tightened around him and he held my head as his mouth covered my cries. Seconds later, his movements became less rhythmic and his breath came out quicker. My body clenched him as my arms wrapped around him. I buried my face in his chest as he groaned out his release and fell forward, resting both our weight against the truck.

Peace surrounded me. Love engulfed me. I was his forever.

With the fire inside me dissipating, a light breeze cooled my bare skin, giving me chills. Luke raised his head and kissed my forehead before slipping out of me and gently letting my feet find footing on the ground. Bending down, he pulled up his jeans, while I stood feeling naked for the first time since he'd pulled my clothes off. He eyed the ground until he found what he was looking for and bent down. He turned to me with a sexy grin and held up my bra and shirt. I reached for the bra, but he yanked it just out of reach.

Instead, he rested the bra across his bare shoulder and helped me into my shirt. "I'll get something for you to clean up with. Be right back."

Watching him walk away, my head became clearer and my nerves threatened to take control. What if he thought having sex with me was a mistake? That tension got too high and he acted before thinking. If he regretted being with me, I would die. I would run away, find a cave to move into, and never come out.

Bending forward to search the ground, I decided if I found my shoes before he came back out, it was a sign to get the heck out of dodge and save face. I couldn't really do it, but it sounded less humiliating than being told, *let's be friends* or *oops, that shouldn't have happened.*

Stop it, Veronica. He loves you, you idiot. Trust him.

Before I managed to find even one shoe, Luke's boots came into view.

"What are you doing?"

Standing, I brushed the hair from my face and tugged at the hem of my shirt. "Um, I was looking for my shoes."

"Here," he handed me a cold, wet rag. "Clean up. I'll find your shoes."

Walking gingerly on the gravel driveway, I moved to the front of the truck, out of view of Luke and the house before taking care of business. Once done, I made my way back to him, still not sure how things were going to play out. He handed me my jeans and I slipped them on.

"I can take the shoes now," I said, holding out my hands for the shoes he held.

He moved forward—closing me in against the truck—and set the shoes on the hood before grabbing me by the waist and lifting me to the hood. While speaking, he lifted each foot and dusted the gravel from them. "Stormy is snoring in the first room."

I smiled, not only at the thought of Stormy snoring, but the way Luke was touching me. He slipped both shoes on my feet, tightening the laces but leaving them free. Spreading my knees apart with his body, he moved in close, rubbing against my tender thighs, but I didn't mind. I didn't mind at all.

He wrapped his arms around my back and buried his face in my chest, his heavy breath warming my chilled skin. Tentatively, I stroked his hair and kissed the top of his head, enjoying this moment because after tomorrow, there was no guarantee we would have another for a long time to come.

"I mean it, Roni. Don't ever try something like that again," he said, his words guttural.

I palmed his cheeks with both of my hands. "I won't, I promise. I wasn't myself then, but I won't go back to that place ever again."

He nodded and I leaned in and kissed him. "How did you hear me?"

"Window is open in the living room and I was sitting on the porch."

Letting my hands fall to the hood, I turned back to the house. "Oh." I reached for my bra but he swiftly stepped out of reach. "Can I have my bra now, please?"

"Hell no. This thing is ugly as shit," he said, holding it up with his fingertips like it was radioactive. "I think I'll burn it. A bra like this needs to be in museums, not on you."

I couldn't help but laugh. The offending piece of fabric really was ugly and nothing like he had witnessed me sporting while on the orchard. This was a plain Jane, no frizzles, thick-strapped granny bra. It probably *should* be burned, but it was all I had.

"I can't go around without a bra on, Luke," I said, jumping to the ground and trying to swipe it from him again. He was too quick and tall for me to snag it away.

"At least don't put it back on tonight."

Crossing my arms over my hard nipples, I lifted my chin. "Only if you leave your shirt off for the rest of the night."

Luke looked down at his bare chest, then back at me with a sly grin. "Deal."

I couldn't stop my mouth from breaking into a wide smile. This felt like it used to between us. It felt right. All we needed now was to get our brothers and return home. I moved in closer to him, close enough I had to tilt my head back to look into his face. He bent down and kissed me, then wrapped his arm around my shoulders and walked us into the house.

We were greeted by the sounds of Stormy's snoring. I smiled. It reminded me of Jacob when he slept, though not nearly as loud as Jacob. I couldn't wait to see him again and to finally meet Adam.

Stepping out of Luke's embrace, I lit a fresh candle and blew out the one that had burned down. The apple scent of the candle filled the air, reminding me of home. Soon, very soon, we would go home. All of us. My family.

I turned to Luke and watched as he leaned over the couch and closed the window, the muscles in his back stretching with his movement. I clinched my hands at my sides to keep from reaching out and touching the fading red welts my nails had left on him. If I did, it wouldn't stop with one touch, and we needed to discuss the plan for getting our brothers.

He turned and my eyes moved from his abs to the tattoo on his chest, past his corded neck, and finally to his smirking mouth. By the time I made it to his eyes, my nipples were hard and I squeezed my thighs together.

"Roni?" he asked, quirking a brow.

"I, uh…" I scratched behind my ear and looked away to collect my thoughts. "What's the game plan for tomorrow? Do you think they're there?"

"I'm not sure. I would bet at least Jacob is with them, but we could get lucky and both of them could be there."

"Wouldn't that be amazing?" I shook my head at the thought. It would be more than amazing; it would be a miracle. "Wait, do you have enough medicine for Adam if he is there?"

Luke sat and toed the bag I'd pulled from the trunk of his car. "There's enough for a little over a week."

"Good. That's plenty of time," I said, my wheels spinning. "How do we do this? I know we can't go in together."

"I'll handle it. You just worry about the little one in there," he said, pointing a thumb toward the hallway.

I scoffed and plopped down on the couch to look at him opened-mouthed. "You can't be serious."

"Dead serious. You can't go. They've seen your photo, and Griffin is a smart man. If I show up, he's going to be watching."

"Then you stay with Stormy and I'll go check things out. He won't remember what I look like if you don't trigger his brain."

"Yes, he will. Yours is not a face easily forgotten." His words would have melted me, but I wasn't ready to not be pissed.

"Then I'll cut my hair and wear a cap," I retorted.

"You're not cutting your hair."

I stomped my foot. "I'll cut my hair if I want."

Leaning forward, Luke rubbed his mouth with his hand to cover his smile.

"It's not funny."

"You're right, it's not, but you're still not going."

Taking a deep, cleansing breath, I tried to look at it from his point of view and explain how his point of view was wrong. "Look, I understand why you don't want me to go. You want to keep me safe, and I get that, but you have to understand you're not alone. They are both of our brothers. You might not like it, but you know as well as I do it would be safer together. We could go in separately. You make up some excuse for being there, and I can find the boys and sneak them out while you have the others occupied. Simple." I moved to him and sat on his lap, wrapping my arms over his shoulders, nuzzling his neck. "I have to do this."

Giving a resigned sigh, Luke wrapped his big arms around me and squeezed. "We need to get some sleep. It's going to be a long day tomorrow."

Lifting my head from his shoulder, I look into his eyes. "Does that mean you agree?"

"It means I don't have a choice," he said before running his hand through my hair and kissing me.

"You know we'll be okay, right?"

He nodded slowly, not making eye contact. "I'll make sure of it."

"*We'll* make sure of it." I smiled, excited about convincing him I was right as well as the possibilities tomorrow held.

Carrying the scented candle, we made our way to the bedroom across the hall from Stormy and went to bed. Luke took his spot closest to the door like he always did. I had asked him once why he slept that way and he told me if anyone came in, they would have to go through him before they could reach me. I smiled at the thought. Crawling over him, I took my spot, tucked in at his side, my head on his chest. With my fingertip, I traced the shadow of the Special Forces motto tattoo on his chest. *De Oppresso Libre*. Free the Oppressed. It wasn't just a motto to him—it was a way of life. It was part of him, and tomorrow he would get to live it.

"I love you," I whispered.

He kissed the top of my head and put his hand over mine, pressing it down over his heart. "All yours, Baby."

My heart both swelled and constricted in the time it took between two beats. He meant it. His heart was mine and I hadn't taken care of it. I wouldn't make that mistake again. I would prove to him I was worthy of him.

"When Wells and Griffin realize they're gone they're going to come after us." His voice vibrated in my ear. "Be ready to run hard and run fast for a long time."

Chapter Eleven

I woke to an empty bed and the roar of a truck engine coming to life. *Oh, hell no!* Knifing up, I ran barefoot through the house to the front porch in just enough time to see the truck backing out of the driveway, and when Luke spotted me, he hit the gas. I ran as hard as I could, but by the time I made it to the road, the truck was barely visible.

"Shit!" I yelled at the top of my lungs, stomping my bare feet on the paved road.

"What's going on?" Stormy called from the opened front door. Her hair was wild and her eyes were wide.

My hands were on my hips and my chest heaved. Starting back toward her, I waved a hand toward the road. "He freaking left."

When I reached her, the fear was evident in her eyes. "He just left us?"

"Yep, the bastard," I said, doing a terrible job of hiding my anger.

"But I thought... I thought he loved you. I thought we were safe with him?" She stepped forward. "He just left us!"

Realizing what she was thinking, I shook my head hard and grabbed Stormy's upper arms to calm her. "No, no. He didn't *leave* us, leave us. He just left to get the boys without me."

Stormy's body relaxed under my grip. "You mean like you were going to do to me?"

Releasing my hold, I looked up to the sky and prayed for patience. "That was different."

"Sure it was," Stormy said, crossing her thin arms over her chest. "So what are we going to do about it?"

Swiping a hand over my face, I let both arms drop to my sides. "I don't know. Last night he said to be ready to run, so maybe gather everything?"

She cocked her head to the side. "Get ready? That's all. Seriously?" When I didn't speak, she shook her head and rolled her eyes. "We're so going to die out here."

Luke was alone. He was an idiot for going alone and would likely get caught, and I would end up having to save all three of them. How in the hell was I supposed to do that when I didn't even have a way to get there?

Pacing back and forth, I scanned the area until I saw our solution. "Come on. Let's get ready. We have a lot to get done in very little time."

Moving into the house with Stormy on my heels, I went straight to the bedroom and put on my shoes. "Go get your makeup. Bring any V-neck tops you have, too."

"You are so weird," Stormy said, walking to the bedroom where she'd slept.

Opening the curtains for more light, I moved the oversized mirror resting on the drawer to a better position and inspected myself. *Gah. I look like shit.* My hair was a mess and the circles under my eyes were dark enough to resemble war paint. I had a lot of work to do if I was going to make myself presentable.

Rummaging through the house, I found a hair brush, dry shampoo, and a bottle of perfume. I also found a bra. It was a size too small but only helped to push my boobs together, making them look larger than they were. Stormy came in with her oversized purse and a handful of shirts.

"What are we doing?"

"We're going to go bring the boys back," I said, brushing my hair and spraying the roots with the dry shampoo.

"Are you planning to dress like a hooker and hitch a ride?" Stormy asked in all seriousness.

I laughed. "No. There were a few cars down the road. Surely we can get one of them started. I'm going to look like a hooker in case I need to talk my way out of anything." I picked through her shirts and found one I thought could possibly fit my larger frame and slipped it over my head. Looking in the mirror, I smiled. "I'm hoping if we get stopped, they'll be too busy looking at the girls to pay much attention to my face."

"What about me? You're not leaving me here alone." Stormy sat next to me and watched me through the mirror.

"No, you're coming with me, but you're going to stay out of view. Hopefully, we both will."

"Can I do your makeup then?" she asked, excited about the prospect.

"Sure, but we need to hurry."

An hour later, we sat inside a sedan, searching for a set of keys. I had already searched the house only to find the remains of the residents but no keys. The keys were in there somewhere, but I couldn't handle looking around any longer.

"Move and let me hotwire it," Stormy said, stepping out of the passenger side and walking around to me. Ignoring her, I reached my hand under the seat, feeling around and coming up empty. "Move."

"You do *not* know how to hotwire a car." I laughed.

"*Move*," Stormy said again, pointing her thumb away.

"Okay," I said, throwing my hands in the air. "But if you screw up this car, you're going to be riding in the back of the truck all the way to Canaan."

Getting out of the car, I watched as she climbed in and popped off the panel at the bottom of the steering wheel. She leaned in, blocking my view. I sighed. She was so going to screw up this car, and then we were going to be stuck here with me looking like a hooker for no reason. In the old reality, my current look wouldn't necessarily make me look like a hooker, but no one wore makeup anymore. It was as useless as a washing machine, unless you were, in fact, a hooker.

Then I heard it—the engine trying to turn over. Gripping the door frame, my eyes widened. "Try again."

"Duh."

The engine whined and I yelled, "Push the gas pedal."

Stormy twisted her body and hit the gas and the car miraculously came to life. I jumped in place and let out a whoop before Stormy climbed out and joined me. Taking her by surprise, I wrapped her in a tight hug. Her body went rigid before she leaned into the hug and put her head on my shoulder. I squeezed her and looked down. "Let's go save the men."

Stormy stepped back with a wide smile and ran around the car and got inside. I slid in and checked the gas gauge; it registered nearly a full tank. *Hallelujah!* I backed out of the driveway and headed toward the battlefield.

"How in the world did you know how to hotwire a car?" I asked in total amazement of this little girl.

Stormy flipped her hair and flashed a sly grin. "I have my ways."

In complete disbelief, I burst out laughing. No wonder she'd made it on her own for so long.

Maybe she really was a ninja.

****

White-knuckling the steering wheel, I swallowed against the lump in my throat as the town came into view. Stormy sat up in the chair, her hands fisted in her lap. This wasn't like Canaan. There weren't road blocks—at least from this side—and not nearly as many people trying to come in and out. What concerned me the most were the people so far seemed to be in a hurry to get wherever they were heading. There wasn't laughter in the air or people stopping to talk to one another.

"Well, here we go," I said with a heavy sigh. I was doing my best to keep my voice calm and neutral, but I was failing miserably.

"Yep," Stormy said, keeping her eyes pinned to the road.

"I'm going to try to hide the car so we can make a quick getaway." I slowed down to a crawl before making a right on the next street, then made a U-turn and parked behind a car with flat tires. I hoped the old warehouse next to it would help to keep it unnoticed. Switching into park, I released the brake and turned to Stormy. "Now, how do I turn it off?"

Reaching over, she tugged on the loose wires and killed the engine. "Like that."

"That works. Okay, so we're going to kind of walk around and see if we can find where all these military guys are. Act natural. Don't run unless I tell you to, and if we see Luke, pretend you don't see him at all. If they realize we're with him, they'll probably kill us or him or someone. Alright?" I hated this. I hated that Stormy was with me and neither one of us had a weapon to defend ourselves if it came to that. *God, I hope it doesn't come to that.*

"What're our names?" Stormy asked.

"What?"

"We need names. You said Luke said they know who you are, so we need names in case we get stopped and they ask," Stormy explained like I was an idiot.

"Hmm, I don't know. Pick one." I was ready to get out there and find them. The fact that all three of them could possibly be there made me want to run until I found them.

Stormy tapped a finger against her chin while she inspected me. "Gina. Gina is a good name for a lady of the night."

"A lady of the night?" I tilted my head back and prayed for patience. "Where in the world have you heard of that kind of thing?"

"I'm fifteen, not three. There were things like television, the Internet, and *junior high* before everyone started dying."

My lips twitched and I swallowed down a laugh. No matter how the world was around us, she was still very much a smartass teenage girl, and I loved that about her. "Gina it is. What do you want your name to be? Tiffany maybe?" I asked, lifting my chin a tad.

Stormy sucked in air and her eyes narrowed. "No, you did not!"

"What? You don't like that name?" I shrugged my shoulders and played dumb.

"Don't call me that. Call me Paula. Let's go," she said, opening the door and slamming it once she was out.

Hurrying so she wouldn't wander off ahead of me, I got out and shut the door. "Stay close, *Paula*."

Stormy put her hands on her non-existent hips and waited until I reached her before moving. Once we turned the corner and four people came into view, the lightness from our previous banter fled and we were in game mode.

Slowing our steps, I took in the group. It was two older women, another woman probably in her early forties, and a man—probably in his forties, too—sitting in a wheelchair.

164

They watched us curiously but didn't seem to be ready to strike. I couldn't imagine what they thought about the two of us walking around the corner. I bet we were quite the sight.

"Follow my lead," I said through the side of my mouth before we were within hearing distance. Putting a hand out in front of Stormy, we stopped walking.

"Hey," I said lightly with a small wave. "Can you tell us where the army guys are?"

The group stared at us, not moving, not speaking. I cleared my throat and twisted a strand of hair around my finger. "See, they recruited my boyfriend and I came by to tell him goodbye before they head out."

"That ain't no place for young girls to go," the man in the wheelchair said firmly before leaning over and spitting on the sidewalk.

"Well, I just miss him so much. I *have* to tell him goodbye," I whined.

"What are you doing taking that girl with you?" one of the women asked.

I opened my mouth to speak, but Stormy spoke up first, "I'm going to work. Child labor laws don't really exist anymore, and I bet someone needs their shoes shined or a button sewed on."

Reaching down, I squeezed her hand. "Oh, she's so funny. My boyfriend is her brother and she wants to tell him bye, too. It's okay, though, we'll just find them on our own."

Still holding Stormy's hand, I began walking us away from the group.

"Go that way," the woman in her forties said, pointing. "They're a few blocks that way then turn left. You'll find them."

"Thanks!" I kept my voice annoyingly high-pitched. "You all have a good day now."

"Guessing it'll be better than yours," one of them said as we walked away, hoping she wasn't right.

Once we rounded the corner, I released Stormy's hand but scolded her. "You can't be a smartass today. Can you please try to act sweet?"

"Try not being such a loser and I'll try to behave," she scoffed.

"Stormy..." my voice dropped in warning.

Tossing her hands up in defeat, she sighed, "Okay, sorry. I'll be a sweet, boring little girl."

"Thank you."

We walked in silence until it was time for us to veer left. Foot traffic picked up as we moved farther into town. I leaned in. "I'm going to find an alley or a shop to walk through. Keep your eyes out for Luke, but don't react if you see him. Okay?"

"Yeah."

Eyes followed us as we moved along the sidewalk. The men's eyes were leering and the women's were glaring. I had an overwhelming urge to pull my shirt up to hide my cleavage but forced myself to stand tall. If all the attention was on me, it meant it wasn't on Stormy.

Down the road, a few men wore military pants and boots with rifles strapped over their shoulders, talking to each other instead of guarding like they were supposed to be doing. At the next side-road between buildings, I tugged Stormy left and started walking faster. "We're close. We're going to stay out of view if we can and try to find out where they're staying."

"Okay. What do they look like?"

"Jacob is a dirty-blond who will probably be walking with a limp and Adam is a younger, thinner version of Luke from what I've seen," I explained as I darted my head around the corner to see down the next road. I quickly yanked myself back and put my hand out to keep Stormy from moving. "There're guys with guns on this side, too."

Biting my lip, I assessed the situation. There were men with guns at each corner on our side, and I imagined it was the same from the other side, which meant there was someone inside the square they wanted to protect or someone they wanted to keep out.

It had to be where the men were camped out, and it had to be where Jacob and Adam were being held.

Twisting my hands, I turned to Stormy, wondering how I could get inside and keep her out of view but came up with nothing.

"Are you chickening out?" Stormy asked with her hands posted on her hips.

"No. Just thinking."

"Could you think a little faster?"

Releasing a frustrated breath, I matched Stormy's stance and narrowed my eyes. I conjured up as much of my mother as I could. "Do you think you can stop throwing attitude at me? I will walk you back to the car."

Her shoulders hunched over and she looked to her feet. "Sorry."

It was obvious she was nervous, though I doubted she would ever admit it. Her already flippant attitude blatantly ramped up to snarky when she was stressed. I got it. It was part of her coping mechanism. Mine was jumping to conclusions and acting before thinking. And that was the reason I needed a solid plan before we threw ourselves inside the lion's den. If I was caught and Luke had to save us all, he would be livid. If Stormy was caught, I would never forgive myself.

Rising my head to the heavens to ask for divine help, I spotted a metal ladder attached to the building. After a silent thanks, I looked from left to right to see if anyone was paying us any attention. "Okay, I have the start of a plan."

"That sounds promising," Stormy said under her breath.

"I'm going to lift you up and you grab on to that ladder." I pointed above us haughtily. Stormy gave a half-smile, a recognizable approval, and nodded. "I should be able to jump and reach it after you're up."

Lacing my fingers together, I turned myself into a human stepstool. "Move as fast as you can once you reach it so no one sees."

"Got it," Stormy said, placing her small foot in my palms. She straightened her leg and used my face as a hand placement until her weight lifted off me.

I kept my eyes moving from right to left, making sure no one noticed us. Thankfully, no one who had passed by paid attention to what was going on around them. Something popped me on top of my head, and I raised my hand to rub my head as I watched a pebble bounce away. I looked up to find Stormy waving me up.

Taking one last glance at the street, I jumped as hard as I could until my hand latched onto the ladder. *Shit.* It wasn't as easy as it looked. My hands were already burning, and my arms wouldn't last long if I didn't get moving. Pulling with everything I had, I managed to move my body up enough to lift my leg and hook a foot on the bottom step.

Once I got my weight distributed, it didn't take long to make it to the top.

Stormy helped me over the ledge, and I plopped down on the graveled rooftop. "Holy hell. I'm really out of shape," I groaned between ragged breaths.

"Come on, old lady," Stormy teased with a light laugh.

"I'm not an old lady," I said moaning as I stood.

"Sure, you're not."

She had no clue my back and thighs hurt from the amount of exertion Luke and I had put them through against the truck the night before. It had absolutely nothing to do with my age. "I'm only ten years older than you are."

Eleven, actually, but she didn't need any more ammunition.

"I know," she grinned.

Getting down to business, I looked around the rooftop. There was a shed-like structure in the middle of the roof, which I assumed opened to a stairwell, and there were three industrial-sized air conditioning units. Plenty of places for cover if we ended up needing it and another way to get out if we were seen.

"Let's walk as quietly as possible to the other side. Sound is going to travel, so keep it down. If we get caught, separate and meet up at the car. If I'm not there in thirty minutes, go back to the house and I'll find another way."

Not waiting for her to argue, I hunched over and began hoofing it to the other side. I looked back to find Stormy in the same crouched position close behind me.

Good girl.

Peeking over the ledge gave us a full view of the buildings around the area as well as the small courtyard which seemed to be the hub of the town. First, I looked from rooftop to rooftop, making sure no one else had the same idea as us. The coast was clear. I found a bit of arrogance in that. They didn't expect anyone to be brazen enough to try to infiltrate their camp and challenge the hold they had wherever they went.

The bastards.

Shouldn't they know those who rule the sky rule the war?

"What are we looking for?" Stormy whispered.

I wanted to laugh. I didn't have a fucking clue what I was doing but thought it best to fake it all the same. "Getting a feel for the layout. Check out the people coming and going and maybe someone will lead us to their base."

"There are people everywhere," Stormy said with worry in each word.

Seeing what we were up against, I let air fill my cheeks before slowly releasing it. "Yep."

"Look, there's Luke!" she whisper-yelled.

My eyes whipped toward Stormy's line of sight, and there he was. All six foot, three inches of pure testosterone strolled along the road with another man beside him. They stopped, and Luke tilted toward the man, his sinewy arms that held me up the night before crossed over his broad chest. The man next to him stabbed a finger toward him. Luke leaned in a fraction and his lips barely moved. Whatever he said must have been a warning because the man's hands quickly dropped and he shuffled from one foot to the next as his head bobbed while he spoke. Even from our perch, the tension between the two sucked the energy from the area.

When the man turned to look behind him, I understood why Luke looked like he was keeping his arms crossed so he didn't wrap his hands around the man's neck. It was the same prick who came to the orchard—General Wells's right-hand man. The man who read the letter I wrote to Luke. The man who stole the photo of the three of us I'd placed in Luke's bag to remind him we were waiting for him to come home.

The man who came for Jacob.

For the life of me, I couldn't remember his fucking name, but I would never—not in a million years—forget that face.

My body was involuntarily rising when Stormy's hand wrapped around my upper arm and tugged me back down. "Are you crazy?" Stormy pinched her lips and hissed. "If the hordes of men with guns don't kill you, Luke will."

If Luke saw us, he would flip out and probably end up getting himself hurt in the process of trying to keep us out of danger. It would be best if Luke didn't see us until we secured the guys and were on our way out. That would be safer for all of us.

"Luke!" someone called.

Luke turned his head and a wide smile overtook his face. His arms fell to his sides as he took a step away from the asshole. Looking across the square, my breath caught and Stormy sighed next to me.

"Holy shit," Stormy said in awe. I agreed, but for probably entirely different reasons.

There walked Adam. It had to be him. He was nearly identical to Luke, except Adam was much thinner, had longer hair, and his skin tone was darker. From what Luke told me about Addison's Disease, both the weight and darkening of his skin were signs he wasn't getting enough hydrocortisone.

If I had a gun right then, I would have gladly taken the asshole out for punishing Adam and Luke without having committed a crime. Hell, even criminals weren't denied medical treatment.

Not good.

What *was* good was seeing the two brothers finally come together. Their arms wrapped around each other, Luke patted Adam on the back and pulled his brother back to look at him. Wrapping his hand around the back of Adam's neck, he put their foreheads together. Luke's mouth was moving and Adam nodded before stepping back. Asshole stood with his hands on his hips watching the pair. At least I thought he was, but since his back was to me I couldn't be positive.

"He's so freaking hot," Stormy moaned. "You did *not* tell me that."

"I told you he looked just like Luke."

"Yeah, but you didn't tell me he wasn't old."

"Well, he's still too old for you," I said, raising a brow at her.

Luke threw an arm over Adam's shoulder and started walking toward a building across the way. Waiting until the guys walked into the building, I turned to Stormy.

"That's the building we need to get inside of."

Stormy twisted to sit on her butt and leaned against the brick wall. "I figured."

I mimicked her position and looked up at a blue, cloudless sky free of lines from airplanes. This world was so different than the one I grew up in. Would it ever go back to the way it was? Would Stormy remember what it felt like to have ice cream on a hot summer day? She would never get the chance to text a friend or go to prom. Would the world we had before die with her generation? Probably. Most likely.

This new world was incredibly silent like Earth was holding its breath, waiting to see what we would do next.

And I was ready to make some noise.

Chapter Twelve

Taking a calming breath, I plastered a smile on my face as I walked toward the two men with guns strapped over their shoulders. I tugged on the hem of my shirt, making sure my cleavage was visible, and stopped a few feet from the men. This had to work. If it didn't, we were screwed.

"Hey, guys," I said conversationally while twisting a strand of hair. Both men had watched me take the last few steps to them and stood a little straighter when they realized I was talking to them.

"Can I help you with something?" the man closest to me asked, but his eyes stayed on my chest.

"Yeah, I'm looking for a place to get a drink, relax a little bit. There a place like that around here?"

The second man took a step closer, both giving me their full attention. I looked to the left of them and watched

Stormy slip by and around the corner. She was in, now I just had to get myself inside.

"You here alone?" the first man asked, dragging his eyes from my chest to my face.

"My aunt's around somewhere." I looked past the men to the square. The men eyed each other and by the grim set of their mouths, that wasn't the right answer. *Guess I need to boost their egos.* "I don't want to be any trouble. I just need a drink something awful. It's been a long time since I've felt safe enough to get good and drunk, but I figure with you guys here protecting the town, nothing can happen."

"Go on in, but don't be making a ruckus or they'll kick you out," the older of the two said.

Smiling innocently as I could, I asked, "Which way should I go?"

He pointed to the right of where we stood. "Over there where the blue sign is. Stay clear of the building next to it. That's where we're all staying and they won't let you in unless you're here for their entertainment."

Bingo!

"I'll just go have a drink then. Thank you, boys." I winked and sauntered toward the bar, hoping Stormy was out of sight and out of trouble. The only thing that made me feel better was knowing the girl had spent the last three years making it on her own and had street smarts I couldn't even begin to have. If anything, *I* would probably be the one getting into trouble and she would end up saving my ass. The girl was remarkable. Stormy was already sharp as a tack. If she were able to continue her education, there was no telling what she could do in the future.

Glancing over my shoulder to find the guards back at work, I sighed. Hopefully, neither of us would be in need of an ass saving.

First I had to get into the bar, take a shot of anything strong if they would give it to me without payment, and find my way through the backdoor and inside the next building. I needed to get it all done in the next ten minutes so Stormy wouldn't be waiting out in the open for too long.

Smoothing the worry lines from my forehead, I squared my shoulders and pushed the door open. The sound of a piano playing softly hit me first as my eyes adjusted to the dim lights of the lantern-lit room. I blinked until the room came into focus, finding every eye in the room was on me. Taking a deep breath, I inhaled smoke from the cigarette-saturated room and coughed loudly. *So much for first impressions.*

I was Gina, the sexy dimwit with no aversion to tonguing a man with smoker's breath and making a few extra dollars in the stalls of the bathroom. *Ugh, I nearly gagged myself with that one.*

Walking through the room, I ignored the leers of the men and the glares from the few women as I made my way to the bar. A balding man wearing a buttoned up flannel shirt with the sleeves rolled up rested his hands on the bar and glowered down at me. "What can I get you?"

Voices around picked up to a normal volume and I leaned in. "Um, what do I pay with?"

The bartender glanced around us then moved in even closer. "How about I give you a freebie, but you gotta get out of here after that, alright?"

Looking in his eyes, I saw the warning and worry. This was no place for a girl, even Gina. I nodded in agreement. He reached down and pulled out a shot glass and a bottle of amber-colored liquor, filling the small glass half full before sliding it to me. "Bottoms up."

Lifting the glass to my nose, I closed my eyes and inhaled the rich oak from the liquid before tossing it back and letting the burn slide down my throat and warm my belly. Wiping my mouth with the back of my hand, I felt someone take the stool next to me. Knowing what was coming next, I fought the urge to release a grieved curse. Instead, I sucked it up and put on my Goodtime Gina face and turned my head with a wicked smile.

The smile froze in place when I laid my eyes on none other than Adam Grislon. He grinned at me sweetly with one elbow on the bar and his other hand on his thigh. My eyes swept the rest of the room expecting to see an immensely pissed off Luke, but the only eyes on me were the same as the ones when I walked in. My eyes moved back to the still grinning Adam.

How was I supposed to play this? Every eye in the place was waiting to see what was about to happen between the strapping young man and the woman ready for a good time. Though this was not how I wanted to meet my, hopefully-future brother-in-law, I had to play this off or get us both in a heap of trouble. Forcing my body to relax into the bar top, I contemplated how to start this conversation when he spoke.

"What's a pretty girl like you doing in a place like this?" Adam asked, his bright eyes mischievous and his smile swoony.

Had I been any other woman—any woman who wasn't in love with his brother—I would have melted at that smile.

Oh. no, please don't flirt. This is so bad. "I was thirsty."

He chuckled and nodded. "What's your name?"

I cleared my throat, wishing for a dozen more shots to get through this act. "Gina. Yours?"

His eyebrows lifted, much like his brother's. "Gina," he said slowly, testing it out. "Pretty name for a beautiful face. I'm Adam."

Scanning Adam's face, I fought the urge to wrap my arms around him and hold him tight. He didn't know I knew everything about him. I knew he grew up without a father and Luke had willingly and wholeheartedly stepped into the role for his entire family. Even though Luke wasn't old enough to do so, he did it anyway. I knew he almost died as a kid until the doctors realized he had Addison's Disease and gave him the medicines he needed to live. I knew when the plague broke out across the nation he had to watch everyone he loved die in front of him while he waited for Luke. I also knew he was a good guy and liked to laugh and live life to its fullest. If Luke hadn't already told me that, I would know just by the sparkle in his eyes and the easy way he smiled, like it was the only way his face could be.

For all these reasons, I had to get him away from this place and back with his brother so they could have the life they deserved—or at least the best life I could give them. And to do that, I had to get him out of this bar and tell him who I was on our way to get Stormy.

God, please let her be where she's supposed to be and not causing trouble.

Letting the thought rest on my mind, I felt the need to hurry this along. "So, Adam," I drew out his name, "want to take me around and show me the town?"

He leaned in, ran his fingers over my forearm, and moved close enough I could feel his warm breath on my neck. "This town is boring. How about I show you my room?"

Oh, no, this just got even more *awkward and I didn't think that would be possible.*

Letting Goodtime Gina take over so I could get this over with, I stood and pushed out my chest. "Let's go then."

He unfolded from the chair, towering over me, and slid an arm over my shoulder, tugging me in close. His hand slid down until he patted my ass. *Patted my ass!* His head dipped down as we started walking toward the front door. "Hope you're ready for this."

Swallowing hard, I looked up into his eyes. "Me, too."

We walked out of the bar and straight to the house next door. Men whistled, making lewd comments and gestures to Adam. Adam acknowledged them with a shit-eating grin, which made me want to throw an elbow into his side. When we got to the room I was going to smack the shit out of him for picking up random girls and taking them back to his room. This had better not be his typical behavior or I was going to smack Luke, too, for not teaching him better.

We stepped inside the house and irritation was immediately replaced by fear. The place was crawling with men. There were women here and there, but the vast majority were mean looking motherfuckers. I leaned in closer to Adam as he started toward the staircase with me in tow.

"Adam," a voice called out, stopping us on the first step.

Adam leaned down and whispered in my ear, "Keep your mouth shut."

He turned his head back. "What?"

Glancing over my shoulder, I spotted Dickface walking toward us. My hands instinctively fisted and my breathing quickened.

"Who do you have there?"

I felt Adam shrug. "Uh, what's your name again?" He laughed. "Gina. That's it." My cheeks felt hot with anger and I hoped it passed off as me being a little embarrassed. "Did you need something, Griffin?"

Griffin, that was it, though I still preferred Dickface. It fit him better. This man was an arrogant prick. It was written all over his smug face and the way he sauntered around like he was used to getting his way. I bet his dick was the size of a tic-tac.

"No, but Gina," his eyes moved to mine, "come see me when you're done playing with the boys."

I nodded. I would go see him alright. I would love nothing more than to look into his beady eyes while I bled him until his eyes went blank.

Without another word, Adam walked us up the rest of the stairs and down the hall to the last door on the left. He pushed the door open and waited for me to step inside. I walked in and instantly, a hand came around and clamped over my mouth. Not knowing how to handle this without making a commotion, my eyes widened as the door closed behind me. Adam stepped in front of me with his palms up.

"Okay, he's going to remove his hands, but you can't yell or get loud, understand?" Adam's voice was low.

What the hell is he doing?

I nodded. The hand released my mouth, and I whirled around ready to fight but found Jacob standing behind me with a smile, his dimples shining like a beacon of light on the haze that had become my life.

"Jacob, oh my God, Jacob. You're alive. You're okay." My shaking hands flew to his face, cupping his cheeks while hot tears ran down my face. I gripped his shirt until my knuckles hurt as he tried to wipe at my tears.

"Hey, sissy," he whispered, cupping the back of my head and tugging me to his chest.

My body shook with raw emotion. Digging my face into his chest, I closed my eyes and breathed him in. I wrapped my arms around him and leaned the side of my head against him, listening to his steady heartbeat. It was the most beautiful sound I had ever heard and was so strong and fast, exactly how Jacob lived his life. His life!

"Roni, he needs to sit down."

I opened my eyes to find a fuming Luke standing behind a nervous Stormy. Stormy's hands were fidgeting and her eyes slid back and forth between Adam and Jacob. Seeing Luke and Stormy were safe, I focused all my attention on Jacob.

Leaning back, I looked up into eyes so similar to mine. "I missed you so damn much."

Still holding my hand, he moved to the edge of the bed and sat, favoring his right leg on the way down. My eyes shot to his leg and my nose stung while fighting to hold in my temper. Jacob pulled me next to him and slung an arm around my shoulders.

"I'm alright. The bullet went straight through." He chuckled sadly. "A real cute nurse stitched me up, gave me antibiotics. I'm good."

"I can't believe you're really here. I thought you were dead," I said low, knowing all the ears in the room were listening to us.

"Yeah, I heard," he laughed. "I can't believe you were trying to hunt Luke down to kill him."

Embarrassed, I glanced at Adam, who was grinning from ear to ear like I was a cute puppy who thought I was a wolf. "Hi, sorry I tried to kill your brother. There was a big misunderstanding, but I swear, I was still going to get you out of here after he was dead."

Luke groaned and Adam and Jacob laughed.

"I like her," Adam said to Luke.

Luke stepped forward, his hands on his hips. "Now that we have to get *five* of us out instead of three, let's wait until later for chit-chat."

Jacob turned to me. "Are you ever going to learn to listen to what he tells you to do?"

Immediately, my spine stiffened. "Excuse me? I didn't listen because he didn't tell me what the hell he was doing. I was supposed to go with him and he snuck out in the morning and took off."

"You really took off without telling her?" Adam asked his brother.

"Spend a few days with her, you'll understand," Luke said, and Jacob agreed with a nod.

I stood, finger pointed to Luke while my other hand fisted on my hip. "What's that supposed to mean?"

"Well, *that's* different," Adam murmured behind me. I didn't bother to ask what he meant since I was too busy shooting daggers at Luke with my eyes.

"Come on, sis, you know what he's talking about."

"What?" I spun, hurt because Jacob was agreeing with Luke when we'd been separated for so long. Maybe I was being naïve, but I thought when I got him back he would look up to me for coming after him, or at least be on the same page instead of siding with Luke. He just shrugged with a sheepish grin on his face.

"Roni, we'll deal with this later," Luke growled a warning.

"There's nothing to deal with," I threw back, but I couldn't stop my stomach from dipping from wondering exactly how he was going to deal with me.

"Oh my gosh, will you all just shut up for a minute?" Stormy said with a frustrated sigh. "I don't know how any of you made it more than a week on your own." I backed off and returned to my post next to Jacob and held his hand while glaring at Luke. "You two, stop it. We all know you're going to be making out in a few hours."

The boys muffled their laughs and Luke's lips twitched. I rolled my eyes because she was right. Denying it, even to myself, would be useless. I was going to make out so hard with him. I was going to do way more than just make out with him, but first things first, we had to get out of the devil's clutches. Then our sort of happily ever after could begin.

"Stormy, I think you're going to fit in with us just fine," Jacob said, and Stormy blushed.

No smartass retort? Blushing? I think someone might be a tad bit smitten.

"Captain wants Roni to come see him when we're finished," Adam said, then his eyebrows drew together. "I mean, he wants to see Gina when we're done." He fidgeted more. "I mean—"

"We know what you mean," Luke said, turning his eyes on me. "You're not going to see him."

"I think I should." I held my hand up when Luke and Jacob both started to disagree. "Listen, if I keep him occupied, the rest of you can get out."

"No way," Jacob said, shaking his head.

Luke took a menacing step forward, making the room shrink with each step. "How exactly do you think he wants to be kept occupied, Veronica?"

A shiver moved down my spine knowing exactly what the Captain would expect. I shrugged my shoulders. "I'll improvise." When they glared at me, I threw my hands up. "All of you put your male instincts away for a minute and think about what's best for all of us."

Sighing, Jacob ran a hand over his face. "I don't like it, but unless you guys are ready to leave, guns blazing, I don't see another way." Jacob shifted his right leg. "Adam can stay with her since he already knows they're up here together."

Luke was already shaking his head when Adam chimed in. "I agree. If we don't talk to him when we leave, he's going to know something's up and shut the town down, and we'll all be stuck here. I do not want to spend another freaking night in this hell hole."

Luke looked down at Stormy as she bit her bottom lip, then he turned to me, knowing what had to be done and not liking it one bit. For the sake of us all, I had to see Griffin. Stepping forward, I slid my hands around his waist and looked up at him. "We need to go home."

Cupping my face with his big, strong hands, he leaned in and softly pressed his lips to mine.

"Gross, will you two at least wait until you're alone?" Stormy chided.

Luke's abs moved with suppressed laughter before kissing the tip of my nose. "He's not a good man, aby."

"I know," I whispered. He was the man who'd looted my home, shot my brother, enforced Adam's capture, and was the puppeteer to Luke's every move. I would love nothing more than to get as far away from him as we could. "We'll get out as quickly as possible."

"Why are you wearing makeup?" Luke asked as if he'd just noticed. "You look pretty without all this crap on."

I smiled at his backhanded compliment. "Stormy did my makeup. I had to get us in somehow."

He rumbled low before tucking me under his arm and speaking to the group. "Stormy, do you remember how to get back to the house?"

She nodded, her lips pursed in confidence. "Yeah."

"You and Jacob will need to go first. I'll wait for these two and we'll leave in the truck."

Thinking about the distance to the car and Jacob's leg, I asked, "The car's about five blocks away. Can you make it that far?"

Jacob sneered. "Yeah, I can make it, but we'll have to do it fast. They keep pretty close tabs on me. Adam, you have to promise if he lays a hand on my sister, you'll put a bullet in his sorry-ass head."

"Promise, man. He won't lay a hand on her," Adam swore, and Jacob nodded.

"Can you drive?" Luke asked.

"I can drive," Stormy announced excitedly.

"*I* can drive," Jacob said, eying Stormy.

"Do you know how to hotwire a car?" Stormy asked with raised eyebrows.

"What? No." His lips parted and his eyebrows rose in question.

"Stormy had to hotwire the car for us to get here," I explained.

"You're kidding, right?" Luke asked, pride shining in his gray eyes.

"Nope." I was grinning like a parent whose kid had just told them she brought home straight As. "She sure as shit hotwired it."

"Damn, girl, you have skills," Adam said with an appreciative nod.

"Thanks," Stormy replied with another blush.

"I'm still driving," Jacob announced, squaring his shoulders.

"We'll see," Stormy said with a smile.

"You two need to go first. Once I get you out safely, I'll double back and wait in the truck." Luke turned to Adam. "I'm parked by the swing set on the east side. Know where that is?" Adam nodded. "You should probably double dose at least."

Adam pinched his lips, probably because he was being told what to do, but he nodded anyway. When we finally made it home, I was going to talk to Luke about letting Adam take care of himself. I shifted my gaze to Jacob, knowing I mothered him all the time. *Or maybe I'll just keep my mouth shut.*

Luke steered Stormy to the back window and raised it. "Ladies first."

"Wait," I said, moving to them. Grabbing Stormy, I hugged her stiff frame and let go. "Be careful." Her reply was to roll her eyes and slide through the opening to the outside. I turned to Luke. "You be careful, too."

He leaned down and kissed me on the forehead. "Don't do anything stupid."

"I love when you sweet talk me." I sighed and batted my eyelashes.

He smiled and turned to Jacob. "Let's go."

"Wait," I said again to multiple pairs of rolling eyes. "Are you going to be able to climb down?" I asked, worried Jacob would fall from the second floor and injure himself more than he already was. That and I wasn't ready to let him out of my sight just yet.

"Sis, don't worry, we got this. Stop worrying about everyone else and worry about getting yourself out of here." He turned to Adam. "Take care of her, man."

"Jacob," I squeaked out. He sighed and turned toward me with his hands on his hips. Taking two quick steps, I wrapped my arms around his waist and held on. "I love you."

Releasing him, he winked at me. "Love you more."

"Not a chance." Blinking back tears, I smiled as I watched him bend down and exit through the window. Once Jacob was totally out of sight, my focus shifted to the two remaining men in the room.

Luke squeezed his brother's shoulder before sticking his head through the window and scanning the area. His body was halfway through when he looked back at Adam. "If you're not at the truck in an hour, I'm coming for you both."

His eyes bounced between the two of us before his full lips pulled into a thin line and he disappeared out of view. Exhaling slowly, I swiveled until I came face to face with Adam. He shoved his hands into his back pockets and rocked on his heels.

"So…" I crossed my arms over my chest. "What now?"

Adam pulled his hand out of his pocket and looked at the watch on his wrist. "We've been up here thirty minutes, so I think that's long enough for him to think…"

As Adam's cheeks flushed bright red, I raised my eyebrows. "Think that's long enough?"

He cleared his throat and scratched behind his ear. "With someone normal that wouldn't be long enough—"

"Someone normal?" I asked. Seeing him squirm was even more fun than watching his brother squirm.

"You're normal. I mean, I've had girls up here longer. Not that I don't think you would deserve to be up here longer…"

The pain on his face was enough to make me laugh. "It's okay. I know what you're saying. I think." Uncrossing my arms, I sat on the edge of the bed and stared at him. "Any advice with Captain Dickface?"

"Dickface?" He chuckled with a shake of his head.

"That's what I call him."

Adam shrugged and sat next to me. "Act like you're totally in love with me and maybe he'll let it go."

Eying the younger man, I wondered if it would work. "Won't that seem strange if I'm all fangirling over you when we just meet and I'm clearly older?"

He chuckled. "I've had older girls than you come up here and want a ring on their way out, so no, I don't think he'll see a problem with it."

Tilting my head to him I glared. "I hope you're being smart and using protection."

"Oh, God, please don't." He was bent over with his elbows on his knees and his head in his hands.

"What? The world needs to be repopulated, but you don't need to do it single-handedly."

Flashbacks of Luke pressing me against the truck the night before filled my head and I hid a smile. Protection had been the *last* thing on our minds. It wasn't smart and we needed to be more careful next time. *If it isn't too late already*, I thought, fighting the urge to put a hand over my stomach. Oddly enough, the thought of being pregnant didn't make me want to take a swan dive off the nearest building.

Pulling myself from my thoughts, I found Adam staring at me with abject horror in his eyes. I reached over and patted his thigh. "Better get used to it, sweetheart."

Chapter Thirteen

Three rapid knocks on the bedroom door sucked out whatever semblance of ease we had created like a high-powered vacuum. My eyes were on the door when I felt Adam stand. Instinctively, my hand shot out to stop or protect him—I wasn't sure which. All I knew was we couldn't screw this up. Everyone was depending on us to do our part and get the hell out.

"Wait," I whispered when he took a step toward the door.

"Adam?" a male voice called from the other side of the door.

"One minute," Adam called back, and looking down at me, raising his shoulders in exasperation.

Jumping up, I ran my hands through his hair and reached down to unbutton his jeans when he slapped my hands away. "What are you doing?" he hissed.

Hands on my hips, I glared at him. "We just had sex, remember?"

"You can't go groping me. Do you know what would happen? Luke would kill me. *That's* what would happen." He shook his head while unbuttoning his jeans, kicking off his shoes, and yanking his shirt over his head.

"Gross! I wasn't groping you. You're like my brother." I did my best to keep my eyes on his face, but wow, he had himself a body going on under that shirt. He wasn't as broad or muscled as Luke, but they clearly had the same genes. Adam's body just happened to be a leaner version. He had the baseball build to Luke's football build.

The beating on the door was harder this time. "Adam, open the door or I'll have to break it down."

"Get in bed and look… satisfied."

"Again, gross." I crinkled my nose. Yep, he was just like his brother—egos the size of hot air balloons. Hurrying, I hopped on the bed and pulled the covers over me. Once I was in position, he took a breath before opening the door. He stepped into the open doorway, one hand remaining on the knob while his other rested high on the door jamb.

"Dude, we're kind of busy here. What the hell do you want?" Adam said in irritation.

His head lolled like he'd just woken from a nap and he sighed repeatedly as he drummed his fingers against the door frame. I was surprised at how well he played the irritated role. Maybe he wasn't acting. Maybe I *was* irritating him like I seemed to constantly irritate Jacob and Luke. *Ha. I knew he would fit perfectly in our family.*

The man tried to step in but Adam's body didn't budge. "What do you want?"

"Griffin wants to see you two, now," the man behind the door said in regret.

If the man coming to retrieve them didn't seem excited about the task, what did it mean for us? *Fucking Griffin. What an asshole to think he can bully everyone around.* That's exactly what he was doing, but sadly, no one could stop him. Yet, at least. Give me a gun and a way out and I would fix that problem. Even as it came to mind, I cringed at the thought of taking another life. Not that I couldn't do it—I'd had to before—but if this world had taught me anything it was life was precious. Then again, it also taught me the good turn bad and the bad turn rotten. If the rotten wasn't plucked from the crop, the sickness would spread until it ruined the rest.

Adam raked a hand through his mussed hair and nodded. "Tell him we're on our way."

Without waiting for a reply, Adam shut the door and turned the lock. "Time to go."

The thin set of his lips was so much like his brother's when he mulled over something, it made me want to smile, but smiles would have to wait until we were out of there and on the road home. I wasn't going to lie, I was anxious. How could I not be when Griffin had the power to tell Luke what to do without threat of Luke killing him in a matter of seconds? The man had a literal army at his beck and call, and he was waiting to see me.

"Any words of advice?" I asked as Adam redressed.

"Try not to talk if you don't have to and don't piss him off."

"You definitely sound like your brother," I murmured under my breath as I climbed off the bed.

"Luke's right. Griffin isn't someone to mess with. He's a heartless piece of shit and doesn't try to hide it." Adam took a few steps until he was inches from me and spoke slowly. "Don't piss him off."

Fighting the urge to swallow hard, I nodded and pushed down the fear. "I won't. Swear."

Adam walked to the nightstand, pulled out a plastic bag, and popped a couple little, white pills in his mouth, washing them down with a bottle of water. He tossed the empty bottle and bag across the floor and reached for my hand. "Let's go."

"Show time," I said, putting my hand in his and followed him out the door.

Side by side we took the stairs, and my anxiety levels skyrocketed. What if Griffin was a human lie detector and could tell if I was lying by my pulse rate at my neck? Tension flooded through me, and I did my best to relax my shoulders so my arms didn't look like they were sprouting from my ears. Trying to control my heart rate, I breathed in through my nose and out through my mouth. After a few of those, I felt marginally better, but Adam was taking weary glances at me. I gave him a weak smile and squeezed his hand. He didn't look convinced but continued down the stairwell to hell.

Reaching the bottom, I could feel multiple sets of eyes on us, but I pretended to not notice. My usual calm was on the edge of crazy, all the while Adam stood next to me as cool as a cucumber. He knocked on a door and I examined him while we waited. It was shocking, really, how much he looked like Luke—same jaw, same lips, same nose minus the slight bend to Luke's from getting his nose broken. The only major differences were the eyes and the bulk. Luke had steely gray eyes that could burn into my soul with one look, and Adam's eyes were a deep green that made me want to crawl up next to him and sleep. Both were beautiful.

Footsteps sounded from the other side of the door and I gripped Adam's hand a little tighter. He winked at me. "Don't worry. I got you."

That made me smile. He was so much like his brother, probably because Luke had basically been his father since their own had died when Adam was little.

The door was opened by a young man, probably in his early twenties, whose eyes darted from Adam to me before stepping out of the way for us to enter. Adam moved first and led me into the large study before halting in front of a desk where dickhead Griffin sat pompously on his throne. I studied him while he ignored us by leafing through a small stack of papers. He wasn't a bad looking man. If I were honest with myself, I would have to admit he was actually attractive, but the devil was in his beady eyes.

The door clicked behind us, and we were left alone with Griffin. Guess he didn't think of us as a threat, and I would assume it was a positive thing. I would take all the positives we could get.

"You wanted to see us?" Adam asked, releasing my hand—probably to get circulation back after my death grip—and wrapped his arm around my shoulders. Thankful for the extra support, I wrapped my arms around his middle like a girl in love. Using the pretense of a lovesick sigh, I took a deep breath to calm my shaking arms.

What the hell is wrong with me? Why am I so ridiculously nervous? I knew how to handle my shit and I was *not* handling my shit at all. It had to be because I was worried about Adam's safety. He was at risk because I was a hothead and had to show Luke what a grown, capable woman I was. Now, if I screwed up, it wasn't just me paying the consequences; it would be Adam, too.

Luke would never forgive me if Adam was hurt. Hell, *I* wouldn't forgive me.

Dickface steepled his fingers, tapping both index fingers against his lips as he scrutinized us. *What an arrogant asshole.* Did it make him feel more dominant to have the peasants wait to hear what the "powerful one" had to say? I wanted to slap my palm against the desk and tell him to speak, but I took a deep breath instead.

This lasted long enough I feared even-keeled Adam might very well snap, when Griffin opened his thin lips and spoke with glinting eyes. "Did you two have a nice *visit*?"

Shifting uncomfortably at the tactless question, Adam sighed. "Yep. I'm about to show Gina where the kitchen is before it closes until dinner."

Griffin's eyes flicked from Adam to me. "Gina, is it?" I nodded. "You're new to town?"

Here we go. I smiled. "Yeah. For a few days at least." I turned to beam up at Adam and he squeezed my shoulder. "Hopefully longer."

"Humph," came from Griffin.

"We better get going before the kitchen closes." Adam began to turn us.

"Hold up," Griffin said, annoyance lacing his words. "Adam, why don't you give me a few minutes alone with Gina?" Although posed as a question, it wasn't a request.

I made a pouty face. "I'm really hungry. Do you care if we grab something to eat first then come back?"

A flash of anger flamed in his eyes before he stood and smoothed his features to appear more pleasant. "I'll only keep you a few moments and you can do as you like afterward. Adam."

Guess I wasn't doing a very good job at not pissing him off. Adam's arm fell from my shoulders and he took a protective step in front of me, so I spoke before Adam said or did something to make matters even worse. "Adam," I said low, "wait outside the door. I'll only be a minute and we can go."

He tilted his head to look down at me with clinched teeth and searched my face before nodding. "I'll be right outside."

"You do that," Griffin said condescendingly.

Griffin and I stood still while Adam left the room. I had no doubts he was right on the other side, listening for any sign of distress so he could barge in and rescue me at the first sign of trouble. Knowing that gave me even more reason to not ruffle Griffin's feathers.

"Take a seat," Griffin said, pointing to a chair to my right.

"It's okay, I'm fine standing." I tried to smile, but it probably looked more like a grimace.

"Sit," he demanded, as if I was a damned dog and he was my master. If I had my gun, I would so shoot him between the eyes without batting a lash. Reminding myself why I had to play nice, I sat. "That's better now, isn't it?"

He stepped from behind the desk until he was in front of me and sat at the edge of the desk, towering over me. Exactly the way he wanted. Looking down at me made him feel more powerful.

Bully. I fucking hated bullies.

"Tell me about yourself, Gina," he said conversationally, as if this was a pleasant meeting instead of the obvious witch hunt it was.

"What do you want to know?"

"You're here with your mother?"

"Aunt, actually," I corrected, wondering if he was trying to trip me up. "She's looking for a place to get some work for a few days." *That sounds reasonable enough.*

"And is that what you're doing? Looking for work?" His eyes perused my body, stopping on my cleavage before flicking to my face.

Bile threatened to rise in my throat. My eyes narrowed and fire burned my cheeks. "I'm not a *whore* if that's what you're asking."

Sucking in his top lip into his mouth, he inspected me. "I thought maybe we had spent some time together before, but I guess not. But why do you look so familiar?"

My palms immediately began to sweat and my blood pumped wildly through my veins. I dipped my chin an inch in an attempt to block his view of the pulse in my neck. "I don't know." I shrugged. "Have you ever been to Texas?"

I raised my eyebrows, waiting, but instead of answering me, his eyes briefly widened before they narrowed. The blood causing my heart rate to rise came to a crashing halt.

Oh, shit, he knew.

He knew and I was about to die.

His head tilted back and he shook his head slowly as he laughed. When I thought perhaps he'd cracked his lid, his head came up slowly and his cold gaze landed on me like a block of ice. "So *you're* the piece of ass Luke fought so damned hard to keep hidden?"

"I don't know what you're talking about." My voice cracked, but I didn't dare look away. Maybe he was trying to call my bluff?

"Don't play stupid. You know exactly what I'm talking about." Moving around the desk, he reached inside and pulled out a letter.

My letter.

My hands gripped the arms of the chair to keep from jumping up and shoving my shoe up his ass. Tossing the letter on the desk as if it were a past due bill, he picked up the Polaroid photo I had left with the letter. Looking back and forth from the photo to me, he smiled. Play time was over. I couldn't talk myself out of this one. I might be made-up, but there was no denying I was the same woman in the photo.

He flipped the photo between his fingers to face me. I glanced at the photo of Luke, Jacob, and me smiling brightly at the camera with true happiness. His grimy hands didn't deserve to touch the photo. "Isn't this you with Luke and that useless piece of shit?"

"You're the only piece of shit I see," I said between gritted teeth.

This time, his smile was sadistically real. The devil was about to show his horns. He wanted this—me fighting with him. "There it is. That's what he sees in you. You have fire in you. Not many women have that, but I see it in there." Shaking a finger at me, he said, "I bet you want to hurt me right now, don't you?"

I pinched my lips tight to keep from making matters worse, but there wasn't anything stopping my eyes from glaring.

"Yeah, you do." He moved back to the front of the desk and sat in front of me. "Let me guess why you're here. You want to be part of the group? Maybe earn your keep by being passed around while Luke's out?"

I gave him a blistering glare but stayed silent.

"No?" he asked when I didn't take the bait. "Did Luke send you in here thinking this little ruse you and Adam have going will free all of you?"

When it was clear I wasn't going to give him a reaction, he swiftly moved until his hands were on the arms of the chair, shaking the chair, me included. "I'm in control here!"

Digging deep—and I mean really deep—I fought the urge to wipe the spittle he sprayed on me during his pathetic act of superiority. Instead, I looked him in his unforgiving eyes. "Why is keeping Luke under your thumb so important to you?"

He leaned back, smoothing out the button-down shirt he wore. "*Nothing* about Luke is important to me. If it were up to me, he would have had a bullet between his eyes for treason months ago. The General wants him and unlike Luke, I follow orders. The rest is purely entertainment."

My lips curled back. "*Entertainment*? You think holding hostage the family of a man who has served his country is entertainment? You're a freaking psycho!"

In a blink of an eye, he gripped my upper arms, yanking me up until I was on my tiptoes, and spun us around until the backs of my thighs bit into the edge of the desk. I squeezed my eyes and clinched my jaw to keep my teeth from rattling as he shook me. His breath was hot on my cheek, but I dared not struggle. This man was clearly unstable, and as much as I hated it, he did have the upper hand.

"I'm in control here. I decide if you live or die. *I'm in fucking control.*"

Suddenly, his grip loosened and his body moved from mine. Opening my eyes, I saw Adam with wide eyes, holding a bookend, and Griffin lying face-down on the floor. Pushing off the desk, my hands went to the sides of my head in horror.

"Oh my God, Adam!"

"Holy shit! We gotta go. Now!" Adam dropped the bookend and reached for me.

I pulled my arm back and bent down, putting my fingertips on Griffin's neck. Thankfully, he had a pulse. As much as I wanted the man dead, I didn't want his death on Adam's conscience. Frantically, I looked around. "He's alive, and we're dead as soon as he wakes up. Look for something to tie him up with and something to put over his stupid mouth."

Running, I went to the door and locked it so we wouldn't get any surprise visitors, then searched for rope with no success. We had to hurry. Griffin would be awake any second, and I refused to let Adam pay for my bad decisions. I rushed to a lamp, yanked the cord from the base, and tossed it to Adam. "Tie his hands."

Finding a tie, I went to Adam and helped him heft Griffin into a chair. Once we got him slumped over, I wrapped the tie around his mouth like a horse bridle, then went back to pulling cords from lamps. Adam was staring down at Griffin's limp body. *Oh God, was he having one of those Addison's crises Luke told me about?* Dropping the cords, I moved to Adam and put both palms on his face until his eyes cleared and he looked at me.

"Adam, do you need more medicine?" How I would get the medicine was a different question, but by God, I would find a way.

"No, no. I'm good. I just…" He sidestepped me and glared down at Griffin. "He's going to come after us. He won't stop until he hunts us down and kills us."

Though it was probably true, I shook my head. "We'll be okay. We just have to get out of here and Luke will know what to do. If we don't hurry, Griffin won't have to go far to find us." Adam nodded in agreement and picked up the cord I'd dropped. "Do you have any more medicine here for the road?"

He handed me the cord and with renewed purpose, then moved to the desk and searched the drawers. With a smile, he pulled out a clear bag with three bottles of medicine. "The asshole loved it when I had to come to him for more medicine."

I tightened the cord holding Griffin's chest to the chair a little extra for being an asshole. "Let's get out of here."

Rushing to the window, Adam stuffed the bag of pills inside his jeans and pulled it open. "Ladies first."

Taking one last glance at Griffin, I yanked the letter and photo from where it had fallen on the floor and tucked them into my bra. I passed Adam, climbed out the window, and waited for Adam to follow. Once out, he eased the window down and grabbed my hand. "Now, just walk normal."

I nodded and leaned into him, my heart racing, but I smiled. I smiled so wide my face hurt. Our family was complete now and I would die before I let anyone take them away from me again. To anyone around us, I probably looked like a lovesick puppy, but that was fine. I was a bit lovesick.

"Luke should be right around the next corner," Adam said, tilting his head slightly toward the right.

"He's not going to be happy with us," I chuckled, and Adam laughed.

"You think?" He smiled down at me. "From what Jacob has told me, and seeing him with you for just a few minutes, he can't stay mad at you."

"Well…" I scratched my head. "I'm a handful, so I try his nerves a lot."

Adam agreed with an appreciative nod. "You did drive through a wrecked country hunting him down to kill him. And even then, he forgave you."

Embarrassed, I turned my face away. "I thought he'd killed my brother. If he thought someone did that to you, he would do the same thing."

"Exactly. You two are perfect for each other." He released my hand and wrapped an arm around my shoulder.

"There're a few guys coming up. Try not to pay any attention to them."

"Hey, Adam, where you going?" one of them called, but I kept my gaze averted.

Adam didn't slow his pace. "Taking Gina to the hotel."

"Let me know when you get back," he yelled.

Adam gave a backward wave. "Will do."

We rounded the corner and Adam stopped moving. "Shit."

"What?" I asked, looking behind us for any signs of trouble but found none.

"The truck's not there," he said. His arm fell away, and he began jogging toward the swings.

I followed, looking around the area for Jacob's truck. "He has to be here somewhere."

"Well, he's not," Adam huffed, tossing his hands in the air.

From a distance, there was a commotion. Men were yelling, feet were stomping, and vehicles were starting. It could only mean two things: they either found Griffin, or he's awake and sent out the troops to find us. "What now?"

"Run!"

Chapter Fourteen

A bullet whizzed by, smacking the wall next to me, sending bits of brick toward my face. Instinctively, I shielded my head with my arm as Adam pulled me into a run. We had only been running for a few minutes and we were both out of breath and sweating. If we didn't get out of this soon, they were going to catch us.

"Go," Adam said between huffs of breath.

Doing my best not to panic, I kept my eyes constantly moving, looking for a way out or at the least somewhere to hide. We could not get caught. He would kill us, Luke would die trying to save us, and when we didn't show up at the hideout, Jacob would come back to find us. We would all be dead and Stormy would be alone again, without the comfort of her home.

More bullets fired and we changed directions. The roar of an engine came around the corner, speeding up behind us. Taking a chance, I glanced back to find Jacob's truck speeding toward us. I stopped in my tracks, yanking Adam to a halt beside me. "Luke!"

The truck came to a screeching stop next to us. "Get in!" Luke yelled through the open window. He reached out with a gun, aimed behind him, and fired off a few rounds while we scrambled inside. He didn't wait for the door to close before peeling out and flooring the pedal.

"Put on your seatbelts," he instructed without sparing us a glance.

Fumbling around, we managed to find and secure the seatbelts as Luke twisted and turned through the streets. Luke reached down and passed me a handgun. "Give this to Adam."

I glared at him until I realized it would be hard for me to shoot anyone while being perched between them unless I wanted to shoot out a window. I handed the gun to Adam, thinking I was going to have to give him a quick tutorial. "Do you know how to shoot?"

Adam leaned forward and spoke to Luke, "Are you kidding me?"

"What? It was just a question," I defended myself.

"Sweetheart, that's like asking a guy if he knows how to drive or needs help opening a jar," Luke said while making a hard right. "You don't."

Rolling my eyes, I gripped on to Luke's thigh to keep myself upright as I noticed a car with gunmen coming directly toward us. "Luke!"

"Adam," Luke said, calm as a cucumber. This man was a freaking badass. The more stressful the situation, the more relaxed he became. No wonder they wanted to keep him so badly. Seeing him in this mode was a big turn on. "When we get clear of this shit, you two are going to explain to me why they're trying to kill us instead of hold us."

"It's my fault," I said at the same time Adam said, "I caused this."

Adam stuck his hand out the window and pulled the trigger, blowing out the oncoming car's right front tire, sending it careening out of control, not stopping until it smashed into the side of a building. Adam had his arm and head stretched out the window, shooting at the car behind us.

"Like I said, we'll discuss it later," Luke said, slamming on the brakes and turning the wheel, sending the back of the truck into a spin. Suddenly, we were face to face with the guys chasing us. "Adam, now!"

Adam pulled the trigger multiple times until the car came to a rolling stop. Luke put his arm around me to the back of the seat and drove in reverse before spinning the truck and speeding off.

Adam sat back in the truck with a grimace. "Think we're clear."

"For now," Luke growled.

Reaching over, I squeezed Adam's hand and gave him a silent "thank you" for possibly taking a life to save mine. Being forced to end someone's life to save yourself and the ones you love wasn't easy, even if there wasn't another option. I knew firsthand. I was the person who had naïvely said I couldn't take another person's life, but that all changed when a group of men came to our house with every intention of raping me before they slaughtered us all. Then, I didn't think twice about unloading a gun on them.

Surveying the area we were headed, I turned to Luke who was taking turns looking from the windshield to the rearview mirror. "We're going the wrong direction."

Luke lazily draped an arm over my shoulder and tucked me in close to him before planting a kiss on my forehead. "We're taking the scenic route."

"Though that sounds lovely under normal circumstances, don't you think we should hurry and get to Jacob and Stormy?"

"Well, my dear, since the entire military force with Griffin will be looking for us right now, we don't want to head straight back to camp." He rubbed my upper arm. "Now, why don't you two tell me exactly *why* the entire military force is trying to kill us."

Biting my bottom lip, I turned to Adam and raised my eyebrows. He shook his head and I rolled my eyes. "Fine, I'll go first."

While I told our story—Adam filling in the holes I left out—Luke's fingers gradually became white on the steering wheel. "Then you ran up behind us and picked us up. By the way, why weren't you by the swing set?"

He sighed and his tan skin turned a light shade of pink. "The truck was almost out of gas and I had to find some." Being unprepared wasn't like Luke and being unprepared while Adam and I were at risk was unimaginable. Luke glanced at Adam and me openly gawking at him. "Okay, okay. I didn't think you two would get out that fast."

In unison, Adam and I started laughing. Of course, the situation was entirely scary and our chances of making it until the next week were slim, but the thought of Luke not being prepared when he bitched at me and Adam all the time was hilarious.

"Alright. That's enough," Luke demanded, only causing us to laugh harder.

After a few more moments, we finally sobered up. "What do we do now?" Adam asked.

Luke's lips pinched before he ran a hand through his hair. "Still working on it."

Unease saturated the cab of the truck at the reminder of the shit storm we just left behind and what we still had to deal with ahead. I wanted nothing more than to take my family home and live the best life we could in this world, but as things were, it was impossible. Griffin knew where we lived and I had a feeling he would gladly hunt us down until he witnessed us hanging from a noose. Not to mention General Wells wanted Luke for reasons unknown to me and would use all of us as pawns to get him back.

We remained quiet until we pulled into the driveway of the house we were staying at for the night. The front door swung open as we climbed out of the truck. Jacob stood smiling in the doorway and Stormy slid under his arm and ran straight to me.

"What the hell took you guys so long?" she asked, doing her best to look angry, but the gleam in her eyes showed her relief.

"Don't say hell," I chided, pulling her in for a quick hug, which she returned, giving me further confirmation of how she felt having us back. "We took the scenic route back."

Letting me go, Stormy held up her fist until Luke bumped it as we walked as a group to the front door and a waiting Jacob. Running the last few steps, I threw my arms around my brother and held on for dear life. I never thought I would have this again, and I was going to bask in it for as long as I lived, or as long as Jacob would allow. His allowance lasted all of about thirty seconds.

"Let's get inside and get you guys settled in," Jacob said, peeling me off him.

"I'm fine right here." I sighed, content for the moment of happiness we had.

"You're skin and bones, so you're going to sit down and eat," he ordered.

Glancing down at my visible breastbone, I tugged my shirt higher. "We have a lot to talk about first. We can eat later."

"No," he announced to the crowd. "You guys eat first and *then* we talk."

"How about we do both at the same time? We need to eat, but we need to let you know what's going on in case we need to bug out fast," Luke said while unloading multiple cans of food from one of the totes and carrying them to the kitchen.

Jacob's eyes went from watching Luke's back to me. "You had trouble leaving?"

Adam snorted. "You can say that."

I cleared my throat. "Let's help Luke heat something up and we'll talk."

With everyone's help, it didn't take long to prepare the canned food, boil water for drinking, and get settled into the living room, where Adam and I took turns reciting the events of the day. As I spoke, Jacob's face grew stony, but he remained quiet until we finished.

He set his bowl down and laced his fingers in his lap. "I swear to God, when we get home I'm locking you up and you're not going anywhere ever again. That's how he knew where to find us? A freaking letter and a photo?"

Ashamed, I dropped my head and nodded. "I didn't tell Luke I had put it in there before he left."

"The guy I was with must have taken it out the first night and handed it over to Griffin," Luke added.

"Are you sure Griffin's not dead?" Jacob asked, looking between Adam and me.

"We're sure," Adam said. "Roni checked his pulse."

"He was just knocked out." I tucked a loose strand of hair behind my ear, still embarrassed I had put all of us in this situation because of my "act first, think later" attitude.

Adam looked to his brother. "You know he's going to get word to the General and they'll all be searching for us."

Luke's full lips went thin and he nodded. "That's why we need a plan."

If General Wells came, he would be bringing his whole army of misfits with him, and that meant big trouble. How could we hide from an army of men? Was there a real army somewhere out there or was the United States forever in the control of crazy men? Then it hit me. "We can never go home again."

Luke pulled me to lean against his side and kissed the top of my head, sending immediate ease through my tense body. "We'll get home, sweetheart. It just might take us a while to get there."

"We'll just take the scenic route," I said.

He smiled down at me, dimples showing, melting my heart. "Yeah, baby, the scenic route."

Stormy sat to the side of us and in the short time we had known her, it was unusual for her to be this quiet. She hadn't said a word since we sat down to eat. I wanted to slap myself for our idiocy. The poor girl was probably scared out of her head and we were openly discussing an army of men coming after us.

Sitting up, I spoke to the group. "First things first, we need to get Stormy with people we can trust to keep her safe."

Stormy's back straightened. "I'm fine with you guys."

Luke shook his head. "Roni's right. It's not safe with us. If they catch us, they won't care if you're a kid or not."

"I'm not a kid," she deadpanned. "I can take care of myself."

"We know you can, but we won't put you at risk. You deserve to be safe," I explained.

She sank back in the loveseat, picking at her chipped nail polish, trying to act like she wasn't worried, but failing miserably. Seeing her worried didn't sit well with me.

"We can go back to Canaan," Adam suggested. "There are good people there and we might be able to get some help."

Jacob nodded. "There's safety in numbers."

"There's also a better chance of someone turning us in," Luke added.

Daisy and Josh came to mind. "There's a small community on the other side of Canaan called Victory. I think you might have stopped near there and punched a guy?" Luke nodded, his eyebrows drawn together. "They're good people, and you should really apologize, but we could go there. I know they would keep Stormy safe and they might help us get weapons. Adam, they actually spoke highly of you when I passed through."

Adam smiled. "You were asking about me?"

"Yeah, I wanted to make sure you were okay since I was going to give you the house after I killed Luke. I didn't want the house to go to waste. Plus, you have a stockpile of medicine there." All eyes were on me, but no one moved. "What?"

Jacob shook his head, exasperated. "I still can't believe you were trying to kill Luke. Did you think you were some avenging angel? Do you know how lucky you are someone else didn't pick you off along the way?"

"To be honest, at that point, I didn't care. I thought he'd killed you and that's all that mattered," I choked out.

"Wait, I was going to inherit a house stocked with drugs?" Adam looked around the group until his eyes stopped on me. "If the offer is still there, I can snuff them out in their sleep."

Laughing, I tossed a shoe at him, missing by a literal foot. Luke reached over and lightly slugged him in the arm.

"There're all the apples you can eat, too," I smiled wide then fake-whispered, "Get with me later."

"So is it settled? Are we going to Victory?" Jacob asked, sitting back and rubbing his bad leg with his good arm.

Luke ran a hand through his hair then leaned forward with his elbows on his knees. "It's a place to start."

"Awesome. I wouldn't mind stopping by the lodge and talking Mrs. Lydia into making me some chocolate gravy," Adam said, rubbing his flat stomach.

"I met her! She's wonderful and gosh, her biscuits…" We moaned in unison.

"Alright, alright. We need to load up the truck before sunset and get some shut eye. No candles or lights unless absolutely necessary. I'll take first watch," Luke said, clapping his hands and standing.

"I want the first watch," Jacob said.

Luke looked from me to Jacob and nodded. "We'll take three-hour shifts. If you start to get tired, wake me up."

Following a stoic Stormy to the bedroom, I sat on the bed while she crammed her things inside the bags. "Stormy, honey, what's wrong?"

"Nothing," she said immediately, shoving a makeup bag into the overstuffed backpack.

"Hey, stop for a minute and talk to me, please." I put a hand on her shoulder.

She stood and tossed the bag down. "Why? Why pretend that you care about me or want me around? Don't worry, I'll be out of your hair before long."

Slowly standing, I reached out and tried to put my hand on her shoulder again, but she yanked herself away. "Honey, we care. That's why we want you somewhere safe. We're just not safe and you don't deserve to be pulled into our mess. These people we're going to are good people, and you won't have to worry about hiding out or running away anymore."

"But what about what I want?" she cried. "I would rather you take me back home than drop me off with more strangers."

My heart breaking, I attempted to move to her again, but she sidestepped me. I let my hands fall to my side. I got it. We were her family now. She was clinging to us because we took her from a solitary existence and gave her hope, and she thought we didn't want her.

Sobbing, Stormy dropped to her knees, head bent so her hair covered her face. I ran to her and wrapped my arms around her tiny body. "Do you really understand what staying with us means? What could happen to you?"

Her tear-streaked face looked up at me. "Since my last brother died, it's been terrible. It's like I've been sleepwalking in a nightmare and I didn't wake up until you guys told me to pack my bags. I don't want you to leave me."

Wiping away tears with the palms of my hands, I plopped down on my rear next to her. I understand how she felt. I lived one week, just one week, without my family and she was right; it was a nightmare. She'd lived like that for years until we came along. She was just a little girl. The people at the lodge were good people, no doubt, but I couldn't hand her over. She was one of us now. I couldn't let her go any more than I could let one of the guys go. We would just have to find a way to keep her safe.

Releasing an over exaggerated sigh, I said, "Guess you're stuck with us then."

"Do you mean it, or are you just saying it so I'll stop crying?" Stormy asked, trying to control her tears.

"I will say anything to make you stop making that horrible noise, geez," I teased, then nudged her shoulder with mine. "You're stuck with us, kiddo. Well, until you realize how crazy you are and make us take you somewhere and I don't know, I think we'll keep you then, too."

"What if the guys say no?" Stormy asked, her voice cracking and her eyes shining.

I patted her shoulder. "Don't worry about the boys, I'll handle them."

After helping her pack the rest of her things, I stayed with her until she settled in for the night. Though she did complain she didn't need tucking in like a baby, she didn't fight hard enough to make me believe it. She wanted to be taken care of, and I wanted to take care of her. We might have only known each other for a few days, but I would give my life to protect hers.

When I did my version of explaining to the guys how Stormy was staying with us, no one fought me on it and to my surprise, they all agreed with a smile. Not sure what to make of it, I stood in the middle of them, ready to fight to keep her but not getting the chance since they seemed perfectly okay with it.

Tugging on my arm, Luke pulled me to him and wrapped his arms around me. "Let's get to bed."

"You go ahead. I want to sit with Jacob for a little bit first," I said, reaching up to my tiptoes to kiss the underside of his chin.

Luke squeezed my ass before patting it, while the guys groaned at witnessing the public display of affection. He looked down at me with a dimpled smile and kissed me quickly. "Come on, Adam. Let's get some shut eye."

"Don't take too long," he whispered in my ear, sending chills throughout my body.

Once Adam and Luke went inside, Jacob and I sat on the steps of the porch watching the glow of the setting sun. He stretched his bad leg and I checked his face for any signs of pain, but there were none. "Do we need to take a look at your leg?"

"Nah, I'm good. It just gets stiff if I don't stretch it out."

Eyeing his leg warily, I asked, "Did they give you antibiotics?"

"Yep," he sighed. "No need to worry about me, sis."

"I'm never going to stop worrying about you," I said with a smile.

"Well, you need to," Jacob clipped.

"Jacob?"

"Why the hell would you put yourself in so much danger? I mean, seriously, Roni, do you have a death wish?" His jaw clinched as he shook his head in disgust or anger; I wasn't sure which.

"I thought you were dead. I thought they killed you and they needed to pay for it. So, yeah, I *did* have a death wish."

"And if I *had* died, you think that's what I would have wanted? For you to go on some kamikaze mission?" He shook his head. "You really think I would have wanted you to give up our home, your future? Do you think that's what Mom and Dad would want?"

"Don't bring Mom and Dad into this," I hissed, keeping my eyes firmly on the ground.

"Why not? You were doing what you did in my name, right? Because you thought I was dead. Do you think I would want to face our parents and be proud you weren't fighting to live?"

"Okay, I get it, now stop." What would he do if he knew how far I actually had gone? He might go ahead and kill me and save myself and the General's men some time.

"Don't you ever do something that stupid in my name again." He leaned back on the palms of his hands. "And right now, you swear. Swear on our parents that if something happens to me, you keep living. None of this 'vengeance is mine' bullshit."

"I swear," I whispered.

"Look at me," he ordered kindly. I turned and faced him, his eyes shining brightly through the dusky sky. "I love you. *Luke* loves you. Don't do something like that again."

"I won't, promise." After a second of silence, I said, "I'm glad you're not dead."

"I'm glad we're both not dead. Now, go get some sleep so you'll be wide awake tomorrow while we're running for our lives."

Chapter Fifteen

"I've been thinking about something Stormy said the other day," I told Luke while staring into the night sky. We had been on the move for two days, trying our best to keep out of sight and off any roads we thought the men might take. Keeping out of sight meant taking the less-traveled roads, which also meant camping out at night. Currently, Stormy was sleeping in the backseat of the car while Adam and Jacob were pretending to be frontiersmen and sleeping on the ground by a fire. Luke and I were parked about half a football field's length away, sleeping in the bed of the truck, which wasn't totally uncomfortable since we'd scavenged sleeping bags to lay down underneath us.

"What was that?" he asked, shifting his head forward, nuzzling the back of my neck.

"She said when her last surviving brother died, she felt like she was sleepwalking." He stopped kissing my neck and pulled me closer to him. "That's how I felt. Like I was

227

sleepwalking through life until you came along. We were alive, but we weren't living. You know what I mean? We weren't doing anything more than making it through the day."

"Sometimes, making it through the day is all some can manage. That's how I lived in the Special Forces. There's no shame in it, it just is what it is."

"When I thought you'd killed Jacob, I felt like that again, only a thousand times worse because I didn't want to wake up. I shut down any feeling I had so nothing could touch me. Well, except anger. I let anger take over and I wasn't me anymore. I'm embarrassed by who I became."

"We all have done things we're not proud of to survive, babe."

"But I don't want to just survive anymore. I want to live. You know? *Really* live."

Luke slipped his hand beneath the waistband of my jeans, the tips of his fingers brushing my clit through my panties. My hips involuntarily moved toward his hand, until he shifted my panties to the side and dipped his finger inside me. I bit my bottom lip to keep from moaning. His chuckle reverberated through me. "You feel alive to me."

"Luke…" I moaned as he kissed from my shoulder, up the curve of my neck, until his teeth nipped at my earlobe. "Luke, we can't. God, they'll hear us."

His fingers continued to work me while he wrapped his other arm around me, pinching my nipple between his fingers, causing my body to shake. "*We* aren't, but *you* are. You can bite onto me to keep quiet."

He sucked on my neck, shoulder, ear, anywhere he could reach. Reaching down, I unbuttoned my jeans and pulled them over my hips to give him better access. Giving a guttural laugh, he adjusted the blanket over me to keep all my parts covered.

"Hey, you started this," I said, pushing his hand back into position. "Now finish it."

"Yes, ma'am." Luke rolled me onto my back, pulling my jeans all the way off and pushed my top up, freeing my breast from the bra he so detested.

His thick fingers moving in and out of me while rubbing my nub, he leaned in and covered my hard nipple with his mouth, flicking his tongue. My breathing became shallow and quickened as I felt the buildup inside of me.

I reached over and rubbed the hard bulge straining against his jeans, begging for freedom.

"Let me touch you," I groaned.

He shook his head, the scruff on his chin lightly brushing over the underside of my breast. "Luke…" I tried to speak between panting breaths. "Please…"

"Come for me, baby," he demanded, his voice low and gravelly.

Gripping the sleeping bag beneath me, I arched my back as he shifted and covered my other nipple with his mouth. "God, Luke…" Unable to breathe, I jerked my head from side to side, and my body went rigid seconds before I crumbled. I clamped around his fingers over and over until his hand moved from inside me.

"You're so beautiful, sweetheart. So beautiful."

Not able to open my eyes, I blindly reached around until my hand found his face and palmed his cheek before he kissed my palm. I yawned and he chuckled.

"Baby wipes are in the tote over there," I pointed.

He cleaned up, then we redressed and laid down, his chest to my back, letting me use his arm as a pillow.

"I love you," I whispered before another yawn overtook me.

"I know, sweetheart." He kissed my temple.

My forehead creased, though I was too sleepy to actually open my eyes. "Don't you love me?"

"Do you really have to ask?"

"Well," I opened my eyes. "I said it and you didn't say it back. That's… I don't know… weird."

"I said it less than an hour ago. I haven't stopped loving you in the last hour, babe," he said, his words low and drowsy.

My eyes narrowed. "I know that, but when you're in love and the person you're in love with says I love you, you should return the sentiment if you do in fact love the person."

Silence.

"Seriously?" I asked.

"What? I'm still trying to figure out what the hell you just said." He shifted to his back, pulling me to his chest. "I love you, too, Roni."

"Thank you," I said, smiling.

"Even if you never hear me say it again, I'm always going to love you. Always, sweetheart."

"I know." And I did and needed to trust in it.

"Now, please go to sleep."

"Okay."

Staying still until his breathing evened out, I rolled my head until I could look up to the starry sky, trying to remember the last time I'd watched the stars after the plague, or even before then, for that matter. I couldn't remember, but I did recall—as a child—wondering if the world was wrapped in black construction paper and the stars were from the angels in heaven poking holes in the paper to look down at the people on Earth.

I wondered what the angels thought of us now. Did they still look through the holes or have they stepped away from the vast destruction? Maybe God took who he wanted and we were left with hell on Earth.

Through sleep, Luke's hand tightened around my shoulder and I smiled. Hell might be on Earth, but in a sense, I'd found a little piece of heaven. If there were any angels left, I hoped they smiled when they looked down at us and put a good word in with the big guy to keep us safe.

Tomorrow would be the day we finally made it to Canaan, and we needed all the help we could get. A few days ago, I'd strolled into Canaan without an ounce of fear. Of course, a few days ago I was also ready to die in a blaze of glory. Since then, my priorities had changed a bit. First and foremost, I wanted to live and I wanted my life to include my messed up, hodgepodge family. I just hoped the people I met along the way were willing to help make that happen and not turn their backs on us in fear.

****

With the truck pulled to the side of the road, my hands on my hips with my head tilted back to look to the heavens I repeated myself for the umpteenth time. "If you don't let me go through first and find the people I already know, we're going to get caught."

"I know a few people. Who do you know?" Adam asked innocently.

Luke glared. "Are you talking about that fucker I saw you kissing?"

"You were kissing someone?" Jacob asked, his eyebrows pulled together.

"Wow," Stormy said with a giggle.

Staring down Luke, I asked, "Are you seriously jealous?"

All eyes turned to Luke and he stood to his full height. "I don't have dick to be jealous about."

I rolled my eyes. "Right, then you agree me going in alone is what's best for the group."

"Not going to happen." He crossed his arms over his chest.

"What part of 'if they see you they're going to automatically go on guard' do you not get?" I asked for the umpteenth time.

"She's right," Jacob said. "You weren't exactly friendly the last time you were here, and being the Incredible Hulk doesn't help you blend in."

"What do you mean he wasn't exactly friendly?" I asked, worried at the possibility of hearing something I didn't want to hear, but I had to know.

"He's considered a badass for a reason."

"And that reason would be?"

"Enough," Luke demanded. "Jacob's right. I can't walk in without knowing who's there, or if Griffin and his men have already made it to town, but you're still not going."

"You are the most infuriating man alive," I said, straightening my arms and fisting my hands while stomping.

"Probably, but I don't give one shit if it pisses you off or not."

"How about if I go with her?" Jacob asked.

"No, you can't do that much walking on your leg and if need be, you can't run," I said, dismissing the idea.

"I'll go," Adam offered, pushing off the rear bumper of the truck. "I've probably spent more time here than anyone."

"Works for me," I said with a smile. "We work well together."

"Fine," Luke said, throwing his hands in the air before scowling at Adam and me. "Don't piss anyone off while you're there." He stomped to the cab of the truck and yanked open the door.

Jacob stepped closer to us. "Get in, scope it out, and then get the hell out. Once we know who's there, we'll know how to proceed."

"Can I go, too?" Stormy asked.

"No," four voices denied in unison. Rolling her eyes, she adjusted the brim of her oversized hat and crossed her arms over her chest.

234

"Let's go," Adam said, moving to the driver's side of the truck.

Patting Jacob's cheek, I assured him we would be fine, then moved to Stormy and squeezed her shoulders. "Don't let these guys chase after us once we leave."

"They don't know how to start the car, so you're good."

Laughing, I lifted the brim of her hat and looked into her pretty brown eyes. "You're the best."

"I know," she said with a smile.

By the time I made it to the passenger side of the truck, Luke stood sullenly against the closed door. "What?"

"I don't like this," he hooked his fingers into the belt loops at my hips and pulling me to him.

"You're just worried David is going to sweep me off my feet and we'll elope before I remember you're here waiting on me?" I asked, wrapping my arms around his neck.

"I'm not worried about that," he said, nipping my bottom lip.

"Why not?" I asked, smiling up at him.

"Because you already have the best," he said low, then leaned into my neck and whispered, "Because he can't make you come like I can."

A shiver ran up my spine at the thought of Luke inside me. "You're right. Guess I'll have to break his heart then."

"Let's go," Adam called impatiently from inside the truck.

Luke turned, opened the door, and helped me inside. He leaned in, kissed me quickly, and then spoke to both of us. "We'll meet back here in two hours. If you feel like anything isn't right, get out. And stay together."

After guaranteeing we would return safely, Adam started the truck and we headed toward Canaan. I was proud of Luke. Giving up control was hard for him, but he knew what was best for us all, even if he didn't like it.

"What's the plan?" Adam asked.

"I was thinking we should try to find my friend Daisy's mom." I wished I would have gotten her name. "She's a nurse, and Daisy said she sets up a tent at the market."

"Maureen?" he asked. When I raised my eyebrows in question, he went on. "Daisy's a pretty blonde? A little hippyish?"

"Yeah. She told me she knew you," I said, remembering a conversation I'd had with Daisy.

"Her mom's Maureen. She's a nice lady. A little different, but nice."

If she was anything like her daughter, I could understand his use of "different." "Do you think they'll help us?"

He sighed. "I think they'll want to, but these towns... When Wells and his men come through, they make a point to put fear in everyone to keep them in line, so they could be too scared to help."

The last thing I wanted was to put these people in danger, but wasn't living under the General's thumb keeping them in a perpetual state of danger? The man thought he could take whatever he wanted, whenever he wanted, even if it included people. If he wasn't stopped, he would eventually take until he had it all and our lives wouldn't be ours anymore.

"Do you think Griffin is there?" I asked. Adam probably knew Griffin better than any of us since he had been forced to spend so much time with him.

"I don't know. I think since we took the long way around, they have probably already been there and gone. If they have, he'll leave men there watching the place, so we're going to have to keep an eye out."

Searching the floorboard, I found the ball cap I'd used the last time I was in Canaan and handed it to him. "This might help." Adam adjusted the band on the back and put it on, then slid his eyes sideways at me. "What?"

"Thanks for taking care of Luke this winter. I mean, besides trying to kill him," he joked. "But really. He's never been an emotional guy, but he's different with you. He's happy and it's been a long freaking time since I've seen him even half that happy."

"Yeah. I'm glad I didn't kill him, too," I said with a wink.

Chapter Sixteen

"Do you know which tent is hers?" I asked as we strolled through the market, keeping our faces down but our eyes open. Getting inside had been relatively easy since we'd decided to leave the truck in the community parking right outside the checkpoint. David hadn't been on duty, but no one seemed to recognize us and no one tried to stop our entry. So far, we hadn't seen any of Griffin's men, but that didn't mean they weren't there.

"It's the big white one with the flag with the red cross on it," he said, pointing to a tent on the far left. "Someone's there or the flag wouldn't be flying."

I was impressed with the whole market setup. Everything was organized in accordance with needs. One side held the booths with food and toiletries while the other side seemed to be a combination of household needs like candles, fuel, wood, and clothes. "Why don't they use the buildings instead of tents?" I wondered aloud.

"Light. The buildings are so dark, they would have to use candles and lamps and that wastes a lot of supplies."

"Makes sense," I said just as we reached the fabric door of the medical tent. Taking a deep breath, I followed Adam inside.

The space was cool and airy, with white vinyl walls held taut with metal rails. I felt extremely dirty standing inside the pristine room. Adam stepped to the next entrance and called, "Maureen, you in there?"

"I'll be there in just a minute," she called out. "Just sign the form on the desk and have a seat, unless you're dirty, then stay standing."

My eyes shifted to the oak desk to our right. I approached it and looked at the long list of names with the day's date. *Is it really mid-March already?* That was crazy. I ran a finger through the list of names and smiled at the normality of the whole place. I wondered if she kept charts for people or not. I bet she did.

Glancing down at my clothes, I figured I wasn't too bad and took a seat. Adam sat next to me and sighed. I noticed since we made it to town his movements seemed a little slower and he spoke less. I wanted to ask him if he needed more medicine but thought better of it. He knew how to take care of himself and with Luke watching over him all the time, he probably needed a break from the constant hovering. I would just have to keep an eye on him. He probably needed to get fluids in him. I didn't have the issues he had and my throat felt bone dry.

"Think she has some water or something? I'm parched."

"Parched?" He smiled and I nudged him with my elbow. "I bet she has something for your parchness, but it'll be back there with her."

I nodded, hoping it wouldn't take too long to get back there. After another ten minutes, I huffed. "Guess wait time at the doctor's office wasn't affected by the plague."

Adam laughed. "It's only been a few minutes."

"Well, it feels longer," I said, inspecting my dry, sad-looking hands. I could really stand to soak my hands in lotion for a while. And what I wouldn't give to soak in a hot bubble bath. That would be the first thing I did when we made it home—right after I found my chickens.

"You aren't a patient person, are you?" he surmised.

"Patience has never been used with my name unless the term 'lack of' was included." I grinned and relaxed in the chair. "Luke told me you were in college before."

He ran a hand over his face and nodded. "Yeah, I was a sophomore."

"What was your major?"

"English."

He must have really been feeling down since over the past few days he'd barely stopped talking and now it was like pulling teeth. "What were you going to do with an English degree? Write?"

"No, I wanted to be an English teacher."

"Really? You wanted to be around kids all day?" I shook my head, confounded. "You really *are* a saint, aren't you?"

"Ha! No, I wanted to teach high school English."

"Oh, okay, I don't know if I would find that better or worse. I didn't like teenagers when I *was* a teenager, but all those sticky hands and kids wiping their noses on their sleeves, yuck."

"Adam? Is that you?" a female voice asked.

My head whipped around to find an older version of Daisy standing in front of us. Maureen looked young enough to be Daisy's older sister. Whatever lotion she was using, I wanted a pallet of it.

"It's me," Adam said, standing.

Her hands moved to cup his face. "Let me get a look at you, boy. How are you feeling? You don't look good. Where's your medicine?" Holding his forearm, Maureen pulled him through the fabric door and out of sight. I rushed to follow them.

The back room held rows of cots separated with light-colored curtains. Like the front, everything was in order and spotless. Maureen stopped at the back of the tent where another desk, a bookshelf, and filing cabinet were.

"Sit," she instructed, and Adam sat. "When was the last time you had your pill?"

"Last night," he answered, keeping his eyes away from me. I sucked in a shocked breath.

"Last night? Adam, why didn't you say something?"

"And you are?" Maureen asked as she pulled a bottle of water from a cabinet, opening a small pack of salt and pouring it into the water. "Drink."

Adam took the salt water and grimaced as he drank it down. "This is Roni."

Maureen picked up a cash box and placed it on top of her desk. She pulled a key from a chain on her neck and unlocked the box while taking glances at me. "Are you the Roni who brought Daisy to town a few weeks ago?"

"I am." I smiled at the recognition. Since Daisy liked me and I helped her out, I hoped it would make Maureen more perceptive to hearing us out and helping.

"You didn't bring a gun in here, did you?" she asked, her eyebrow quirked high.

"No, ma'am, I didn't," I said, holding my hands up. Maybe not *everything* Daisy remembered about me was good.

She turned to Adam and handed him a bottle of pills. "I found these a few weeks back and hoped I would get a chance to get them to you."

He opened the bottle, shaking out two pills into his hand before popping them into his mouth and gulping down the water. "Thanks."

"Now," she sat on the edge of the desk and eyed both of us, "tell me why that asshole and his men came through town madder than a cat with its tail on fire hunting you two?"

"We need your help," Adam said matter of factly.

"Figured as much." Maureen sighed and crossed her arms over her chest. "I was planning on heading back to Victory tonight, so you two can go with me and get—"

"It's not just us," I said. "Both of our brothers and a teenage girl are waiting for us outside of town."

Maureen's lips pursed and she momentarily closed her eyes. "Okay then. Let me think."

"We don't want to cause any problems. We just need somewhere safe to sleep for a night or two so we can come up with a plan."

"You guys know they're not going to stop looking for you," Maureen said to Adam.

"I know," he said low. "That's why we have to stop them."

"It's about damned time. I'm completely against violence, but those men… It's like they're glad the world is suffering so there's no one to stop them from doing whatever they want. They're nothing but a bunch of terrorists." She went silent, in thought. "You know they took Karen's boy this last time? He's sixteen years old, for God's sake. Told them if he didn't go, they would burn their house down. It's a shame. They have to be stopped."

"We'll stop them," I said, trying to convince myself along with her.

"You two need to get out of town and head toward the lodge. Try to stay out of sight until sundown and I'll let everyone know you'll be coming so no one gets spooked by a group of people showing up at night." Maureen pushed off the desk, put on her stethoscope, and listened to Adams heart. "Feel better?"

"Yes, ma'am." He grinned innocently.

"Good." She wrapped the stethoscope around her neck and pulled out two bottles of water, handing one to Adam and one to me. "Stay hydrated and don't be stingy with the meds. Take them like you're supposed to. We can always find more."

Once we were back in the truck and on the road, I turned to Adam with an annoyed glare. "Why did you lie?"

Scrunching his eyebrows, his eyes moved from the road to me then back to the road. "What are you talking about?"

"This morning, Luke asked you if you took your medicine and you told him you did. Why didn't you say you were out?" I asked, more than a little peeved. What if Griffin had been there and we needed to run? The thought made me sick to my stomach.

After a few minutes of me staring at him and him staring at the road, he spoke, "Luke has worried about me for as long as I can remember. Everything he's ever done has been for me. Even before I got sick, he was my dad. *After* I got sick, he was with me through it all. My sickness became his life. Sometimes even more than it's mine.

"Being a burden to someone you love sucks ass and before you say it, I *am* a burden, especially in this freaking world. None of us would be in this situation if Luke hadn't been protecting me, taking care of me. If I didn't have Addison's, he would have never joined the Army. He wouldn't have had to do the things he's done to make sure I got medicine. And if he knew I didn't have any this morning, he would do something possibly stupid to find me some, and he *definitely* wouldn't have let me go with you to Canaan."

"First, you are *not* a burden. Do you think Luke would do less for you if you hadn't gotten Addison's? Like you said, he was like a father to you even before you were diagnosed and it wasn't because he had to be. He *wanted* to be. He loves you so much. His face lights up when he talks about you and it's Luke we're talking about. He's not a light-up-face kind of guy."

Shaking my head, I went on, "I can't imagine what it's like for you to depend on medicine, but Wells would have found another way to use you or keep Luke under control. And you can say they wouldn't know about Luke because he would have never joined the Army, that may possibly be true, but being in the Army is a part of him. I think he would have joined no matter what. And now, if you're a burden, so am I. So is Jacob. So is Stormy. You know why? Because he loves us and would do anything for us. Each of us would do anything for each other. We would fight, steal, or beg, whatever we had to do, to keep each other safe. One thing's for sure, though, we have to depend on each other or we'll never make it. We have to trust."

Letting the words soak in, we kept our eyes forward as our family came into view. Adam slowed the truck, pulling it to the side of the road. Just as I was going for the door handle, Adam stopped me. "You know, I'm not the only one who makes his face light up."

My eyes moved to Luke's smiling face as his eyes zeroed in on me. I turned to Adam and my smile grew before I opened the door and hopped out of the truck, running to my man and jumping into his arms like I used to when we were on the orchard. "I missed you."

"Really? I can't tell," he said, kissing me quickly as he carried me to the truck. "Were they there? Is that why you're back so soon?"

"Nope," Adam said. "We need to load up and head to the lodge. I'll explain it to Jacob on the drive and Roni can tell you."

I slid off Luke and hugged Stormy and turned to my brother. "Did you all eat?"

"Yes, Mom," Stormy said sarcastically.

"Whoa, I am not *that* old."

"Then stop acting like it," Stormy said, and Jacob bent over laughing.

I slugged him and he held his hands up, still laughing. "What? She's freaking hilarious."

She was, but not when it was at my expense. "Load up, we need to get going. Stormy, who do you want to ride with?"

Stormy's eyes flashed to Adam and then to the ground. "I'll ride in the car so I can lay out in the back."

I fought to keep my eyebrows from rising, but I couldn't help the slight grin I sported. Turning to Luke, I tucked my arm into his and smiled up at him. "Let's get on the road then." Looking over my shoulder, I said, "Oh, make sure Adam eats something." I winked at Adam. Maybe I *was* the mom of the group, but someone had to be.

We all loaded up and headed toward the lodge, Luke and me in the truck, and the others following in the car. I recited the events of the day, leaving out the part where Adam had lied to him and was feeling down, but I did tell him Maureen checked him out and gave him another bottle of hydrocortisone.

"And that's all?" he asked, eying me.

"Yep," I swallowed. I hated not telling him about Adam, but what good would it do? I knew and Adam knew I knew, so the only purpose it would serve would be to get Luke pissed off and grumpy. No one liked a grumpy Luke. "Why?"

"Nothing."

Tilting my head, I searched his face and then it dawned on me. "Are you wondering if I saw David?"

"No, I'm not," he said a little too quickly.

"Well, just in case you want to know later... we didn't see him or anyone else, actually. Though I did see a camping stove that I would love to have for my birthday."

His eyes slashed down to me. "Birthday, huh?"

"Yes. You do remember when my birthday is, don't you?" I batted my eyelashes at him. He shifted in his seat next to me and I bit the inside of my mouth to keep from smiling. "Well?"

"It's in June," he said with more confidence than he showed.

"Close."

"May," he said quickly, like he just remembered it.

"Are you sure about that?" I asked, still holding my head slightly askew. He cleared his throat and looked so miserable, I couldn't hold back any longer and laughed. "My birthday is June the tenth and yours is April the tenth. See, easy."

He glared down at me but put a hand on my thigh and squeezed. "You're a girl. Girls remember that stuff."

"Sure, blame it on my gender, but I bet David would remember my birthday."

"Since he's a pussy, I bet he would," he growled.

Chapter Seventeen

"There she is," I whispered, pointing to the willowy figure standing on the darkened porch of the lodge.

"About time," Jacob said, grunting as he pulled himself into a standing position from the ground. "After listening to you two talk about the food here for the last three hours, I'm freaking starving."

Taking a few steps forward, Luke grabbed my arm to stop me. I twisted my neck and watched his constant surveillance of the pitch black surroundings. Every muscle in his body was taut and ready for anything that went bump in the night. Spinning around, I moved in close to him and tilted my head up.

"Nothing is going to happen here."

"They could be setting us up."

"They're not. You have to trust me on this, and you really need to chill out. If you walk up there all badass, they aren't going to take kindly to it at all. Plus, if you keep clinching your jaw like that, you're going to break a tooth, and I don't see any dentists around." Placing my hands on his hips, I tugged at his hips trying to loosen him up.

"She's right. They'll make you sit outside while we go in and eat good food," Adam said, walking past us toward the porch with a limping Jacob tagging along.

"Let's go," Stormy said to both of us.

Raising his eyebrows, Luke took a long breath before grabbing my hand and moving. It wasn't lost on me how Stormy stayed close to Luke's side, her eyes searching—just like Luke's had been—while we made our way to the porch.

With hands on her hips, Maureen eyed Luke suspiciously. "Anyone carrying a weapon?"

"Nope," I lied since no one had been able to talk Luke out of carrying a handgun on his ankle. "We left them somewhere safe."

Maureen turned to Stormy and smiled genuinely. "And you are?"

When Stormy leaned toward Luke, he slipped a protective arm around her and Adam stepped in. "This is Stormy and this is Jacob." He pointed a thumb toward Jacob. Remembering his manners, Jacob stuck an open hand out and shook Maureen's hand. "Jacob is Roni's brother. Stormy's our…"

"She's our sister," I provided. "Can we sit down? Jacob was shot in the leg a few weeks ago and he tires easily."

"Oh yes, yes. Everyone is waiting in the dining area," Maureen said, hurrying us into the foyer. The voices carrying through the walls of the house went silent as the large door closed behind us.

We followed Maureen through the living room and into the dining room. At least twenty sets of eyes stared back at us as we filed in.

"You have got to be shitting me," a male voice said, angered, as the sound of chair legs scraping on the floor filled the air. "We are *not* helping him."

My guys stood guard in front of Stormy and me, but I managed to wiggle my way between them to find Josh standing in the middle of the room bowed up like a bear protecting his honey. I moved to step around Luke, but he reached back and put a hand on my hip, stopping me.

"Get your hands off her," Josh said, taking a step forward.

"Roni, is that you, girl?" Daisy said from the side of the room.

"Hey, Daisy," I waved above Luke's shoulder. "Josh, can we all sit down and talk?"

"This is my brother," Adam explained, pointing a thumb toward Luke, not understanding what Josh's deal was.

Josh's hands flung up in the air. "Well, this day just keeps getting better and better."

Sliding around Luke, I smiled at the crowd of confused faces. "Hi. It's good to see you all again. Thank you for letting us come. Now, if you all don't mind, we'll all sit down and then we can explain everything. Josh, I know Luke was the jackass who punched you, but if we sit down and talk, then hopefully he can explain why he did." *I hope.*

Daisy looked at Luke like she was just now noticing he was in the room. Her hand went to her hip. *"You're* the one who hit him?"

"I was in a hurry," Luke murmured.

I spun my head around and glared at him. He raised an eyebrow at me and I shook my head in frustration. "Everyone, sit down."

When no one moved, I stared at my group and pointed to the table. "Now!"

Like they were waiting for the magic word, they all moved to the table and sat, leaving Maureen and me the last two standing. I smiled and scooted in next to Luke so I could pinch him under the table if he needed it. Maureen sat across from Josh, giving him a stern look on her way down that could put fear in any man. With everyone seemingly calm for the moment, I told our story, letting Adam and Jacob jump in as needed. When we were basically finished, all heads were cast down and a silent anger reigned over the room.

"Now, we have two choices: never go home, or stop them so they can't screw with more people's lives," Jacob said, tapping his knuckles on the table.

"How exactly do you plan on stopping them?" a man I vaguely remembered seeing the last time I was there asked. Our group turned to Luke for the answer, and I hoped he had one.

"Still working on it, but one thing I know, we can't do it alone," Luke said, his eyes moving around the room.

These people didn't understand what it took for Luke to ask for assistance. He was a proud man who was entirely capable of protecting himself, but he had the rest of us to think about.

"Personally, I think you're going to get yourselves all killed," another man said. "Along with anyone who helps you."

"How many men have they drafted from here alone?" Luke asked.

"Five," Lydia answered.

"Did the men *want* to go?" he asked, and they shook their heads. "Right. The majority of the men they have with them don't want to be there. They're there because they were forced to be and if given a real opportunity, they would fight to leave. Is there a chance someone gets hurt or dies? Yes. There's a real chance, but I can promise if you don't do something now, they will keep coming back and eventually someone will die anyway."

"If they aren't stopped, imagine what it will be like in ten years when they're too big to stop," Adam added. A lump formed in my throat at the thought. "We are at a place where two futures are possible. One is being controlled, hiding our sons when General Wells's men come around, and the other is being free. Right now, we get to choose our future, we just have to be brave enough to choose what's right."

Luke watched his brother with pride in his eyes and I could imagine his heart swelled. He might not be Adam's father, but he sure did raise one hell of a man. My eyes moved to Jacob and we smiled at each other from across the table. I was thankful to have such great men in my life.

"This is exactly what I've been saying," Maureen said. "At first, they took our food, then our men, what will they want next? I have to hide medicine, not from the people of Canaan, but from the soldiers who have been ordered to take anything I have. What will we do if they want the girls next?" Her hand reached out and took Daisy's.

"Griffin would kill any one of us without batting an eye," Josh said, tight-lipped. His head turned to Daisy then back to the group. "I'm surprised they hadn't started taking the women, too."

"The larger they get, the more reckless and entitled they'll feel. If we can stop just Griffin's group, there's a chance Wells will leave it alone and move on since he's been in a rush to get to Atlanta." Luke ran a hand over his scruffy beard.

"What's in Atlanta?" Maureen asked.

"That's where he's from," Adam provided.

"Really? All this to get home?" Jacob asked, his lips curled back in disgust.

"I think it's more than that. He wants to be centralized there so he can rule or whatever from his back yard." Adam turned to Lydia. "Do you mind if I grab a glass of water?"

"Oh, sure, honey, go on in the kitchen. Actually, if you're all hungry, there's plenty of stew and biscuits left."

I moved to stand with Adam, but Stormy stopped me. "I'll go with Adam and we'll bring you all back something." When I nodded, Stormy turned to Adam. "I mean, if that's okay with you."

"Of course," Adam said, and Stormy smiled at him like he was the lead singer of a boy band.

Luke's eyebrows furrowed and I smiled. I'd wondered how long it would take him to realize Stormy was crushing on Adam pretty bad. I thought it was cute, but by the scowl on Luke's face, he didn't. Chuckling, I turned my attention back to the group.

"To put it simply, we need help," I said putting my palms up. "I hate to ask, and if you can't or don't want to, we understand, but if you do, we won't go into this like a bunch of idiots. Luke was Special Forces. He knows how to do this with the least amount of risk."

"You want us to put our lives in the hands of the man who came through our town, demanding we give him gas, punches Josh, and leaves?" Daisy asked as her nose crinkled and her upper lip rose to show her gums. "He's one of them."

Tilting my head to the side and raising my eyebrows at Luke, he rolled his eyes and laid his forearms on the table. "I *was* in a hurry the day we stopped by." Daisy and Josh both shifted in their seats. "Jacob had the bullet hole in his leg, and I was trying to get him to a medic to stop the bleeding."

Josh stared at him while slowly sucking a breath between his front teeth. "I guess I can see where that would warrant the act of aggression."

"Griffin isn't a patient man, and he would have had one of them shoot you if I hadn't decked you and gotten what we needed." Luke relaxed into the back of the seat. "You're lucky he didn't force you to go with us."

"So, essentially, you saved his life," I said, knowing full well he had. He'd punched Josh so he would shut his mouth and not get himself killed. My man was a damn good man. I leaned over and kissed him. "I love you."

He winked at me and his cheeks flushed pink, but he grabbed my hand on the table and rubbed the palm of my hand with his thumb. Yeah, he loved me.

"Okay, you two. No one wants to see that," Jacob said, leaning into his open hands and covering his eyes with his palms, rubbing them.

Stormy and Adam came back into the room, each carrying two bowls, and set them in front of us. I thanked them as I dug into my food. The people from the lodge gathered together on the other side of the room, letting us eat in peace. Stormy sat next to me.

"What did we miss?" she asked.

"That Luke's a super hero and saved Josh by knocking the shit out of him to keep him from being killed," Jacob provided.

Adam laughed and Stormy's chin dipped as she looked at me in question. "It's true. I think we should find him a cape. Maybe we could make one from a bedsheet."

"Stop it," Luke said in a growl, but the corners of his mouth twitched.

The group at the other end of the table broke apart, and a few people stood and left the table, giving a nod on their way out. Lydia leaned in. "We decided to help. Lots of the people here tonight had a son or brother taken and we want them back. We want this to stop."

"We want it to stop, too," I said, squeezing her hand. "Thank you."

"Darren and Becky are getting a house ready for you all now. We'd love to keep you at the lodge, but we never know when they will show up, so it's best if you all are out of sight."

"We appreciate that," Luke said for all of us.

Lydia's gaze traveled over each of us before stopping on Adam. Reaching across the table, she patted his hand. "I'm glad you're back."

His eyes sparkled and a smile spread across his handsome face. "I'm glad to be back."

"And you, young lady, aren't you just beautiful," Lydia said to Stormy.

Stormy's eyes flicked to Adam before replying, "Thank you."

We finished eating and I stacked the bowls, then carried them to the kitchen with Daisy close behind. I put the bowls in a soapy bowl of water and began cleaning them. "That's the guy who had you so tore up, isn't it?"

Keeping my eyes on the task at hand, I answered, "There was a big misunderstanding. I thought he'd killed my brother, when in fact he shot him to save him." I looked at her. "Like he did with Josh."

Daisy huffed. "He shoots and punches people to save them? Sounds messed up to me."

Setting down the last clean bowl, I turned to face her while drying my hands. Anger simmering in my veins, ready to boil over. Sure, Daisy was being flippant with reason, but I was tired and more than a little sick of Luke repeatedly being shit on. I tossed the hand towel on the counter. "It *is* messed up. It's really messed up that Griffin and Wells held Adam's medicine over his head to make him do whatever they wanted. And it's really messed up that no matter what he does to protect the people around him, he's treated with disdain and suspicion. It's messed up that he's a freaking hero but is constantly looked at like a villain."

Daisy's hand went to her chest. "Did they really keep Adam's medicine?"

"No, I lied," I deadpanned. She would either believe me or not, but I wasn't in the mood to state the obvious again.

"Those assholes." Her hand fell to her side and her bottom lip dipped. "I'm sorry. It's just, you know, hard to trust people and he's so… big," Daisy said with wide eyes, then she smiled. "You look happy, though."

Smiling, I nodded. "I am happy, and I plan on doing whatever it takes to stay that way."

Sighing, Daisy slid a strand of hair behind her ear. "I know what you mean. I would do just about anything for Josh and Momma."

"In this world, I think if we want to be happy, we're going to have to fight for it. All of us."

Letting my words soak in, Daisy stared into the darkened room before smiling. "Looks like the only thing you're fighting tonight is keeping your eyes open. Let's get your crew and I'll show you guys to the house they're setting up for you."

I followed Daisy into the dining room where everyone seemed to be in quiet discussion with one another before I herded the guys and Stormy, and we followed Daisy out the back door. Adam and Jacob went first, followed by Stormy and me, then Luke took up the tail end, keeping his eyes on our surroundings. We walked alongside two houses directly behind the lodge, then cut across a road, past another house until Daisy stopped.

The house before us was almost impossible to see in the dark, only being silhouetted by the dim light of the half moon. No lights shone from inside to indicate anyone was there. Daisy handed Adam the lantern and pointed to the eerie house.

"There you go." She took a step back. "The windows have been blacked out so no one can see light from the outside."

"That's smart," Luke said from close behind me.

"Well, this isn't the first time they've kept people hidden," she said with a shrug.

"Thanks, Daisy. We'll see you in the morning," I said, grabbing Luke's hand and pulling him toward the house. Once on the porch, we waited for everyone to join us before Luke opened the door, sending a dim light spilling onto the porch. Poking my head inside, I found a cozy craftsman-style living room, complete with filled bookshelves.

Filing inside, Stormy went straight to the couch and plopped down. Jacob and Adam took the lantern and checked out the rest of the house.

"Think we need anything from the cars tonight?" I asked, slipping an arm around Luke's waist as we stood and took in the room. For the first time in a really long time, it felt like a real home and a safe place to lay our heads at night.

"Yeah, we need water and no way are we sleeping without being armed," he said low. Guess he wasn't feeling as secure as I was.

Jacob and Adam came back in the living room. Jacob put his hands on his hips and smiled. "Three bedrooms, all clean. One of us can sleep on the couch."

"I don't mind sleeping on the couch," Stormy said bravely.

"Nope. I already called dibs, didn't I?" Jacob said, jabbing Adam with his elbow.

"Yeah, he did," Adam agreed.

"Guys, let's get the vehicles and find a garage or building to put them in," Luke said, taking the lantern from

Adam. They headed out the door, leaving Stormy and me to ourselves.

"Let's check out the rooms," I said, tugging on her arm until she stood. Taking a candle from the coffee table, we walked through the house and decided on our rooms. Using the candle in hand, we lit candles in each room.

It didn't take long for the guys to come back, carrying more than enough supplies for the night. Jacob, Adam, and Stormy sat at the dining room table with a deck of cards while Luke and I called it a night. I was exhausted, but I wanted—no, I *needed*—time alone with him.

Finally alone, we went to the bathroom and shared a freezing shower, quickly washing each other before heading to the bedroom and taking our time slowly and quietly making love. We lay out of breath on the clean sheets. My head rested on his heaving chest, his arm wrapped around me. The muted sounds of our family laughing made me smile. It was the first time in a very long time I felt a semblance of normalcy, and it was beautiful. We were all together, the way it was supposed to be.

"It's been killing me, not being inside you," Luke said, kissing my forehead.

"Once all this is over, you and I aren't leaving our bedroom for a week," I said, groaning at the thought. "We won't even leave to eat. We'll just live off love."

He chuckled, the sound vibrating through my ear on his chest. I loved the sound and didn't get to hear it nearly enough. "*You* might be able to live off love alone, but I'm going to need pasta."

My smile widened, remembering a time when he taught me to make homemade pasta. I missed those days. I missed being home. Whispering, I asked, "Do you think we can do this?"

He squeezed my shoulder. "I'll keep you safe, sweetheart."

Kissing his chest, I snuggled in closer. He *would* keep me safe, I knew that. I was more worried about who was going to keep *him* safe.

Chapter Eighteen

Two weeks flew by in a flash, and this day was no different. It started out busy and hadn't slowed down through lunch. Jacob, Adam, and Luke spent nearly every day with Josh, scouting the surrounding area, talking to other people, mostly men, who wanted to join in on stopping Griffin, while Stormy and I were sent to the lodge to help feed all of those men. I wasn't happy about being left out of their discussions, but I would have felt equally as bad to leave the women of the house to handle all the hard work. I was surprised, though, with how great Josh and Luke ended up getting along; they even joked around with one another. Luke had offered for Josh and Daisy to come over a few nights before and play cards. The guys ended up playing while Stormy, Daisy, and I painted our nails and talked boys.

Today, I had to keep an eye on Stormy. She woke up in a bad mood and was doing her best to become every teenage stereotype there was out there in one day. She whined, got pissed off, back talked, and came to the point of

266

tears when I told her she had to help out at the lodge. Stormy wanted to hang out at the house by herself and when I refused, all hell broke loose.

Currently, she was half-assed washing the lunch dishes and refusing to speak to anyone. I picked up a bowl she'd cleaned and inspected it before tossing it back into the wash water.

When Stormy turned to me with a glare, I'd had all I could take for the day. "Go, I'll finish these."

"Fine," she said, shaking the soapy water from her hands while stomping through the kitchen and out the back door.

Maureen scooted into my place to rinse as I began scrubbing the dishes. "I'm sorry for her attitude today. I'd like to say it's not like her, but well…"

Maureen, Lydia, and Daisy all laughed. Lydia and Daisy were at the small, square kitchen table with a small sewing kit, replacing buttons and sewing small tears.

"Oh, to be a teenager again," Lydia said with a wistful sigh.

"I bet this is a lot for her to take in all at once," Maureen said, looking out the window to where the men stood, talking. More men had shown up to help with the fight against Griffin.

Earlier that morning, I had explained to them how Luke and I had found Stormy and how she was now a part of my family, for better or for worse. Like me, they were shocked at her ability to manage on her own for so long.

"I bet she's on her period," Daisy said, and I turned back to look at her and she shrugged. "I'm a raving lunatic when I'm on mine."

"Huh, that makes a lot more sense," I said, turning back to the dishes.

"I have some pain reliever you can give her." Maureen left the room and came back with a little, white pill and a candy bar. "The pill is for the cramping, but the chocolate makes everyone feel better."

Lydia stood and moved me out of the way. "Go make that girl feel better."

"Thanks," I said, giving them both a hug before heading out the door.

Once outside, the group of men stopped talking, and all heads turned toward me. I heard a low whistle and my spine stiffened. Three male voices yelled at the offender to shut the hell up. Glancing to the side, Jacob's chest was puffed out as he stared the man down, while Luke jogged toward me.

"Where are you going?" he asked, moving alongside of me. He looked down at the candy bar in my hand and smiled. "Please tell me you didn't steal that."

I shoved at him with my free hand and laughed. "It's for Stormy. She's not feeling well."

His eyebrows furrowed. "Yeah, she came out a few minutes ago and when we asked her where she was going, she told us to fuck off in Mandarin and hand gestures."

I laughed and moved in closer, nodding my head toward the group behind us. "How's it going?"

Shoving his hands into his front pockets, he sighed. "They seem to be willing, but none of them have any experience. We're going to need more."

Stopping, I put my hand on his upper arm. "You have us women, too. Daisy, me, even Maureen." He shook his head and I stopped him before he said something to piss me off. "Don't you dare say the women aren't getting involved. We're already involved. We're going to help whether you want us to or not, so unless you want us to start our own all women brigade, start including us."

When his head dropped back and his eyes closed, I glared, waiting on him to argue.

"I'm working on a plan and I promise to include you," he said, surprising me.

Leaning in, I brushed my breasts against his chest and smiled up at him. "Thank you."

"Oh, there are plenty of ways you can thank me." He gripped my butt, pulling me to him until I felt his hardness against my lower belly and groaned. "Go before I drag you behind those bushes over there and let you *really* thank me."

"Let me go then," I said, teasing as I leaned in closer, kissing the base of his neck while slightly brushing my hips against him.

He bent down and took my mouth hard and fast before releasing me and taking a large step back. "You're gonna pay for that tonight," he said with a wicked grin which made my insides quiver, and I squeezed my thighs together with anticipation. His gray eyes turned silver as he watched me. "Go."

Winking, I turned and hurried to the house, hoping my suddenly overheated body didn't melt the candy bar in my hand. Once inside, I found Stormy lying in the fetal position on her bed, until she saw me and sat up.

"What do you want me to do now? This is child labor, you know."

Ignoring her words, I picked up her water bottle and sat on the bed. "Are you on your period?" When Stormy's eyes shifted to her fingernails, I had my answer. "Why didn't you just tell me?"

"It's none of your business," she spat, her lips pursing like she had sucked on a lemon.

"You're right, it isn't any of my business, but I could help. I do know how it feels." I held the small pill and bottle of water out for her. "Take this, it'll help with cramping."

I waited for her to take the pill and drink the water before I held up my ace in the hole. "This helps, too. Well, not really, but it's worth it."

Stormy's eyes widened as she took the candy bar like she had just been handed the Holy Grail. "Where did you get that?"

"Maureen gave it to me to give to you," I said, brushing the hair from Stormy's forehead as she opened the packet and took a small bite. "We're a family, right?"

Stormy gave a weak nod as she settled back to her side. She broke off small pieces of the chocolate bar and let them melt into her mouth before breaking off another.

"Since that makes me your big sister or aunt or whatever, it's okay to talk to me about these things," I said easily, trying not to turn this into a really bad after school special. "When I get my period, our whole house will know."

Her eyes widened in horror. "Oh my God, please don't tell them. I would die."

"Don't worry, I won't say anything, but it's nothing to be embarrassed about. It's part of being a woman, it's natural." I wondered if I should slip this conversation into a more detailed one and decided I might as well go for it. I tried to remember how my mom talked to me about sex. "Do you know about babies and sex?"

Stormy's head fell back and she groaned. "Stop it. You're ruining my candy bar moment."

"So that's a yes?" I waited until she gave me that "duh" look she had perfected. "Okay, well, that's another thing you should really come and talk to me about if you ever need to."

"With the amount of boys my age alive, I'll probably die a virgin," she said without looking at me.

I laughed. "You'll find someone someday. Just don't rush that day because you think you won't get another chance."

"Are we done with this conversation now?"

"Yes," I said, sighing with relief. "I'm going to head back to the lodge. Do you want anything else?"

"No, I'm good." She smiled for the first time all day. "Thanks."

"No problem. That's what families are for." I ruffled her hair and stood up. "I'll come back and check on you later."

Pulling the door almost closed, I stepped into the room Luke and I were using and sat on the bed, trying to calculate the last time I had actually had a period myself. Gnawing on my bottom lip, I counted the days it had been since my last period and then counted the days since the first time Luke and I had made love against the side of the truck. Was it possible? Yes, it was entirely possible since we hadn't been careful at all that time. Twisting my hands between my knees, my mind warred with what to do next. No way could I tell Luke there was even a remote possibility I could very well be pregnant with his child. He would go into Neanderthal mode and lock me in a room while he battled the world. He would end up getting himself killed, then I would be a single mother to a child who would never know his or her father.

Standing, I paced back and forth on the carpeted floor while chewing my thumbnail. No, I couldn't tell him until this was over and Griffin was taken care of. Maybe I wasn't even pregnant at all. Perhaps I hadn't had my period because of the amount of stress my body had gone through in the past month. Yeah, that was completely possible and probably what was going on. Feeling a bit of relief, I took a deep breath and left the house. I needed to find Maureen and see if she had a pregnancy test and could keep her mouth shut about it. Surely she would still believe in the whole "medical privacy" thing.

I walked across the yard without seeing anything around me. Jacob called my name as I passed them, but I waved him off and went inside the lodge. I walked, my legs feeling much like jelly, to the kitchen and stood in the open door, wringing my hands as I stared at Maureen.

When she turned around, she stopped and asked, "Roni? What's wrong?"

"Can I talk to you for a few minutes?" I squeaked out.

Maureen dried her hands with a towel and spoke to the other women before taking my hand and walking down the hall to an office and closed the door. "Is Stormy okay?"

I waved and sat down. "Yeah, she's fine. It was her period, but the thing is… well, I got to thinking about the last time I had *my* period and well…"

Maureen's delicate arms crossed over her chest and her head tilted to the side. "You think you might be pregnant?"

I swallowed hard and nodded. "But you can't say anything to anyone."

"No, dear, I wouldn't say anything. But first, take a deep breath, then tell me everything," she said, pulling a notepad and pen from the desk and sitting down next to me.

I gave her my best estimated guess on dates and waited while she wrote a few things down and nodded. "It's possible you are pregnant, but you're going to need to take a test to be sure."

"How do we get one of those?" I asked, crying and scared to death at the possibility of having to wait to see if my stomach started to grow before we had an answer. If I remembered right, in the medieval days, they peed on a rabbit or something to see if it died. If it died, they were either pregnant… or not. I couldn't remember! *Oh my God! I do not want to pee on a rabbit.*

Maureen chuckled and patted my hand. "Calm down. I have a few left here. How about I get one for you, you take it real quick, and we'll know one way or another."

"Really?" I asked, letting some of the tension out of my shoulders. When she nodded and stood, I puffed out my cheeks with a long breath. "Thank you so much."

"Do you want me to get Luke?"

"Dear Lord, no!" I shook my head emphatically. "I'm good. Well, maybe ask Daisy to come in here? Wait, can Daisy keep something this big a secret?"

"If I tell her to, she can. Now, you put your head between your knees until I get back. And don't forget to breathe. Either way, you're going to be alright." She opened the door just enough to slip through and closed it behind her.

Taking her advice, I put my head between my knees and did my best to slow my breathing to a normal pace. When I felt marginally better, I slowly sat up and leaned against the back of the chair. The door opened and Daisy slipped in with an enormous smile, followed by Maureen. Maureen held out a small plastic stick.

"Mom just told me what's going on." Daisy beamed down at me before bending and hugging me tight. I closed my eyes and leaned into the hug, thankful for the support.

"Go pee on this and bring it back in here when you're done," Maureen instructed.

With a trembling hand, I took the stick from her and stood. I left the room and walked down the hall like I was on death row. In the bathroom, I made quick work of peeing on the stick and wrapping it in toilet paper before I walked back to the office.

"What now?" I asked, holding the mummified stick out like it was on fire.

Maureen laid a paper towel down on the desk and pointed to it. "Unwrap it, set it down, and wait."

"This is so exciting," Daisy said in a squeal.

Unwrapping the stick, I avoided looking at the little window that would tell me my future and took a giant step back, plopping down in the chair. "Yes, so exciting," I murmured.

I watched as Maureen stood over the test and then turned to me, her face void of any emotion. "It's ready. Do you want to see for yourself or do you want me to tell you?"

"Just tell me... no, wait. Ugh, I need to see for myself," I said, swallowing hard as I stood.

Daisy moved to take a look, but Maureen held her back and moved to the side. Fisting my hands at my sides, I looked straight ahead as I walked to the desk, closing my eyes before I bent my head down. Taking a deep breath, I opened my eyes and looked at the test. It showed two blue lines. *What the hell does that mean?* Wasn't there supposed to be a positive or negative? A yes or a no? "What does this mean?"

"It means, honey, you're going to be a mom," Maureen said, and Daisy clapped. I leaned my arms onto the desk to keep from falling flat on my face.

Daisy wrapped her arms around me and hopped up and down, jolting my body, making me queasy, or God, was that morning sickness? No, surely not.

"I need to sit down," I said low, my voice foreign to my own ears. Daisy held my arm and walked with me to the chair until I sat down.

"You are going to have the most gorgeous baby. Are you two going to get married now?" Daisy asked dreamily.

"Well, uh, no..." I squirmed. "We hadn't talked about it." I bit the inside of my mouth, wondering if it was even possible to get married anymore.

"Geez, child, give her a second to let it soak in," Maureen said. "Roni, drink this." She shoved a glass of water in my face.

I took the glass and drank down half of it in one gulp, letting the news sink in. I was going to be a mother. I was going to have a child. I had a part of Luke growing inside of me. How could I not be happy about that? Scared? Hell yes, more like petrified, but I was also miraculously, instantly, in love already.

What was Luke going to think? Would he be happy or upset? One thing was for sure; he couldn't know until we were all safe from Griffin's grasp. "This has to stay between us. No one can know. All hell would break loose."

"Is it not Luke's?" Daisy asked, wide-eyed.

Maureen scolded her and I couldn't help but laugh. "It's Luke's. I just don't want him to know with everything going on right now."

"We won't say a word, will we, Daisy?"

Daisy mimed zipping her lips and throwing away the key. "My lips are sealed."

Maureen moved in front of me and sat on her heels. "All the vitamins I have are expired, and you need to cut back on the canned food when you can and replace it with fresh. Try to eat a lot of eggs. They're rich in amino acids and choline. Both are important to have while pregnant."

My mind went to the chickens I had left behind at the orchard. Hopefully they were safe and enjoying their freedom and would be around when we made it back, and I was more determined than ever to make it home.

"Okay," I said, licking my lips. "I can do that. We better get back out there before people start noticing us missing."

"Do you need help up?" Daisy asked.

"I'm pregnant, not injured," I said as kindly as I could manage. I was beginning to doubt Daisy's ability to keep my secret for long, but I wasn't going to say a word for as long as I could. The men had enough on their shoulders, and I didn't want to add the extra weight to it.

Leaving the office, we moved back to the kitchen and continued doing chores. Replacing Lydia at the sink, I looked out the kitchen window, finding Luke immediately. It wasn't difficult to do when he was so large and gorgeous. He had his hands in his front pockets, laughing at something Adam said. Adam was grinning sheepishly while looking at the ground.

Maybe we shouldn't fight. Maybe we should give up on the orchard and move out of Wells's reach. We had been happy in this town for the past few weeks, why couldn't we be happy somewhere else? My eyes scanned the other smiling faces in the crowd and I sighed. Because we couldn't leave these people to be at the mercy of a couple of mad men.

De Oppresso Libre. Free the oppressed. That was the Special Forces insignia tattooed on Luke's chest. It wasn't just a saying to him, it was who he was. It was as much a part of him as the love he had for his family. That was who we all were now, and we couldn't walk away while others suffered fates possibly worse than our own.

If I'd learned one thing from the end of the world, it was that we needed each other to survive.

Chapter Nineteen

We were about halfway through our evening meal at the lodge when a loud banging at the front door startled everyone at the table. My eyes immediately find Stormy's staring back at me with trepidation. Luke stood and pointed to our family to be ready to move out. He pulled a handgun from the holder he kept strapped at his waist.

Lydia's husband pushed his chair back and left to answer the door while the rest of us waited to see if this day was going to end good or bad. I strained my ears to listen to the front of the house. At first, I could only hear murmurs, but the voices and footsteps grew louder as they made their way toward the dining room.

George walked in first and when I saw his smile, I relaxed until I saw the person standing behind him.

Oh, hell.

"Roni?" David asked, one side of his mouth quirked up.

"Hey." From my peripheral vision, I could see look Luke's head move from me back to David before his chest puffed up.

David stepped around George and stood across from me, still smiling. "It's good to see you. I've been worried about you."

"That's sweet of you. I've been good," I said, trying to ignore Jacob and Adam leaning in a little closer while Luke took a step next to me.

"No need to worry about her, she's well taken care of," Luke said.

David's eyebrows rose and his head tilted ever so slightly. "And you are?"

"David..." When I said his name, Luke growled, but I went on, "This is Luke, my... boyfriend?"

It felt strange calling him my boyfriend. He was more than that. He was the love of my life. He was my soulmate. He was the father of my child and hopefully, one day, he would be my husband, but those weren't really introduction terms.

"Luke, this is David," I said lamely.

David lifted his chin in recognition. "Roni and I ran into each other in Canaan a few weeks back," David said, grinning down at me with a twinkle in his eye.

Luke took a step forward and I had to do something before Luke asked him to duel at dawn or they both whipped out their dicks to see who was superior. "David, this is my brother, Jacob. This is Luke's brother, Adam, and this is Stormy." I pointed to each as I spoke.

"David and I know each other," Adam said friendly enough before they fist bumped. "Why don't you have a seat and tell us what's up?"

"David." Josh half stood and shook his hand as they both sat down.

"Hey, pretty lady," David said to Daisy with a wink. Daisy slapped at his shoulder but giggled at the compliment. "Come sit down, boys." He waved the two men who came in with him to the table. David introduced the two men as Lawrence and Tyler and each shook the guys' hands before sitting next to David.

Luke sat and slung his arm around the back of my seat, making a point. I wanted to roll my eyes, but I didn't want David to think Luke was annoying me. David didn't know our history and probably assumed we had just met. That or he thought I was a cheater and if I could cheat once, I could again.

"Okay, you don't come here for no reason," Jacob said. "What's going on?"

"Lately, I've been hearing there was a group of people looking to recruit for some sort of resistance, and when Griffin and his men showed up in town this morning asking about you guys, I put two and two together and decided to come see for myself." Everyone at the table sat a little straighter. My eyes went to Luke and I fought the instinct to cover my belly. The time we had been planning for was upon us and though they might be ready, I wasn't.

"You sure you weren't followed on your way out here?" Luke asked, his voice changing from conversational to authoritative. He was in military mode now and ready to do battle at any second.

"I know what I'm doing. No one followed us. No one even knows we left town," David said defensively.

Feeling the tension, Josh piped in. "David's former military, served in Afghanistan. Anytime we've needed to hide people, he's been our man."

Luke nodded with appreciation, but since it was David, he wouldn't say it. "How many men does Griffin have with him?"

"At least thirty, maybe a little more. I don't know what happened, but he's pissed way the hell off."

Adam laughed. "Roni and I got away from him. That's what happened."

"I wouldn't doubt if he doesn't head this way in the next few days. Right now, they're going door to door, searching buildings and interrogating people to find you guys. When someone opens their trap and tells him about the recruiting going on, and you know some idiot will, they're going to start spreading out their search perimeter. Roni came to town with Daisy before and Maureen hasn't been in town all week, so I figured my best bet was to start here."

Well, David's powers of deduction were good, at least. I turned to Luke. "What now?"

He wrapped his arm around my shoulder and pulled me close to his side. "Now, we make our move."

Fear filled me and bile rose in my throat, choking me. I wasn't ready for this. I looked around the table to all the faces I cared about. "When?" I whispered because it was impossible to speak normally.

He turned to Josh. "Are all the guys still here?"

"Pretty sure most of them are." Daisy leaned into him and he kissed her forehead. "I'll gather them now."

"I'll go with you," Daisy said, grabbing his hand and holding onto his forearm as they walked out of the room. She had just as much to lose and was just as afraid as I was.

"You want in?" Luke asked David. Luke wasn't one to watercolor things. He was black and white, in or out. If David gave the wrong answer, I was sure Luke wouldn't let him leave until the conflict was over.

"We're in," David said with a wicked grin, with Lawrence and Tyler agreeing. "Most of my men would gladly stick a boot up Griffin's ass. What's your plan?"

"Take them out while they're small, give the ones who were drafted a chance to change sides, and stop Griffin before he can call in reinforcements to Wells." Releasing me, he put his forearms on the table. "How many men do you have?"

"Eight who would be willing to put their neck on the line," David said matter of factly.

Luke rubbed his chin. "Twenty against thirty isn't bad odds at all. Especially considering at least ten of the men Griffin has with him didn't choose to be."

"When you say now, you don't me *now,* do you?" I asked, still feeling like I was going to lose every bit of dinner I had.

Instead of answering me, Luke asked David, "How quickly can you get your men ready?"

"I can have them ready by tomorrow," he said, leaning back in his seat and tapping his fingers on the table.

"It'll be easier if we go at night," Jacob said. My head whipped to him. His leg was getting better and better every day, but he wouldn't be able to run for long if he needed to.

I wasn't ready for this, but then again, would I ever be?

"You are not going tonight," I demanded, my voice coming back full force. Luke's hand covered mine. "I mean it."

"We'll go tomorrow night. That'll give David enough time to brief his men and we can wait until lights out before we go in." Luke put his finger under my chin and turned me to face him. Leaning in, he gently kissed my lips and looked into my eyes. "We're going to be okay."

Doing my best to believe him, I blinked back the tears welling in my eyes and swallowed hard. "Okay."

"Why don't you take Stormy to the house and we'll be there in a bit?" Luke asked, his voice as smooth as butter.

Stormy sat beside me, staring at Adam while picking at her painted fingernails. She was just as worried as I was and though I wanted to stay, I knew it would be best if I took her home. "Okay. I am wiped. Stormy, you ready?"

"Sure," she said, standing.

"Lydia, do you mind if we sit out on the dishes tonight? I'll come cook and clean in the morning."

Lydia waved a hand at us. "No, no. You two go on and get some rest. Maureen and I can take care of it."

"Thank you," I said, my lips flattening. "David, good to see you again. Thanks for coming to warn us."

David winked at me. "Good to see you again, too."

Luke's jaw clenched and his hands moved to fists, so I leaned in. "Walk us out?"

Luke stood and put his hand on the small of my back and walked us out the back door. "That guy is really going to miss his pretty face."

Laughing, I slung my arms around his waist and laid my cheek to his cheek. "I only have eyes for you."

"I'll be home soon." Luke palmed both sides of my face and kissed me until Stormy made gagging noises.

"Don't forget to include me in the plans for tomorrow night. I won't be left behind again."

"I don't think—" he started to argue, but I stopped him.

"I don't care if I'm just sitting in the getaway car outside of town. I am going, one way or another, and we both know you trying to keep me out of it is only going to piss me off and I'll go anyway."

Looking to the heavens, Luke sighed. "Alright. Go get some rest. We're going to have a long day tomorrow."

Luke watched as Stormy and I took off across the road before turning around and heading back inside. Stormy stayed close but remained quiet on the way to the house. Once inside, she went straight to her room and I sat on the couch. A few minutes later, Stormy came back into the living room wearing a pair of purple pajamas and tossed herself down next to me.

Pulling a half-eaten chocolate bar out, she broke off a square and handed it to me. "You look like you need this as much as I do."

What I needed was a stiff drink, but that was no longer an option. I popped the chocolate in my mouth and closed my eyes, savoring the taste. "Thank you."

Tucking her feet under her, she eyed me. "What's up with you?"

Picking at a thread on my jeans, I asked, "What do you mean?"

"You've been acting weird the last few days." She narrowed her eyes. "Have you changed your mind about keeping me with you guys, 'cause I'm not staying here if you did."

"No! We didn't change our minds. I told you, you're stuck with us now."

"Then what's going on?" she asked, her voice wobbly, like she didn't believe me.

Just a few days ago, I told her she could trust me and I needed to trust her in return. The only thing I worried about was her ability to keep my secret between us.

"Just tell me already," she said, tossing her hands up. "Were you a drama teacher before?"

Laughing, I shook my head. "No. I was an accountant."

Her eyebrows shot up. "Seriously?" When I nodded, she shook her head. "God, that's boring." She broke off another chocolate square and held it up. "Now, tell me."

Taking the chocolate square from her, I put my feet up on the coffee table and leaned my head on the back of the couch. "Can you keep your mouth shut?"

"Duh," she spat, staring at me.

"I'm serious. You can't say a word. You can't act different. You will have to pretend you don't have a clue."

"Okay, sure."

"I'm trusting you," I said, tilting my head toward her. Her head bobbled and her face went stony. "I found out I'm pregnant."

"You're what?" Stormy squealed, and she hopped on the couch. "What did Luke say?"

"Luke doesn't know. He *can't* know. At least not yet."

"Why not? OMG, is it not his? Is it that David guy's? He said he ran into you a few weeks ago, but you could tell he meant more than talking. He's hot. The baby will still be cute," Stormy rambled as she pulled her hair into a ponytail and secured it with an elastic band.

"God, no. I did not have sex with David. I just kissed him once. The baby is Luke's, but you know Luke. He'll go into hyper protection mode and won't let me out of the house. Whether he wants to admit it or not, they need me out there. They can't hold us back because we have boobs and a vagina."

Stormy's lips curled back, showing all of her pearly whites. "You're not going to have anything to knock you out."

"What?" I asked, lost in the conversation.

"When you have the baby. You're going to feel *everything*. That's going to suck." She shook her hands, excited. "Oh, can I name it?"

I huffed and looked sideways at her. "You named yourself Stormy. You are *not* naming my child."

"Stormy is a kick-ass name," she said, offended.

"Sure, for a rock star. And don't say ass." I yawned and closed my eyes. "How did you come up with the name, anyway?"

"My brothers and I used to watch X-Men all the time, and Storm was my favorite," she said with a shrug.

My heart hurt for her. "Stormy is a kick-ass name."

"I know."

With a tired hand, I reached over and squeezed her arm. "Our secret, right? Well, besides Maureen and Daisy. They were with me when I took the test."

"Our secret. Thanks for telling me."

"You're not naming my kid."

"I'll wear you down," she said with a yawn of her own.

****

I woke as Luke was laying me in bed. He moved to take a step back, but I reached out for him. "I'm awake, don't go."

"I'm not going, just getting undressed." I watched as he simultaneously kicked off his boots and pulled the t-shirt over his head, a multitude of ab muscles rippling with the movement. I moved to sit on my legs and tugged on his belt loop until his thighs rested on the side of the mattress.

Pulling up to my knees, I palmed my hands on his chest and outlined each muscle, following my hands with my mouth. Luke growled and slid his fingers into the back of my hair, tilting my head back.

"You're killing me, sweetheart."

"I plan on doing a lot of things to you, but killing you isn't one of them." I smiled up at him while unbuttoning his jeans with one hand. Fisting my hair, Luke tugged me to his mouth in a hot kiss. He moved to lay me back against the mattress, but I shook my head and pushed against his chest. He glared down at me, only making my smile widen. I was so unbelievably hot for him. My clit throbbed, and I could feel the wetness pooling between my legs, but I wasn't ready to have him inside me just yet. I wanted to savor every last inch of him.

Taking my time, I slowly unzipped his jeans, his underwear-clad cock filling the space. My eyes widened. It didn't matter how many times I saw him, the size of him still amazed and excited me. I watched him as I pulled his jeans down over his ass, letting them rest on his thighs, and dipped my hand inside his underwear, wrapping my hand around his heat. The rapid pulse beat beneath my fingers and I felt him grow as I pumped him gently.

"Roni," he warned, tweaking my nipple through my shirt, sending the sensation straight to my clit. I released his dick, looping my thumbs inside the elastic, and pulled down his underwear, watching him stand at attention, waiting for me to please him. Luke stepped back and removed his jeans and underwear before coming back and tugging at the hem of my shirt. Lifting my arms, I let him slide the shirt off me, his hands brushing my skin the entire time. He moved to wrap his arms around me but I shook my head and reached back, unsnapping my bra, letting it fall to the bed. My breasts felt heavy and my nipples puckered as I watched Luke watching me.

I wasn't so graceful pulling my jeans off, but he didn't laugh. No, by the set of his jaw and the hardness of his entire body, he wasn't in a laughing mood. All that intensity was for me. Because he wanted me. I was going to give him everything I had.

Back on my knees, I sat my bare bottom on my calves and leaned in, wrapping my hand around the base of his massive erection to guide my mouth around the tip. His body shook and his groan was guttural, sending vibrations through me, giving me motivation to keep up the good work. I flicked my tongue under the head while I slid my hand up and down the length of him, using the moisture from my mouth to lubricate my hand.

My body ached to be touched, to be satisfied. Filling my mouth with him, I suctioned him on the way out, beckoning his release. Almost without thought, my free hand moved between my legs, rubbing my clit, moaning around his dick as I pleasured both of us. Luke gripped my hair and cupped my breast, massaging me.

"Fuck, sweetheart. Fuck... This... I..." His hips moved back and forth, fucking my mouth as my fingers moved quicker over my clit. Releasing his cock, I let his hips do all the work. I cupped his balls, loving how tight they were against his body. As soon as I squeezed, he pulled his hips back, pulling himself from my mouth before picking me up under my arms and spinning me around until my ass was hanging from the side of the bed and my elbows rested on the mattress. He yanked my hips back and leaned over, his hot breath on my neck. "Hold on, baby. You're about to be fucked hard."

My ass involuntarily pushed back against his hardness as I gripped the blankets. He cursed and wrapped his hand on the nape of my neck before slamming inside me. The movement was jarring, sending my body forward, but his big hands pulled me back as he filled me.

"Touch yourself, baby," Luke demanded, and I obeyed. I worked myself while he slammed inside me over and over.

Leaning over me, the slickness of his chest rubbed against my back as he pulled me closer to him. He tugged my head back until he crushed his mouth over mine. Once he released my chin, he gripped my hips and I pushed my head down until my check laid flat on the mattress. I couldn't hold back anymore. Using my free hand to cover my cries, I held my breath and felt heat course through my body as a climax rippled waves through my body like a typhoon hitting land. Luke must have felt the clinching of my walls because he lost whatever control he had left. Digging his fingers into my hips, he pumped over and over, his head thrown back in pure fucking ecstasy which, combined with his movements, forced my body to respond with another climax.

His hips jerked and his fingers bit in my sides before he quickly pulled out, fisted himself and came on the small of my back.

Luke's breaths came out ragged, filling the quiet room. My legs were jellied, and I slid until I was flat on the bed. My body was spent, my limbs useless, my soul wonderfully satisfied.

Leaning down, Luke kissed my shoulder. "I'll be right back."

I tried to nod, but I couldn't. All my energy and concentration was focused on taking the next breath. I listened as he put on his pants and almost soundlessly left the room. My thoughts remained fogged and my body limp until Luke came back with a wet rag and cleaned my back. Gently, he turned me over and repositioned me under the covers before sliding in next to me and pulling me to his chest.

"I don't think I've ever come that hard," he said, his voice light and relaxed.

"Glad I could help with that," I said, tracing the outline of his tattoo with my finger.

"Baby, you don't have to do anything to get me going, but watching you take me in your mouth while touching yourself... It was all I could do to last as long as I did."

"I couldn't watch you strip and not do something with all that hotness," I teased. "I love you."

"I love you, too, sweetheart." He kissed my temple and brushed the hair from my face.

Scooting in closer, my breasts felt tender pressed against his side, reminding me I was pregnant. I ached to tell him. I wondered what his reaction would be. Would he be angry? Would he be happy? Scared?

I would find out how he felt in the next forty-eight hours.

If we were both still alive by then.

Chapter Twenty

"Sis, I really wish you would sit this one out," Jacob said, loading the back seat of the car with a box of water while I loaded the extra ammo inside the trunk. Luke was true to his word and included me in the plans. Of course, he took the least dangerous option of me sitting in George and Lydia's car, ready to haul ass if need be, but at least I was being included. Daisy got lucky enough to be posted with me, though that was about as close as she wanted to get to the action.

I figured Daisy asked to go just because she knew I was with child and thought to keep me out of trouble.

"I wish you would sit this one out, too, but that can't happen for either of us," I said, closing the trunk and leaning against the bumper. Reaching over, I rubbed his upper arm. "We need as many people as we can get."

Shifting his weight from one foot to the next, Jacob kicked at the gravel with the toe of his boot. "I know, but I don't have to like it." He looked across the field, the wind blowing the curls forming on his head. "These are good people. I just hope no one gets hurt."

Looking at everyone saying goodbye, I watched George hugging Lydia, Daisy wrapped around Josh's back, both laughing as they walked to the back of the lodge. Luke stood with his feet apart while holding a handgun talking to Adam who listened intently. So many people were sticking their lives on the line to stop Griffin because they trusted us, trusted Luke, to keep them safe.

"Me, too," I bumped my shoulder to his. "Don't get shot again, okay?"

He laughed and relaxed into the car. "I hope to God I don't. That shit hurts."

"I'll take your word for it," I said, smiling. "I'm going to find Stormy and make sure someone is watching after her when we leave so she can't sneak in with us."

"That girl is something else," he said, shaking his head but smiling. "I'm glad she's staying. She needs us."

"Yeah, I think we need her, too." I pushed off the car and headed toward the lodge, smacking Luke on the rear as I walked past.

Handing Adam the handgun, Luke turned and ran toward me. I ran and squealed in return while laughing as he wrapped me up from behind and spun us around and around. When he put me down, he stepped in front of me, bent down, wrapped his arms around my thighs, and lifted me up until my head was higher than his. Laughing, I leaned down and kissed his smiling mouth.

"Where are you off to?" he asked, his eyes twinkling.

"To check in with Stormy and maybe grab a peanut butter sandwich. Want one?"

He smacked his lips to mine before easing his arms and letting my body slide down until my feet touched the ground. "I wouldn't mind a peanut butter sandwich. Do you mind making one for Adam, too?"

"Sure." I sighed. "I'll be back in a few."

"You look extra pretty today," he said, his eyes roaming my face. "Are you wearing makeup?"

Blushing, I smiled. "No, I'm not wearing makeup, and you know you don't have to say things like that. I'm a sure thing."

"I wouldn't say it if it wasn't true, and you're beautiful, sweetheart."

"Thank you. Now, go do manly things so I can get our sandwiches made before it's time to go," I said, walking away and into the lodge.

Stepping into the kitchen, the smell of yeast filled the air. I found Teri at the table kneading dough while Stormy sat to the side, her face slack with her chin resting in the palm of her hand. When she saw me, she sat up straight. She opened her mouth, but I held a hand up, stopping her.

"We haven't changed our minds. You're staying here, kiddo," I said, resting my hands on my hips. "Come help me make some peanut butter sandwiches."

Rolling her eyes, she slouched in the chair. "I'm good."

"Adam was hoping you would help me out," I said in a low blow.

Standing, Stormy moved to me. "I'll help, but I still think it's stupid that you won't let me go."

My lips twitched while I fought back a smile. Teri gave me a knowing look and shook her head. "The peanut butter is in the pantry over here."

Stormy retrieved the bread while I got the peanut butter. We lined up an assembly line of sorts, both using butter knives to make the sandwiches. I gave her a sideways glance. "Do you know how to play chess?"

"No, I used to when I was little, but I don't remember how," Stormy said, smearing a thick layer of peanut butter on the bread before laying another slice on top and smashing it down.

"Lydia said there's a chess board upstairs. Want to play me tomorrow?" I asked, sliding a sandwich into a bag.

She shrugged. "I guess."

"Well, I'm pretty good, so get the board tonight and ask Lydia to give you a refresher. Loser has to do the other's chores for three days?" I challenged.

Stormy's lips pursed in contemplation and Teri chimed in. "Girl, I would take that bet. You're on bathroom duty this week. Plus, I can play you tonight, get you ready."

"Deal," Stormy said, smashing another sandwich together and twisting the lid back on the jar.

I stuck my hand out and she shook it. This would assure me she would be well watched over and her mind would stay occupied and not dwelling on what was going on with us.

"I'll take Adam his sandwich," Stormy said, holding a bagged sandwich to her chest.

Handing her another, I asked, "Can you take this one to Luke?"

She took the bag and hurried out of the room. I began cleaning up the mess we'd made. "Thanks for keeping an eye on her tonight."

"No problem. You guys just stay safe out there and we'll take care of everything here," she said, still kneading the dough.

"You think you could teach me how to make that bread, too?" I asked, hopeful. It smelled divine.

"This is for cinnamon rolls in the morning, but I sure can." She moved to the side to let more light in. "You mind lightin' that lantern before you go? I can't see a thing and my hands are gooey."

I lit the lantern, said my goodbyes, and hurried outside. The sun was setting fast and we needed to get on the road. The group leaving was huddled together near the trucks. Adam spotted me and waved me over with his sandwich. Stormy was between Adam and Jacob, looking as content as I had ever seen her. When I reached the group, I saddled up next to Luke as he opened the sandwich bag and took a bite. He gave me a quick kiss in thanks and turned to the trunk of the car where Lawrence had a hand-drawn map laid out. Leaning in, I listened to Lawrence explain where the bulk of the men were staying, including Griffin.

"Where should we park?" Daisy asked.

Luke pointed to the far side of the map, about as far away from where Griffin was staying as we could get. "Really? Why so far away? If you need us to get out quickly, we need to be parked over here." I pointed to a blank area about two roads away from Griffin's place.

"Yeah, there's a used car place over there where we can blend in," Daisy said, pointing close to where I'd indicated. I grinned up at her with silent girl power. She smiled back and put her fist on her hip, begging the men to argue. Following suit, I crossed my arms over my hips and in a surprise move, Maureen stepped up.

"That makes sense to me," Maureen said, putting an end to any sort of argument that could arise. "George and I are going to go in first and meet up with David, letting him know we're in position. Since David has guards at this post, we can tell them to let Roni and Daisy pass. Plus, at least two of you men can ride with them in and not have as far to walk. I'm thinking Adam, so he doesn't wear himself out before we get started, and Jacob, to save his leg."

Luke crossed an arm over his chest and rubbed the stubble growing. The same stubble I felt on the back of my neck the night before. I squirmed at the thought. I sure hoped he didn't decide to go easy on me once I told him I was pregnant. If anything, I wanted it more and harder now than I did before. My eyebrows pulled together. *I wonder what that is all about.*

"Anyone have any objections to the plan?" Luke asked the men.

My eyes followed his to each man. None looked happy about Daisy and me being behind enemy lines, but they couldn't fault the logic. When no one spoke, Luke sighed. "Alright, let's roll."

Everyone scattered to their prospective vehicle and piled in, leaving me standing next to Luke and Daisy on the other side of the car hugging Josh.

"Be careful. Don't worry about me, I swear I'm staying out of sight." I wrapped my arms around his neck and pulled up to my tiptoes. "I love you."

"So help me God, if you don't stay in the car, I will bend you over my knee when we get back," he warned, and I wiggled my eyebrows.

"Don't threaten me with a good time," I teased.

"I'm serious." Growling, he kissed me and then stepped back. "See you soon."

I watched as he climbed into the driver's side of the truck with Josh and Lawrence already inside. I gave a weak wave and took a calming breath before giving Stormy a quick hug and ordering her inside. I waited until she was inside the door before getting in the passenger side of the car. Daisy put the car in gear and followed the lights of the two trucks in front of us to guide the way. Jacob reached around the headrest and squeezed my shoulder. I patted his hand and looked over to Daisy, her face illuminated from the light of the dashboard.

We might not have looked like a force to be reckoned with, but we were all survivors and would do whatever it took to keep each other safe. Griffin was about to learn the hard way what kind of people we were.

"Anyone have a bottle of water handy?" Adam asked, shaking a few pills from a bottle.

I reached into the duffel perched between Daisy and me, pulled out a water bottle, and handed it to him. I was glad to see he was taking extra. I could only image what something like this was doing to his lack of adrenaline.

Unwrapping my sandwich, I was just about to take a bite, but stopped. "Jacob, did you get anything to eat before we left?"

"I ate."

"Daisy, what about you?"

"Oh, no, I couldn't eat if I wanted to. You know… nerves. But you need it more than any of us, eat it." Her fingers tightened the steering wheel when she realized what she'd said. I stared straight ahead, eyes wide. "You skipped lunch, didn't you?"

Uh oh, she was going to end up making it worse by trying to fix it. I needed to nip it in the bud quick. "Sure did. Hey, guys… how long do you think this whole operation will take?"

Taking a big bite of the sandwich, I swiveled in the seat to face them. Adam gave Jacob a look and Jacob watched me with narrowed eyes, but if he suspected something, he was going to leave it alone for now.

"Hopefully, about an hour. If it lasts longer than two, then we're probably not doing so well," Jacob said, and Adam nodded in agreement.

"Okay," Daisy said, turning the car left while the others continued going. "We're on our own now."

I turned my head, watching the lights from the other vehicles until they were out of view. My heart squeezed as I prayed for their safety. The car remained mostly silent for the remainder of the trip—each of us worrying about each other and knowing tonight would be our only chance. Once we got close to town, we pulled to a side road and shut the engine off. We had to stay put long enough for Lawrence to tell David we would be coming through so he could let his men know. If we got there too soon, we could have trouble getting through with a carload of ammo. If we got there too late, Adam and Jacob would be on their own once we got inside.

Opening the door, Jacob reached up, cracked the cap off the interior light, and pulled the light out, sending us into almost complete darkness. "Pop the trunk."

Daisy reached down and pulled a lever, and we followed him out. Jacob moved to the trunk and Daisy and I stood to the side, taking turns watching the road and watching the guys. When they got what they needed, Jacob pulled the trunk down and waited until it was almost closed before pushing it down quietly.

"Get in," Jacob instructed, and we all filed inside again.

"What were you getting?" Daisy asked.

Hearing the unmistakable sound of a clip sliding inside a gun, I swallowed hard.

Jacob held out a gun for me, handle first. "Here." I took the gun, preferring the feel of a 9mm rather than this Glock, but I wasn't going to complain. "Daisy, do you know how to shoot?"

Licking her lips nervously, she nodded. "Yeah, Mom and Josh taught me, but I don't like them."

Jacob stopped what he was doing and eyed Daisy while thinking before handing me a second gun. "Roni can hold it for you unless you need it."

Visibly relieved, Daisy's shoulders sagged. "Thanks."

"Listen," Jacob said sternly. "When we get in there, you don't play around. You don't get out of the car. If there's any trouble, you leave. Got me?"

Daisy nodded, but I glared. "You realize I'm your *older* sister, right? I'm a big girl and I know what to and not to do."

"Roni... not now," Jacob growled.

I bit my bottom lip to keep my mouth shut. If I said any more, one or both of us would end up pissed off, and I didn't want him heading for danger with us mad at each other. And if I were honest, this was an argument we'd had since the day the plague killed our parents and one we would probably have until we were old and gray.

We waited another fifteen minutes before turning on the car and heading for the checkpoint. When the men standing guard came into view, my hand tightened on the handle of the gun and my finger rested right of the trigger. Hopefully, if things didn't go our way, we could incapacitate them instead of anyone firing a weapon and drawing more attention.

"We should've brought rope," I said, my eyes never leaving the men getting closer and closer by the second. Adam tossed something at me and I picked it up—zip ties. "That'll work."

"Daisy, do you recognize them?" Jacob asked.

"Yeah, I do," she said, relieved. We pulled to a stop and one of them stayed at the front of the car, staring inside, while the second man came around the side to Daisy's open window. "Hey, Andy. Did David tell you we were coming in tonight?"

"Daisy," he said with a nod, then leaned in and looked at us, his eyes stopping on the gun in my hand. "He did. You're clear to go to the car lot."

Like a balloon losing its air, the tension in the car visibly deflated. Andy tapped on the window frame and stood. The man in front of the car moved to the side with a grin and a wave.

"Take care. See you soon," Andy said calmly, assuring us they were on our side.

Adam tapped the back of Daisy's headrest. "Let's get going."

"Okay, okay," Daisy said mostly to herself, and hit the gas, sending us back in the seat before releasing the pedal. "Oops. Sorry."

The car filled with laughter as we made the quick trip to the lot. With Adam's instruction, Daisy turned off the headlights when we got close to the lot. Both men got out before pulling in and guided her into a spot where we could stay hidden and still make a quick exit if needed.

They came back to the car and we handed them the duffel carrying water and ammo. Jacob had a silent exchange with Daisy before both their eyes glanced my way. Ignoring them, I reached out the open window and grabbed Adam's hand. "You holding up okay?"

He smiled down at me, sporting the same dimple Luke had on his cheek. "You're getting as bad as Luke."

"I am not!" I scoffed and smiled back. "For real, be careful."

Jacob walked up next to Adam, both of them distracted by their surroundings. "We gotta go."

My heart felt like it was lodged in my throat. "Don't take any chances."

Jacob leaned in and squeezed my shoulder. "That's what I was going to tell you."

Blinking back the tears welling in my eyes, I smiled. "I love you guys."

Rolling his eyes, Jacob sighed. "Love you, too."

"Love you, too, Adam," I said, enjoying making him squirm.

Rolling his eyes, he stepped to the car and leaned in. "If Luke loves you, then I love you."

Putting my palms on each side of his face, I choked back a cry. "You're a good man, Adam. I'm so glad you're my family now."

"Let's go," Jacob said.

"You boys be careful," Daisy whisper-yelled from the driver's side.

With one last wave, the guys walked away, melding with the darkness around us.

My patience lasted all of about ten minutes when I started feeling antsy. If we didn't do something to distract ourselves, I wouldn't make it. Keeping my voice low to still be able to listen for any noise and to keep anyone who happened to walk past from hearing, I asked, "Do you want to learn medicine like your mom?"

"No," Daisy said, staring into the night. "I kind of want to be a teacher. I love all the kids, and that's what I've been doing since we have been staying at the lodge, anyway."

Being a teacher was a good fit for her. She was easygoing the majority of the time and had a sweet disposition, and kids needed that around them. Especially these days. Kids needed to learn science, math, and English, but they also needed to learn to be kind and respectful. For a moment, I wondered if I should try to help teach. I was great at math, but I wasn't sure I could. I had tried tutoring in college, but it came so simply to me I would get irritated when my student didn't understand what I was trying to explain.

My eyes squinted, wondering how my child would learn if I didn't learn to teach. Adam could handle the English side. "Do you think I could help with the math class? I could use the practice being around small kids."

Daisy's smile was genuine for the first time that evening. "Absolutely. Are you nervous? About the baby, I mean."

Taking a deep breath, I nodded before slowly releasing it. "I'm equal parts happy and terrified." Shaking my head, I brushed loose strands of hair behind my ears. "It's a life... inside of me! It's going to depend on me for, like, *everything*! And this world... It's just crazy scary and... what if it doesn't like me?"

"Oh," Daisy said, laughing as she leaned closer and patted my arm. "You're going to do great. I think all first time moms feel like that, even before the plague, and that baby is going to love you. Plus, you have Dad, uncles, and an aunt to help you out."

Looking to the dark street, I prayed this baby would have them all. "Thanks, Daisy."

This child was already blessed. Jacob would bring laughter, Adam would bring strength, Stormy would bring joy inside bravery, and Luke would bring safety. Each one of us would bring love—love for one another and unconditional love for him or her. Resting my hand protectively over my flat belly, I vowed to give this baby a life of happiness and love.

"So what are you going to name it?" Daisy asked, bringing my thoughts back to the present.

"Oh, wow, I hadn't even thought of it. I don't know." I bit the inside of my mouth. "Definitely after one of our family members, but Luke and I have both lost so many loved ones it will be hard to choose."

"Yeah. Or if you have a girl, you can just name her Daisy," she said, winking. "What were both of your mom's names?"

"My mom was Carol and his mom was Elizabeth." It still hurts to say Mom's name. I doubted there would ever be a time when it didn't break my heart, and now to know she would never hold mine or Jacob's kids was too painful to think about.

"Carol Elizabeth or Elizabeth Carol are both pretty," Daisy said. "I like those a lot."

"He also lost two sisters, Rebecca and Mary," I said sullenly.

"Well, guess you two will have to have more kids then," she said, laughing.

I smiled. "I don't know about that. I need to leave a few names for Jacob and Adam to be able to use, too."

We were relaxed and smiling when we heard the first ring of a gun being fired filling the air.

Chapter Twenty-one

We both jumped even though it had to be at least two blocks away. Three more shots fired before we had time to think. My first instinct was to open the car door and run toward the fire and help our people, but it wasn't our job. Our job was to wait for them in case they needed to leave fast.

"Oh my God," Daisy said, her chest heaving and her hand covering her mouth.

"We knew there would be shots fired. They'll be okay," I said to myself as much as I said to her.

Both of us stayed still as statues, trying to listen to anything and everything. The sound of a pair of boots hitting pavement in a run grew louder. I gripped a gun in each hand, taking off the safety. "Scoot down. Don't make a sound," I whispered while my eyes roamed the air until I caught site of a figure moving on the road. He didn't stop, he didn't even slow down, he ran right past the car with a gun slung over his shoulder.

When he was out of sight again, I took a deep breath.

"Do you think he was one of ours or one of his?" Daisy asked, her voice shaky.

"I don't know," I said, hating the fact that I could have just let a person intent on hurting one of ours go.

More shots were fired—this time probably a block over—before the sound of engines filled the air in the distance. My chest constricted and my breathing shallowed, causing my chest to rise and fall rapidly.

Waiting was pure torture.

Daisy's hand moved to the car keys in the ignition. "No, we can't yet. We need to wait."

"What if we drive just a block closer?" she asked, her hand not leaving the keys.

"They expect us to be *here*. If they come this way and we're not where we told them all we would be, they could get stuck or caught."

"Well, give me a gun then," Daisy said, holding her hand out.

"Uh, are you sure? I can shoot with two hands and you can't drive and shoot at the same time," I said, trying to keep both of us rational while more gunfire sounded.

"True… I just hate this. I can't stand not being able to do something."

"Yeah," I said, knowing the feeling.

"Get down," I said as headlights rounded the corner to the left and roared down the block before making another tire-squealing turn. I lifted my head, trying to see the vehicle and caught a glimpse of a tan truck. That was Josh's truck, I was sure of it, but Daisy's head was still down and hadn't seen anything. Another vehicle came from the opposite direction. "Stay down."

What I thought was an SUV made a hard right at the same corner Josh's truck had.

"I think we're good for now," I said just as three figures ran across the street straight toward us. "Shit, be ready to start the car."

I held up both gun, my fingers resting on the triggers, ready to defend Daisy, myself, and my baby. I sighed in relief and lowered the gun when I spotted the visitors.

"Son of a bitch," Jacob said as he got to the car and hopped in the back, sliding into the middle while being flanked on both sides by Tyler and someone else I didn't recognize. "They fucking shot me!"

"What?!" I shrieked and whipped around to put pressure on whatever wound he got this time.

"It's just a graze," Tyler said. "We need to go."

"Go where?" Daisy said, frantic.

"Where did you get shot?" I asked, more demanding this time.

He held up his arm where he held his forearm with his other hand. "In my damn arm. My good arm."

"It's just a graze," Tyler said again and pointed to Daisy. "Get us to the market. It's safer there now and you can drop us off and head to the medical tent."

"Daisy, go," I said, reaching back and feeling Jacob's arm. There was blood, but it wasn't gushing. I grabbed the bottom of his shirt and started to tear.

"What are you doing?" Jacob asked as Daisy started the car and took off.

"Wrapping your arm, idiot," I said, yanking off the material and pushing his hand away to wrap it. I was pretty sure Tyler was right, but the bleeding still needed to stop.

"This hurts like a son of a bitch. Freaking shot again. *Again*!" Jacob said, madder than anything.

I tied off the ripped up shirt and turned around, readying my guns in case we needed to use them. "What's going on out there?"

"We've got the west side of town cleared, but Griffin and a few of his men are holed up like pussies," Tyler explained, his voice dripping with venom.

"This shit is burning like a mother," Jacob said between gritted teeth.

"Is everyone okay?" I asked, afraid of the answer.

"I'm not," Jacob yelled indignantly.

"Shut up, you big baby," I yelled. "Is everyone else okay?"

"A few people are wounded and with Maureen, but everyone will live," Tyler answered.

I said a prayer for the ones who were injured and though it wasn't right, prayed it was anyone other than Luke and Adam.

"The fight was heading toward you guys, so Luke sent us to move you somewhere safer," Jacob said.

Daisy drove hard and fast, getting us to the market. When we made it to the point where we couldn't drive any further, we stopped the car and got out. Following the men, Daisy and I ran behind the booths until we hit the medical tent. Tyler went in first, checking for safety before nodding for us to go inside.

"Stay here. We'll be back as soon as we can," Jacob said, leaving before I could say anything else.

"Daisy," Maureen said in relief as we stepped inside.

"Mom," Daisy ran to her and they wrapped their arms around each other.

"I'm going to wait at the door and keep watch," I said, gripping both guns.

Maureen nodded. "Thanks. Daisy, you come with me and hold the light so I can stitch people up."

Standing just outside the tent door, I was entirely submerged in darkness. Gunfire still sounded but, thankfully, not at the rate it had been while we sat in the car lot. At least here, I felt closer if needed. Suddenly, an explosion reverberated through the air, sending a searing pain to my ears seconds before a large ball of fire filled the sky in the same direction Jacob had headed. Without thinking, I ran across the road and through the streets, not taking the time to look around me for danger. All I knew, all I felt, was the need to get to them.

The closer I got, the sounds surrounding me made my stomach clinch. Cries from the injured and yells from one man to the next were all around me. When I came around the last corner, I stopped dead in my tracks. The building Griffin was supposed to be in was completely engulfed in flames. Men were lying on the ground on fire, other men using their shirts to beat the fire off them.

Doing my best to ignore the heat against my skin and the smells infiltrating my nose, I looked from left to right but didn't see them. *Where are they? Oh, God, please!* I begged as my legs wobbled and I began to move again, but arms wrapped around me from behind, spinning me to face away from the horror in front of me.

"Roni, don't look," Adam said. I turned to him and put my head against his chest, thankful he was alive.

"Luke? Jacob?" I asked between heavy breaths, terrified of what I was about to hear.

"They weren't in there," Adam squeezed me tighter, "but we lost David and Lawrence."

"Oh my God, no." *David. Poor, sweet David.* I squeezed my eyes shut and buried my face in his chest again. Both of them were good men hoping for a better future and it cost them their lives. *Damn Griffin. Damn him to hell for what he's done.*

Stepping back from Adam, I inspected his face and body to make sure he didn't have any injuries. Other than a few minor scrapes and bruises, he looked in good health.

"I'm good, Roni. You need to get back to the tent," he said, looking over my head.

My eyes followed his gaze to find Luke and Josh each holding one of Griffin's arms while marching him to the street. Griffin's face was covered in soot and his clothes looked bedraggled, but even in defeat he stood with his head high in superiority. His head turned toward Adam and me and with the blaze from the burning building, the smile he wore shifted until it looked sinister.

Adam and I both took a few steps closer and Jacob jogged to our side.

"Roni, you need to get back to the tent," Jacob repeated Adam's earlier request.

"I'm staying, so save your breath," I said, keeping my eyes on Griffin, wanting nothing more than to raise my gun and put an end to his arrogance.

"How did the house blow up?" I asked, flabbergasted at the destruction.

"Gas lines. Griffin and his men broke the lines before finding a way out. When the guys went in, either Griffin set it off or one of the guys fired the gun, but that's all it took," Adam said grimly, his eyes on the burning structure.

"Did anyone make it out?" I choked out.

"A few, but not many," Jacob answered. The three of us moved until we were about twenty feet away and Jacob stopped our progress. "Stay here. I'm going to help get the guys with the injured."

Nodding, I swiveled my head to Adam. "Go ahead and go with him. I'm just going to wait here until Luke's ready." He looked torn between wanting to help the men and keeping me safe. "Seriously, go. He needs your help."

"Okay, just," he sighed, "stay away from the building. We don't know if the other ones are going to blow or not."

"I will. I promise," I said with a nod for reassurance. I didn't plan on going anywhere, but the hounds of hell couldn't pull me away from these men.

The danger was over.

I was just a witness to the devastation left behind.

Adam left and I stepped closer, watching as Josh and Luke pushed Griffin to his knees and wrapped his hands with zip ties around his back.

"It's too late," Griffin said smiling. "It's too late."

A cold chill ran up my spine at his words. Luke knelt in front of Griffin.

"What do you mean?"

"Wells already knows. He's going to come for me. For you. When he does, you're all going to die," Griffin said with malice lacing each word.

Just as Luke was about to stand, I saw a man to the side of the building behind them raise a gun, waiting for a clear shot at Luke. On instinct, I dropped the gun in my left hand and pulled the gun in my right up with both hands.

"Get down!" I yelled.

I could see Luke, Josh, and Griffin's heads rotate toward me. There wasn't time. They didn't see him and the man would kill one of them. A split second before I pulled the trigger twice, light from the muzzle of the man's gun flashed. The man crumpled to the ground. Adrenaline filling my veins, I turned with wide, fearful eyes to Luke. He was bent over Josh, lying on the ground.

"No," I murmured before picking up the gun I'd dropped and running to their side.

Josh was on the ground, blood pooling on his shirt. Jacob was at my side in an instant, tearing the shirt away from his body, showing a small hole in his chest where blood oozed out. My eyes moved to Josh's face. His eyes were open, looking up into the night, blood at the corner of his mouth.

Spinning, I yelled, "Someone get Daisy and Maureen, *now*!" Turning back to Jacob, I asked, "What do I do?"

Jacob was holding a shirt over Josh's wound. He glanced up at me, fear in his eyes, and whispered, "Talk to him."

Staring at Jacob's face as he worked on Josh, I knew he was working an impossible task. Even Maureen wasn't capable of handling this traumatic of an injury. Brushing away the tears falling down my cheeks with the back of my hand, I moved to Josh and lifted his head into my lap. His eyes focused on me and then blinked to Jacob.

"Take care of her," he choked out, more blood forming at the corner of his mouth.

I nodded my head. "We will, I swear."

"Tell... her, love her," he managed to say, his words garbled by the blood blocking his airway.

Leaning down to his ear, I said, "She loves you, Josh. She loves you so much."

Rising up, I ran my thumbs against his cheeks, watching as he took his last breath with a sad smile on his face. Letting the tears take over my body, I shook with the pain I felt. Jacob reached up and closed his eyes and I kissed his forehead.

"Josh!" Daisy screamed as she ran across the street, her beautiful blonde hair bouncing with each movement. Her kind of beauty should only be surrounded by happiness, not this road of heartache and broken dreams she was on. The pain contoured her face as if invisible fists were taking wild swings at her.

I held Josh's head as I moved and rested it gently on the ground. Daisy skidded on her knees in front of him, throwing her body over him, wailing. "No. No. No. No. No. No!"

The pain in her cries was so guttural; the words reached into my body and clawed their way into my heart until I struggled to take a breath. The air had been sucked out of the universe, given to Daisy to fill her lungs, to release the pain.

I wanted to comfort her. I wanted to beg forgiveness for not firing the gun a second before. I wanted to scream to God, *enough*! *Don't you have enough of us*? But I couldn't do any of those things. Instead, I stood, my feet anchored to the ground while my body shook in violent tremors.

Maureen pulled on Daisy to move back, but she clung to his body, his blood soaking into her clothes. "Momma, help him. Help him."

"Shh, baby," Maureen cooed, brushing Daisy's hair from her face.

"Momma, please," she begged, and my stomach churned.

I spun away, running from the group until I was behind a car and released the contents of my stomach. Adam came up beside me and put a hand on my back. Staying bent over, I shook my head, still hearing her wails of anguish.

"Drink this." He thrust a water bottle in my hand and guiding me to lean against the front of the car. I took a sip and rinsed out my mouth before taking a small drink. "You okay?"

Not able to speak, I nodded and pushed off the car, feeling light-headed. "I need to get back over there," I said, looking back, trying to keep my eyes from Daisy and focus on Luke.

He was still holding on to Griffin, his face hard as granite. I needed him so much. I needed to feel his arms around me, but I couldn't do that to Daisy. Not now. Maybe not ever.

Walking on weak legs to the men, Maureen spoke quietly to Jacob and he nodded before scooping Daisy's fighting body in his arms and holding her tightly to his chest.

She finally went limp in his arms, her cries never stopping, but her will had. His mouth in a grim line, he pressed her face to his neck and nodded to us before following Maureen away from Josh's body and toward the market.

George stood over Josh, his eyes closed, tears running down his face while his lips moved in prayer. That's when Griffin chuckled and I lost it. I took the few steps it took to get close enough to him to ball my fist, reach back with everything I had, and punch him as hard as I could. I felt his nose shift under my fist, giving a satisfying crunch. Griffin fell to the side, and I reared my leg back to kick him in the ribs, but Luke yanked me back and tugged me across the street while Tyler stood over Griffin, pointing a gun to his head.

"Baby, no. We need him alive," he said in my ear so no one else could hear. "Wells is coming. We have to have him for leverage."

"No," I said, shaking my head. "No, we can run. Kill him now and we can run. I can't lose one of you. *I can't!* I can't go through what Daisy is going through. I just can't, Luke. Don't make me watch you die, too."

"You and I both know what will happen to these people if we run," he said, pain in his eyes.

Pulling out the only card I could think of to get him to leave this all behind, I said, "I'm pregnant."

The hand running across his face stilled, and his silver eyes stared into mine. His body went rigid; the only movement was the rise and fall of his broad chest.

"Luke, did you hear me? I'm pregnant!" I took a step closer, he pulled me to him, burying my face in his chest, and felt his body shake against mine. I pulled myself from his embrace and pleaded. "We can't fight Wells. You said that yourself. We have to run."

"Goddamn it. It wasn't supposed to happen like this. Not now, not when you're in danger. We're supposed to go home so we can raise our kids without all this over us." His eyes were red and glassy from unshed tears. He shook his head and threw his hands up before resting them on his hips while staring at the ground. "No. There's no other way. I have to find Wells and kill him before he can get to you. Before he can get to our baby."

Panicked by the determination in his words, I gripped the front of his shirt. "No, Luke. You and I both know you'll never make it back. He will kill you! You can't leave me to raise this baby on my own. I can't do it without you. I don't want to do this without you." Tears poured from my eyes as I desperately pleaded with him to see reason.

He closed the few inches between us and covered my lips with his before pulling back. "It's the only way I can protect both of you," he said, putting a hand over my flat stomach.

"We'll find another way," I pleaded.

"There *is* no other way. He will never stop. He would hunt me to the ends of the world just to make a point. He would take you all from me and hurt everyone else along the way."

"You're just one man, Luke. You can't save the world," I whispered, begging, terrified he would leave us behind and I would never see him again. That he would never hold his child.

"You are my world. You're everything to me. You're carrying our child, Roni. The whole world could burn down around us and I'll make damn sure you're the last one breathing clean air. Do you understand me, Roni? Nothing matters without you. Not a damn thing. And if I have to set the fire to keep you safe, I'll strike the goddamned match."

Acknowledgements

My team, Paula LaFevers, Teresa Morris, Liz Hallford, Susan O'Sick Cambra, Cristina Carter, Andrew Hess, and Heather Alberston, thank you so much for everything you did to make Endure a better book. I don't know what I would have done without your support.

Thank you to the fantastic indie authors that have listened, helped, and supported me on my crazy journey of being an author.

A huge shoutout to Alan Haney for letting me borrow his awesome truck and to Carrie Sanders for letting me use her legs. You guys rock.

About the Author

Amber R. Polk was born and raised in a small town in Eastern Oklahoma. Since then, she moved to Colorado, back to Oklahoma, and now resides in Western Arkansas. Although her husband disagrees, she will always consider herself an Okie and proud of it. She is a great cook (don't fact check with her children) and loves spending her time getting kicked off go-cart tracks for aggressive driving. If you have any questions or comments you can find her on Facebook (she's always there).

Amber R. Polk
<u>The Dynamic Divas</u>
Super Chick

Book One

Can you keep a secret?

Megan McAlister will do just about anything to keep the people of Hope, Oklahoma from learning her secret. But, when she witnesses a kidnapping her hopes for a normal life could come crashing down around her.

Finding herself confronted by the one man she wants to avoid, Detective Drew Calloway, she realizes the only way to get him out of her life is to use her power to find his sister—without becoming a government lab rat. When a mysterious stranger arrives in town with knowledge of her secret, and has secrets of her own, her once quiet life is tossed into chaos.

Questioning everything she thought she knew, she has to decide if she wants to go back to the safe life she had, or the life Drew is offering.

Meet C.K. Green

Author Bio: C. K. Green

C. K. Green grew up in a small town in the heart of Tennessee but has lived in different states across the US with her husband and three children. She started her journey into the world of writing when random scenes started plaguing her every waking moment of the day. The only way to make them stop was to get them out of her head by writing them down. It was like putting a puzzle together with the wrong pieces. Nothing seemed to fit until one day everything clicked together. From the tangled mess her debut novel Damaged was created.

To learn more about C. K. Green and her future books, please visit www.authorckg.com.

Damaged Synopsis

Kiera has a great life built for herself until someone from her past threatens to destroy the walls she has struggled to build. She doesn't want the pain that comes with remembering. How can she let him be part of her life if all he does is bring those memories back to haunt her?

That one case changed the path of Ethan's life forever. Meeting Kiera again brings all the questions back to the surface. He just wants to know what happened to her on the night he found her bloody and beaten.

Neither of them counts on the past changing the course of their future Will there be anything left of Kiera if she is forced to face a past she has tried so desperately to bury? Will Ethan still want her around after he learns the truth?

36596552R00188

Made in the USA
San Bernardino, CA
28 July 2016